CONTRACTING W

DRUGS, DEMONS AND DELIVᴖᴖᴖ

believe you have made a contract with the Devil at work? Have you sold your soul for the Devil's coin and paid the Ferryman his fare to transport you to the Purgatory of your work. Well think yourself lucky you don't have to face the Demons that Jack, Kitty and The Big Yin face as they fight to escape The Ferryman and his demonic employer's hellish eternal grip.

Across North America and Europe they are haunted and pursued by Psychotic American Special Forces, Ancient Welsh Druids, the Corsican Mafia, Dutch gold bullion dealers, Glaswegian hit men, Norwegian shipping magnates, IRA paramilitaries, Turkish hangmen and of course the normal lunatics from Middlesbrough, UK. In a tale of tragedy and humour they are bound together in a fight against good and evil as they seek Deliverance from their demons and find the elusive Secret to Paradise.

Davey J Ashfield introduces a cast of bizarre, frightening and incredibly funny characters in a story of violence, profit, love, and the final hope of redemption.

'The new Tom Sharpe'

By Davey J Ashfield
A Turkey and One More Easter Egg

CONTRACTING WITH THE DEVIL

DAVEY J ASHFIELD

'The Path to Paradise Begins in Hell'
(Dante's Inferno)

Contracting With The Devil
Copyright ©2019 APS Publications
All rights reserved.
The moral right of the author has been asserted.

ISBN 978-1-78996-023-5

APS Publications,
4 Oakleigh Road,
Stourbridge,
West Midlands,
DY8 2JX

www.andrewsparke.com

DEDICATION

To my wonderful children for still loving me despite all the precious
time spent at work and play when I should have been with them

ACKNOWLEDGEMENTS

This story is for all those good people who work for living. There is a bit of every one of you on every page - I praise you all.

For those who hired me, counselled me, paid me, supported me, and also fired me – I thank you all.
For those who worked with me and struggled, laughed, cried, and succeeded or failed with me–I miss you all.
And those who may still not forgive my failures; please try, life is much too short. It was never personal. I tried to make it fun for all - and for sure one thing is true…The Road to Hell is indeed paved with good intentions

BOOK ONE

JACK'S INFERNO

THE NINE CIRCLES OF HELL

1
CALIFORNIA, USA
CHAIRMAN MEOW

The beginning of the end…

The loud snap which could only have been the cameraman's arm was clearly heard over the background noise. The camera fell but continued recording and in the hazy footage Jack could see that The Mule had the film director placed firmly in a Japanese stranglehold. The rest of the NBC TV news crew were running in panic towards what they believed to be safe ground. The Mule was shouting at them, *"I have a particular set of skills…."* Then the footage went dead.

Jack switched off the TV. He sat on his hotel bed, put his head in his hands and shed a small tear. *For God's sake how did he get into this hell?*

The day after the news report Jack was looking out the bedroom window of his downtown hotel, still wondering how he had ever got into this mad house; this purgatory. And to make things worse he had just received a bizarre phone call from his Chairman which had made him question his reasons to live. As he thought about the call, and last evening's horrific TV programme which was the reason for the call, he recalled how he had first met the new Chairman of the company. In his misery he couldn't even raise a smile when he remembered the first question the man had ever asked him.

"Do you ride?"

Do you ride? Jack thought was a reasonable question to break the ice and he answered positively. "Yes, of course," he replied.

"Oh. Which hunt?"

Oh dear Jack thought. *Here we go, I've put my bloody foot in it yet again.*

"I'm sorry Philip, but I thought you meant a bicycle not a horse. I do have a bike and I ride a bit on weekends with my little daughter along the pier," said Jack sheepishly, expecting to be humiliated in response. He was.

"Oh. One would have expected a man of your seniority to ride to hounds. Do you know the Duke of Rutland?"

"Eh! No. Not really Philip. I once drank in a pub that he owned on Rutland Water," stuttered Jack.

"I ride with him regularly at the Belvoir hunt. He's a private equity investor in the hedge fund I manage." The chairman looking his new director up and down through his half- moon spectacles. He continued. "You can always tell a man by his friends. We were at Marlborough together you know?"

Jack looked at his tormentor and realised yet again that he really didn't gel with extremely posh people; psychotic maniacs, yes, but public-school bullies, no. He replied simply but sardonically. "How nice."

As Jack looked over the bay towards the iconic bridge he was repairing he chuckled as he thought of the luxury of having public school and establishment friends. Most of *his* chums and certainly *his* colleagues should have been locked up in Alcatraz prison just over the horizon. Yes, his first meeting hadn't gone too well and the recent phone call about the TV horror show wasn't great either.

"Why was he in this torture? The nine circles of Hell, Dante's, or now Jack's, bloody Inferno. Well, it was quite simple," he mumbled to no one but himself, *"that crazy Norwegian boss, KT, sold the company and my job to the new chairman. Why put me through more bloody purgatory?*

Chairman Meow was the nickname KT, Jack's old boss, had given Philip the new chairman, believing that, as Philip didn't have any experience of the business, he would be a 'pussy cat. *Some bloody pussy cat* Jack grumbled, *more like a tame mouse.* He was soon to realise he couldn't have been so far wrong. And sure enough Jack found his corporate life lay well and truly in the balance after that television program and the phone call.

The week before Jack had been told to cross the Atlantic and sort this bridge repair out because after only a few months the job had as usual gone badly wrong. As he looked out of his bedroom window he wondered *who in their right mind would send The Mule over here to run it.* Granted he was American and ex Special Forces but he was no diplomat, and certainly no tree hugger. For God's sake the job was fraught with environmentalists challenging its legitimacy, protesting and lobbying Senators and Congressmen. And then The Mule brains a Greenpeace member with a scaffold pole and throws one off the barge into the bay. Dear God, didn't they know how he worked? Jack still had the last law suit from the attempted lynching of a client on his desk back at head office.

Trying to sort out the visas for The Mule's favourite sub-contractor Abdul the Turk's Islamic rope-swinging abseilers from Rotterdam had been a nightmare. The Mule building them an illegal Mosque on the bay-side out of laundered stainless steel didn't go down well with either the planning authority nor Homeland security. And, *oh dear,* Jack whispered to no one but himself, *KT asking the Big Yin to talk to the Teamsters Union for the dock access and storage!* He could still hear the Yin telling him how it had gone.

"They threatened me big man. They threatened me. Nay wan dis that wi me. I told them I'll send Big Tam to sort the *******'s oot."

"How did that go big man?" Jack asked, already knowing the answer.

"They told me that Tam wid end up wae concrete boots like that Hoffa gadgy. Ah tald them; **** that, if they wanted tae fight ah'd chib the lot of them and hoyed the heed on the biggest of them."

"That's when the police arrived I guess?" Jack asked getting the anticipated answer.

"Aye big man; and those poliss cells are nay like Glasgee; darkies everywhere."

"Your visa's revoked then?" Again a rhetorical question.

"Aye it is, the bastards. We've sent that English engineer over tae talk tae the unions. He'll bore the bastards stupid anyway and then I'll send our red-faced sales director in with the whisky next week. He'll drink the bastards into a deal."

And now the TV documentary: He could have done without that. It had been shown the night before on NBC, networked across the UK and Europe. A fly on the wall of *The Bridge too Far.* The network had taken film footage and interviews with the workers and supervisors on the bridge under an agreement that they'd show nothing controversial. He had watched horrified. It had featured Abdul the Turk's mountain climbers hanging in mid- air, praying to Mecca, swinging around enjoying themselves as if at a fairground. One being interviewed and saying how they sometimes dropped the odd paint can, or angle iron or welding rod into the bay, and pleading that he had never been the one who killed Flipper the dolphin. Jack cringed and looked for a table to hide under as he watched. He moaned to himself. *And now we're under attack from the Federal environment agency and the whole of the Californian tree-hugging brigade.*

One of his supervisors was telling how they used the rescue boat to fish illegally for lobsters and crabs. The boat should have been under the bridge at all times to rescue falling workers. He'd been chased the night before by the river police illegal fishing patrol. He was proud he'd escaped by braining the police man with his company supplied steel capped rigger boots.

Then innocently and foolishly they had tried to interview The Mule. Jack shivered again, a little angry now as again he spoke aloud in the loneliness of his hotel room, *who the hell thought it was wise to put that crazy son of a bitch in front of a camera?* True to psychotic form, The Mule had snapped the microphone in two and karate chopped the camera man after putting the film director into a Delta Force regulation Japanese strangle hold. The only footage shown was of the screaming film director in his vice like grip and The Mule shouting after the fleeing crew, "*I have a particular set of skills. I will find you. And I will …*" The footage ended with a crunching sound, à la Bruce Lee in '*Enter the Dragon*', as if a neck had been broken.

On the bridge in one of the small shelters dotted across the bridge for eating and rest breaks the fish poaching superintendent demonstrated how to cook Lobster Thermidor and a nice spicy Black Pepper Crab. He masqueraded to the viewers as a three-star Michelin chef, tossing the crab in his wok, mixing in the condiments and spices and pulling steaming red lobsters out of his stainless-steel boiling pan. Jack had watched aghast as his highly paid workforce tucked into an illegally caught, haute cuisine, gourmet feast for a long lunch. This free time he was paying for and it was time he didn't have as now he faced company life threatening liquidated damages for the habitual late finish of all his projects.

He dreaded the calls that would come in. And they had: KT threatening him with disembowelment with his battle axe on the banks of the fjord and a ritual Viking funeral pyre; the Big Yin apoplectic, threatening to send Big Tam from Glasgow over, with concrete overcoats, dead fish in bullet proof jackets and razor slashes galore. Jack's brain melted, *he'd soon be sleeping with his gourmet chef's lobsters and crabs.* And then there was the Chairman's call.

"Jack, I had several people from the City around at my Rutland home for dinner last evening. The servants had just brought our first course into the dining room when Jones minor, the Chairman of the International Wealth Fund and an old school chum said:

'Philip, isn't that rough dirty Norwegian business you've bought on telly tonight?' "Crikey I said. I do believe it is. Should we retire to the TV lounge and watch it. I believe they're fixing up some airport or oil rig in America somewhere." Chairman Meow continued. "So we all retired to watch it."

Oh God, Jack thought, *that's all I need, the bloody city of London, most probably investors in the company, watching how his new company is going to be thrown out of America for killing dolphins, maiming its citizens, stealing its natural resources and failing abjectly to finish on time. I'm dead; I may as well ring The Mule and ask him to use 'his particular skills' to get it over with quick.*

"Jack it was absolutely shocking. Terrible and I felt so ashamed," his aristocratic nemesis continued down the transatlantic line.

"I'm so sorry Philip. So was I." Was all he could bring himself to say, waiting for a tirade of criticism over the environmental nightmare, safety breeches, lack of work, grand larceny, poor productivity, cost escalation.

"But Jack, the health and safety, it was terrible. I thought we were world class, best in class at health and safety?" stated the Chairman.

"Yes we normally are," Jack replied wishing it was over. *What was he going to pick out?*

"Even Jones minor, who has never worked anywhere but in a merchant bank, said it was absolutely horrendous. It shocked most of my guests. I can't have that you know. I'll have to speak to KT about this. Jones minor said what we all felt, that it was frightening and unprofessional."

Just put me out of my misery please, get it over with man… Jack cried out in his tortured mind – and sure enough his chairman did.

"We couldn't believe when we saw the supervisor cook the lobsters without washing his hands. He also was wearing his dirty overalls and so were the working chaps. They didn't even change for dinner. Very poor hygiene management, dear boy. I think you may well have to face the music for that, old chap."

Jack lay back on his bed and breathed sigh of relief. *For God's sake! Was that all he saw wrong with the program, the lads didn't wash their hands or put on clean dinner jackets! For crying out loud it wasn't the bloody Ritz! Never mind the fact that they were lazing in luxury, eating stolen produce; stolen by the company life boat and on company time. Dead dolphins, assault and battery, bone idleness and mountain climbers who play and pray rather than work - all lost on his new ultimate boss and provider of funds.*

He put the phone down and lay back on the bed staring at the ceiling, thinking carefully. *This was ether going to be great news, if Chairman Meow would never bother him as long as he made sure his lads wore dickey bow ties and clean dinner suits - or bad news, as clearly he was expecting something, and somebody, quite different to what he'd acquired and bought and paid for.*

He decided it was inevitably bad news.

As Jack drove along the bay side towards the bridge project which would possibly be his personal Calvary he thought about his probable fate on return to corporate headquarters and drifted back to that first fateful and frightening day in Teesside when he met KT and his fall into the darkness and the first circle of Hell began.

He could think of only one requiem song - by Iron Maiden ...
PURGATORY

2
TEESSIDE
KJEL THE TERRIBLE

Some Time Ago

The door to the office flew open and in rushed two large men. One leapt across the desk and shouted loudly, thrusting his outstretched arm and a small black wallet into Jack's face:

"Police! Don't move you bastard. Serious Crime Squad. You're all nicked!"

So began his life in Purgatory.

Two hours before on that fatal morning he had been introduced to what he thought was a route to a new career and endless happiness by his new boss Kjel the Terrible, KT to his friends. Just two hours before the police raid KT had told Jack of his pride in his Viking ancestors who had murdered all the monks, raped several nuns and destroyed Finchael Abbey, just a few miles away on the banks of the River Wear. That was his family's last rape and pillage of the good folk of the Northumbria. As his new boss tucked into a nice plate of scrambled eggs on toast, Jack thought this was rather a novel and surreal discussion because soon he would be raping and pillaging metaphorically with the good folks of Teesside whom he now employed.

They had met just outside Teesside, at the excellent five-star restaurant *The Tontine* at which his boss had stayed the night before. They had breakfast and his boss had driven him in a large new Range Rover the short distance up the A19 to the construction site

He had been introduced to the project team and its associated business by KT as the man responsible for leading them all to complete the most successful project in history. Jack was feeling pleased and satisfied as his boss had left to rape, pillage and torture the steel fabricator's managing director. He was more pleased when Nicki his lovely young pretty secretary was introduced and she delicately poured him his first cup of coffee and gave him the morning's post. As he sat in his porta cabin office, in a complex of many other porta cabins on the huge desolate site he reflected on his morning breakfast meeting with KT.

He liked his new boss. He had met him in Stavanger some months before with the other Norwegian bosses of the company they had recruited him to lead through its massive new offshore oil developments. The actual office interview had been brief and followed by a huge piss up with KT and his team in the bars and restaurants of that bleak, chilly, rain-sodden part of Western Norway. He was learning that in Norway little work was actually done. Unlike his periods in the USA where they rise up from their beds at 4 am. and are in the office by five and never ever leave until happy hour in the bars at about 6 pm, in Norway the work day is like the daylight, extremely short. The drinking is of course, like the darkness, very long. Jack thought he'd enjoy working for Norwegians.

He just sat back in his comfy office chair and begun to look at the morning's post when the doors burst open, the Feds leapt in and his life was changed forever.

Initially and entirely naturally startled when the doors burst open, Jack had jumped up as the large man flew across the room at him. The assailant's partner was standing against the door preventing Nicki or anyone from coming to his assistance. They could have been anyone - and this was Middlesboro for God's sake - here they were all crazy sons of bitches he was told by anyone and everyone he'd ever met. He was poised to defend himself when the man thrust a huge fist and warrant card in his face. He slumped straight down again in fear and trepidation - what the hell had he done to be arrested so soon in his new job.

"Ok mate? Don't worry, we won't hurt you," the policeman said calmly. Putting his warrant card away in his back pocket, he sat down next to Jack.

Don't worry! Jack thought, *why the hell not!*

The man continued as if nothing was the matter. "It's not really you we're after. Well, it may be, but we don't think so as we've been watching this office for a while now and haven't seen you before. Who are you?"

Jack took a deep breath. *Was this a positive thing that they didn't think it was him?* But his next thought was, *what the hell did they think he might have done and why does the serious crime squad have his site under surveillance. We're only knocking bits of steel and wires together for God's sake, not smuggling tons of cocaine. Or shit, the horror hit him … were they?*

16

"I'm Jack. I've just joined this outfit, man. Just started here two hours ago," he answered hopefully, and shouting to his secretary past the hard-faced growling policeman holding her, "Isn't that so Nicki?"

She pushed her head and assets through the outstretched arms of the lawman and answered in the affirmative just as a tall, bald, be-suited man came running into her office, pushing up against both her and the door guard. He too inserted his head and half his body through the inner office door and said: "It's all right Jack. I can handle this. Let me take these guys to my office. It's just a little thing. I sort these things out every day. That's why I should be running this thing. Leave it to me."

"Like hell I will," Jack howled at the commercial manager he had only just met with KT that morning – a man constantly claiming that he was the one keeping the business alive, from which Jack instantly deduced that he was pissed off at KT bringing in a complete stranger to run the business when he was the only sane and obvious choice as the man who knew everything. "Get your arse in here and tell me what the hell is going on."

And turning to the policeman he added, "Can you lads sit down now and just tell me what you're here for?"

They sat around the T-shaped desk, Jack at the head of the T, the others on either side. The talkative policemen gave an explanation of sorts, the other just stared menacingly.

"We've had an international gang of transport thieves under surveillance for months now linked to organised crime on the continent, using local UK nationals at Dover, Felixstowe, Hull and Grimsby to steal trucks, cargoes and launder money. Maybe some illegal immigration too."

Jack was quietly relieved. Surely this had nowt to do with Middlesbrough and building oil rigs and he told him so. "So what the hell has this to do with us man?"

Jack looked for reassurance to his commercial manager, Nigel hoping he'd confirm his new-found hope but Nigel couldn't look at him. Jack's heart missed a beat.

The cop just looked at them questioningly and said bluntly: "One of the trucks is in your shot blasting sheds, getting blasted right now. We followed it all the way from Hull."

Jack looked at the open window and wondered; *Should I jump? How the hell could this happen to him? Two hours and that crazy bastard KT had put him up as a fall guy for a Rumanian Gyppo white slave smuggling gang. For God's sake it shouldn't be like this.*

"It's ok Jack. Just let me handle this I can explain to the lads. Come on boys come back to my office. It's not really what it seems. I run everything here I can explain to you," Nigel said, trying to force a smile as he looked from face to face searching for agreement that he was indeed the man.

"No one goes anywhere until I know what the hell is going on," Jack interrupted the Nigel appreciation society with some force in his voice. "Nigel, I think you need to tell us all why a stolen truck probably full of gold bullion and Albanian white slaves is doing in our blast sheds."

Nigel looked for some comfort from the cops but they just stared back at him. He shrugged his shoulders and revealed all. "It's not what it seems. The paint shop lads often blast clean the underside of trailers and trucks for the lads. They only charge them a few bob and it goes into the tea money fund. Nobody makes any money out of it, just doing the locals a favour and our lads get tea and biscuits out of it. No one would be into people smuggling or real crime man here. We're all canny lads. And I can sort it all. Jack, there's no need for you worry. As I said I handle everything here. It's just another problem for me to sort out. They never stop. I did everything for the last manager cause he was useless too. I'll do the same for you. Just let me get on with it. Come on lads come through to my office and we can sort this."

Jack just stared at the *'look at me I have the knowledge and the experience to do your job and you should just **** off to whatever University you came from and let us real contractors do the work'* expression on his morose face. Jack made one immediate determination. *'You're not gonna beat me'* he thought. *I'm tougher than that.* It might prove a difficult task but he'd establish his true position in the pecking order. "No Nigel I don't think so. We'll all go and see 'the lads' and find out what's real and what isn't." and he went to get out of his chair.

'No need to do that Jack," the talkative cop added quickly before Jack could fully stand. "It's not your lads we're interested in. Nigel's probably right. The driver could be one of their mates and hasn't a clue who, what or why he's driving. It's not him or them we are after, it's the big boys. Let us track the lorry to its final destination and we'll lift them all then. You just sort your own lads out. It's a local plod matter anyway even if we decide to bother to arrest you."

Nigel smiled for the first time. It was a supercilious *how clever and correct I am* sort of smile. This was not going to be easy Jack now knew but secretly he was pleased this had moved from grand larceny to a minor disciplinary matter. He would be free from Durham jail and employed for a few more hours at least.

"Well if that's what you want. I'm sorry we gave you this bother. We'll sort our end out, so no police matter surely. Hope you get your men." Jack got up and they shook hands.

Nigel was beaming now and asking the police to follow him to sort out the paperwork and next steps.

Jack remained unconvinced that no one was financially involved - these were contractors after all, and he was in '*the Boro*' and being brand new, he must surely show some sort of ethical, legal and moral leadership? But at this stage in his life he was new to contracting, sub-contractors and life on the streets of hard knocks - he had yet to find Paradise and end up in Asia and a life of pure bliss with the masters of real contracting. He was to say the least a touch naïve and out of his depth so he bit his tongue and issued instructions to his pompous commercial manager. "Nigel will you talk to the lads and give me a report on what you find. I want to interview the superintendent in charge of everything on site. Can you send him in to see me please? I think he'll have to be fired."

Nigel was visibly shocked. He told the cops to follow the lovely Nicki to his office and then closed Jack's office door and stood over him. "Jack, listen. You don't know this place and how it works. I can handle it. You can be sure I'm straight and only looking after the money and KT trusts me implicitly."

Jack interrupted the self-appreciation. "Nigel, I don't doubt that you know your business. I will need your help to get this on track and if we can do it together then that's how I work. I'm sure you don't gain from this tea money fiddle but I can't have the bloody police bursting into the site every day and I have to do something so I'll fire the man responsible."

"You can't fire him. It's dangerous, "Nigel interrupted, looking like a big puppy dog now with pleading eyes.

19

"Why the **** is it dangerous?" Jack asked, astonished.

"Because Ernie runs the whole of *the Boro* man: If you fire him we could have trouble here and at all the other sites. He's connected. KT loves him, thinks he's great as he's as hard as that Norgie bugger. KT likes hard men. You don't really want to annoy KT or Ernie. Let me handle it Jack. I live here with them all and know how it all works."

These were early days in Jack's education and he had been brought up to do the right thing, make tough management decisions, solve difficult problems and show strong leadership integrity. He might soon learn otherwise but that would be after his period in purgatory. Now he was determined to act fairly, honestly without fear for his legs or of disappearing into the murky, green and yellow, River Tees.

"Just send this Ernie over please. I'll talk to him and see what his explanation is first. If he's on the take I'll fire him, hard man or not."

"Ok, but don't ask me to get you out of the shite Jack. I'm sick of saving all my bosses' arses. I'm a fully chartered QS, much higher qualified than the bosses I've had. They just didn't listen to me. This place would die if it wasn't for me. KT knows that."

Worn down, Jack just nodded and waited for the Don Corleone of *'The Boro'* to arrive.

Nicki showed Ernie in some time later. Jack realised that Nigel would have briefed this accused and told him how useless his new boss was but, *what the hell, let's do the right thing* as he was taught at business school.

Ernie was wearing traditional site dress, overalls covered in paint, rigger boots and hard hat. Jack immediately noticed how big a man he was; not massively tall but with a body that looked as if it had been worked hard at work and in the gym - the tell-tale signs of slightly puffed up face and huge muscles probably the result of anabolic steroids that hard men took to maintain their fighting lethality. His face was puckered by scars and his chin and nose were that of a boxer. He took off his hard hat and placed it on the table opposite Jack. He stood at the end of the desk and grabbing his balls, lifted them slightly and kept gently massaging them while speaking quietly and very politely.

"Hi boss. Nigel tells me you want to see me about the lorry blasting. I'm sorry if it's caused you a problem with the Old Bill but we just use the money to pay for the lads' tea. The driver comes from across the river in Brambles Farm. He's a mate; he didn't know the lorry was stolen or anything dodgy in it." He kept nodding and bowing his head as if Jack were some sort of Czar of the Russias.

Jack became more confident that he wasn't going to die there and then. Maybe this management thing worked. "Ernie, to be honest I really don't believe that but frankly I have more to do today than chase up and down finding out the answer. I'll let the cops do that. You know I can't really let you use the company's resources to fund your own tea party for God's sake?"

Ernie, grabbed his balls a bit harder, lifted them, shrugged his huge shoulders and bowed his head again. "Aye: but boss, we have to make a bit from somewhere, man. The pay is shite and we have nowhere to sit and have our bait. The kettle's broken and Nigel won't buy us another one. Red Tom is coming to see you soon with all our grievances. We were hoping the new boss might give us a pay rise and improve our bait cabins. We need the tea money, man, to help get a day's work in. Sorry for saying that." And he bowed his head once more and gave his balls another rub.

Jack looked at the huge man who looked as if he could kill him with one blow and wondered at his placidity. It pleased him that his new-found power could tame genocidal maniacs. But he was curious and also compassionate about his new workforce as he had been taught and he also believed in team work, inclusiveness and communication. He had still not learnt 'the paradise secret'.

"I'm not happy, Ernie, if your lads are not being treated well. If we can sort something I will. But who the hell is Red Tom. I didn't think we had unions here do we?"

"**** no," Ernie replied. "Last one who came to talk to me, Empty Heed threw him into the wheel abrader. KT hates unions. Red Tom is just our handyman. He was our headmaster at school in *the Boro*. Bastard used to cane us every day so now we torture the bastard every day. Wrapped him in cling film the other week and left him overnight in the paint store. Hah!"

Jack looked at Ernie who was chuckling away and had temporarily taken his hands off his balls to wipe away the sweat coming down his shaven head.

"We love him really and he's the only one who can actually read and write and talk properly so the lads use him to write down their grievances."

Jack thought he mustn't have been a very good headmaster if none of his pupils could read or write. He also wondered what the hell he'd stepped into. In his last job he was dealing with people educated at Harvard Business School and now he was in the midst of the clearly deranged. Jack looked at his watch. Shit, it was nearly lunchtime, and he had yet to visit the site and meet his full team. He looked at the hulk chuckling in front of him and for some reason, unknown to him but probably fear and self- preservation, he liked what he saw. Gut feel and all that, or just a love of characters. He decided to end the show and give the lad a second go.

"Ernie, you're in charge of the lads, mate so it's your responsibility for anything that goes wrong. Blasting Albanian slave dealers' trucks on company time and money just isn't on man. Is it?"

Ernie looked sheepishly guilty, bowed his head and scratched his balls one more time. "No boss. I'm sorry it won't happen again."

"Okay Ernie. Let's get on with work eh? I'll going to ask Nigel to give you a written warning but I'm sure we'll sort that out as we get to know each other. I'm Jack by the way."

Jack stood up and gingerly moved to the giant Mike Tyson, hoping to God he wasn't too upset. He put out his hand. Ernie gave him his ball-groping hand and shook it in a vice like grip. He smiled at Jack with a knowing and satisfied smile, picked up his hard hat and said; 'Thanks Jack. I'll not let you down, mate. Come and have a cup of tea and a few of those Hob Nob biscuits in the tea cabin that Big Ed just bought with the new tea money and I'll introduce you to Red Tom, Empty Heed and the lads. They're gonna love you."

And he left.

Jack sat down, slightly worried at his performance as a hard, strong leader of men. Somehow he thought that didn't go as it should have. *They are gonna love you'* worried him a lot.

Nicki brought him his lunch and he sat down for a read of some planning reports and organisation charts. He had just started on his sandwich when the phone rang.

He picked it up and a familiar voice howled down the phone. "Get your arse across the river and see that crazy Dane. He's going mental at us. What the **** have you done! You've only been there ten minutes, the police arrive, Ernie is disciplined and I've had Nigel on to me, and now the ******* client is pissed off. Get yourself out of there and see him now."

Jack held the phone someway from his ear and took a deep breath. Things weren't supposed to be like this. Three hours ago KT was eating scrambled eggs and talking about how they both were going to get along so well. Now he was a raving lunatic and what the hell was it for. He answered back quietly and calmly. "KT what's wrong, man? I haven't seen the client this morning, only when you took us to see him in Esbjerg two weeks ago."

"I know that, you daft English bastard. It's that mad project manager you've got over there, The Mule: he's hung the client's paint inspector."

3
HARTLEPOOL
THE MULE

Same day...

After picking himself up from the office floor and taking another abusive burst of management advice from the terrible Nordic Viking, Jack had taken himself off across the River Tees and its quaintly flowing waters. He drove past the smoking, smog-filled metropolis that was the Imperial Chemicals Industry's finest toxic city and up the A19 to that place where monkeys were an endangered species. One hundred and ninety years ago Hartlepudlians had hung a monkey as a French a spy when it had been washed up off a shipwrecked French warship. It now seemed his project manager on this site had decided to hang his own simian French spy, but this time it was his human client...what next? He could only hope he could get back to his North Yorkshire haven in sane mind and body by evening.

He was invited into the client's office to meet Knut, their UK representative. He was Danish and had a fearsome reputation. A few weeks past Jack had met him with KT and they had passed the time talking about how they had destroyed a Singapore shipyard and put it into bankruptcy with a huge ship built for them. How they chuckled at the fact that they'd put two hundred welding inspectors on the job at huge cost just to make them find weld defects and tell the shipyard to repair every one, time and time again. They chuckled at how they'd tortured them. Jack remembered how they told him how they had laughed at the project where they had insisted the yard took the five thousand tonne module they were building and dipped it in acid to just to enforce a one hundred-year paint specification they had cleverly slipped past the eyes of the yard's bidding team.

Knut was sitting at his desk in his overalls. Nothing but Inspection and Test Plans and welding and paint specifications littered the desk. Jack noticed there were no planning documents, key performance indicator charts or financial spread sheets, only the instruments of his torture.

Knut asked Jack to sit down. "Well Jack we're in a mess now. That crazy man of yours has caused a riot down there in the dock. But first, have a *Gamell Dansk*." He opened up a small fridge and took out a bottle of Danish liquorice spirit and poured two shots into the small glasses he kept on the side of his desk.

"Bet you haven't eaten yet? Here try one of these I know you love them," he said to Jack as he opened his drawer and took a large tin out, opened the lid and gave him a circular black object.

Oh shit, Jack thought, *not bloody Piratos again.* He had endured two days of chewing the salty liquorice in Esbjerg and was violently sick after. He was never sure if it was the alcohol in the *Gammell Dansk* he'd imbibed or the entire Siberian salt mine from the liquorice poison which caused the projectile vomiting. But he had to take them now as this Great Dane was his customer. He knew the liquorice torture determined if you lived or died with Knut and he was trying valiantly to bond with the Scandinavian contractor destroyer.

Jack chewed on his emetic and swallowed the horrible liquor, hoping this would appease his new long-term buddy, all thoughts of Health and Safety and prohibition of drink on site long gone.

Knut picked up his phone and asked his secretary to call Jack's site manager and tell him to come upstairs. Jack had yet to meet the notorious Mule, otherwise known as Jimmy, but he'd asked a few questions before he'd arrived at Knut's torture chamber and it seems he was well respected despite a tendency to practical jokes and also periods of extreme temper tantrums. He had appeared one day in Aberdeen with KT who introduced him as an American kick ass from the drilling rigs. It appeared he had spent much time in various war zones during his time in the military and was skilled in all forms of violent mayhem and armed and unarmed combat. He was indeed well suited to KT and to the contracting business. His name across the industry was The Mule, Why? It was simple. If he was in a tantrum and wished to make a point to anyone; he kicked their door down like a mule and hit them with any object that came to hand. One lad had his bedroom door kicked down one night offshore and brained by a lampstand. Windows were not exempt and lads told of passing his house on Saturday morning after a night on the drink and seeing the sofa lying in the garden, his curtains blowing through the broken windows. *Another one to sort and I've only been here five hours,* Jack thought.

"I like Jimmy, Jack," Knut explained as they waited for him to arrive. "He gets the job done and keeps to my spec. but more than that he does what I tell him to do and doesn't argue. Mad as a Finn mind but I like them like that. He loves the sweets and the *Gammell Dansk* too. He battered a guy with a fire extinguisher who annoyed me in a bar in Newcastle and drove us both home pissed. Great company man: You should be proud. He's given me one of your company cars to drive from bar to bar if I want. Great lad, but crackers, but can't have him hanging one of our lads though. We'll have to give him a roasting at the least."

For God's sake what next Jack thought? Pissed, assault and battery, company property used as a potential bribe and for illegal purposes, now hanging a client….

The Mule came in. He too wore overalls. He put his hard hat on the desk and sat down opposite Jack before leaning forward to offer Jack a handshake.

"Hiya Jack. Nigel phoned me to say you were coming. Didn't know you'd taken over from the last daft sucker KT employed. He was ****** useless, couldn't tie Nigel's bootlaces. I hear you've nearly sacked Ernie? Careful mate, Ernie is connected, know what I mean?" And turning to Knut: "All right Knut? I'll take a glass of that shit Danish drink off you buddy…..Skoll….hah hah…."

Jack watched as Knut poured the drink, laughing with Jimmy in prefect harmony. Jack reflected that news travels fast and he'd underestimated Nigel's influence on this merry band. What a tangled web. He broke the jollity and drinking in an attempt to bring them back to the issue in question, namely the death of a client by strangulation.

"Jimmy tell me what happened please," Jack asked.

"Jack, buddy. The man was a son of a bitch. He tortured us all through the project. The lads hated him, even his own lads. Isn't that right Knut?" Jimmy looked to Knut for confirmation.

"Yes. He was German. Not one of mine, I think that new big boss Jon - they call him the Iron Chancellor in head office - sent him; he's a German too. Son of a bitch that one, he's only new but he's causing mayhem in head office. He expects the job finished on time and how can we do that and keep to the spec. Germans, I hate them,"

"Okay Jimmy, but what actually have you done?" Jack got back to the point.   Danish-German diplomatic relations were not his problem here. Homicide and massive law suits were.

"Jack, boy ah was only joking man. We decided we'd have a laugh at the sail away of the first rig. So the lads grabbed the mother and I tied a rope around his legs and threw him off the quay into the dock. He was supposed to land in the water and I'd keel haul the son of a bitch for a laugh and then drag him out. We thought it would be a ****** hoot and he'd be fine with it all. That right Knut?"

"Yes Jimmy. It should have been just the boys having fun. But you should have checked the rope length first, buddy," Knut said with a wry smile.

"What was wrong with the rope?" Jack asked.

"It was a bit short, man."

"Yes it was, wasn't it, Jimmy?" asked Knut and then answered his own rhetorical question. "Problem was Jack, instead of him splashing into the water, the rope was just a foot short and he stopped head first dangling upside down, his head submerged in the dock. Poor twat nearly drowned. His back has jerked two discs free we think."

Knut looked at The Mule, and The Mule looked at Knut. They both looked grim faced for a moment before bursting out laughing. Knut looked over at Jack, shaking his head, his blond flowing locks temporarily hiding the huge grin. "Jimmy's some boy Jack. He did a great job on that first rig. I need him for the next one. I'll replace the German after he gets out of Hartlepool Accident and Emergency with one of our own. Don't go too hard on Jimmy. You've one more to finish yet. You know what I mean?

Jack looked at Knut, and then at a smiling Jimmy, and it dawned on him that yes, he did know what he meant. If he wanted an easy time, go easy on The Mule, keep the drink and cars flowing and eat the liquorice. Things would be alright.

Jack drove back down to *the Boro*. He was tired. It had been a long day. His car phone rang. He picked it up and heard Nigel's laconic, doom-laden Eeyore voice.

"Do you want the good news or the bad news?"

4
THE 'BORO'
BIG ED

Same day

Jack held the car phone to his ear and replied to his gloomy Quantity Surveyor genius. "Nigel, just the good news please"

"KT has arrived back and is going mental," was his frightening answer.

"And what's the bad news?"

"Big Ed is still here and KT might have seen his van."

"Why is that bad news, Nigel?" Jack asked, giving up hope now.

"Because KT thinks we fired him ages ago. He hates him."

"Why didn't you fire him then?" Jack naively asked.

"Because Ed is one of the lads, if you know what I mean. He's our buyer and can source anything, even when it's not available. He knows how to get things but don't ever ask how. KT doesn't understand that. And Ed is a great friend of Ernie, so you should know that means a lot. You have to also know that Ernie and the lads have the guns buried in Big Ed's wife's garden, under her rose bush so it's best not to upset the apple cart if we don't have to. Ed's lass knows nothing about the guns. She works in a bank so it's a very sensitive subject and we try to keep all this away from her. So Jack it's best you let us hide Big Ed from KT. If he asks you about the van, just say you'll investigate and get back to him. I'll make sure we re-spray it as a supplier van to hide our logo. The Mule's mate, Davie, the supervisor on site up there in monkey hanging land can do that in his car laundering garage in Newcastle. Don't worry I'll handle it. Why don't you just go home? I'll see KT to his hotel soon"

Jack shook his head and stared at the traffic in front of him. This was becoming more like *'Once upon a time in America'* as the day went on. But he couldn't give up...could he?

"No Nigel I'll be back in twenty minutes. Tell KT I'll see him when I get there. See you then." Jack put down the phone.

When he arrived Nicki greeted him at the door. "Jack, KT's in your office. He's had a chat with Nigel and then went to see Ernie. I think he's in bad mood. Mind, that isn't unusual. I'll bring you a coffee. You'll need one."

When Jack entered his office, KT grunted a hello. "I've spoken to Knut. Seems you've sorted out Jimmy and all that. Knut seems to like you. If he's happy, I'm happy. The Mule is one of our old lads, Jack. Just needs a slap and kick up the ass every now and then. Keep him off the piss. He's crazy on the piss. I don't want to bail him out again. And keep him away from my stainless steel. I'm sure him and his Geordie mate, are building steel barbecues to sell on the open market. For ****' sake I think my wife bought one off the bastard last week for our new house here."

Jack sat and said nothing. Very little would surprise him anymore he thought. Oh to be back with normal people. Nicki brought his coffee in. KT smiled at her and watched her leave. As she closed the door he looked Jack straight in the eyes and said: "You tried to take her out yet?"

Jack sat back stunned. His mind flashed back to his last boss, an immaculately dressed, ex-Rugby Public Schoolboy, an ex-Grenadier Guard's officer, Oxford and as queer as Oscar Wilde but as politically correct as you could get. Scandinavians were a little different he was finding out.

"No KT, I'm married and it's work and she's engaged to be married. Seems a lovely girl and not like that," he carefully answered as he really didn't know, or trust, why he was facing this question so early in their new business relationship.

"You should. Take her out to Branson's place where I stay. Book a room and treat her to some champagne and dinner. Put the lot on expenses. I'll pay for it. I've just sacked the boss from Denmark. He spent a fortune on expenses on girls but that would have been okay if he was any use but he wasn't, he was useless. Anyway you need to chill out sometimes. We Scandinavians, men or women, don't see anything wrong in shared love. You Brits are just prudish boring bastards. No wonder we took your women and sheep."

Jack just sat in wonder thinking; *this guy tortured people and was a stickler for hard work and loyalty. Every pound of his was a prisoner. Heaven forbid you spent or stole it for your own pleasure. And he's berating him for not spending hundreds of pounds on a secretary he'd only known one day. This just didn't tick. Was it a trap? Who knows he concluded but I'm not falling into it.*

The paranoia was starting...

KT got out of his seat at the side of Jack's desk and held out his hand. His solid gold Rolex glimmered in the dimming sunlight through the dirty, oil-stained windows in the porta cabin. "I'm off now. I'm planning to head up to Aberdeen to torture the drilling contractor. I'll call you."

As he left, Jack lay back in his office chair and relaxed for the first time. It was nearly home time. Nigel knocked and entered the office.

"I've just opened the afternoon post. Do you want the good news or the bad news?"

5
STAVANGER
EMPTY HEED

A month or so later….

"The project is ********." You were supposed to fix that after I sacked that last useless Danish bastard. You are too soft with them; Fire the ****** lot of them. And you let them piss away our money at every turn. Why do you need more equipment? And don't get on at to me about scaffolding. You let them steal and lose it daily, you useless son of a bitch. You have to get hard with them or I'll have to come and sort it out."

Jack sat in the board room facing an inquisition from KT and the rest of the big bosses in the company. He felt like John Wayne at the Alamo, surrounded by Mexicans and with only one bullet left. It had been a tortuous few weeks trying to get his feet under the table, analysing the strengths and weaknesses of what he had inherited and still ensuring his raging berserker Viking boss was kept happy. As he sat enduring the agony of the business review listening to character and professionalism assignation, and awaiting imminent crucifixion, his mind drifted off to those first couple of weeks of his tenure where everything was bad news. He decided one day he'd write a book about it all and call it, *'Three Crosses, Outside Middlesbrough, Teesside.'* Maybe it would make an Oscar-winning movie.

From day one he'd discovered that his quantity surveyor nemesis Nigel never had anything but bad news when he brought the post, his offer of good news being merely an attempt at Quantity Surveyor humour. Jack was learning that QS's had no sense of humour whatsoever. They all thrived on sadism and a maniacal desire to prove anyone wrong. They all believed that they should be running everything as the sole recipients of the universe's profound knowledge. They hated anyone else who might be correct. Only they knew what the contract actually entitled the parties to and in their eyes all project managers and managing directors were just thick.

Early on Jack suggested to Nigel that maybe he needed help. Of course he said he didn't but after a few heated discussions Nigel brought a young QS in to be interviewed by the two of them and introduced the young man to Jack.

"Good morning. Jeremy this is Jack. He is currently the boss. I am Nigel, the commercial manager and you will work for me and as we know, most of the decisions are sorted by us and we run the real business."

Jeremy, smiled, and nodded understandingly at Nigel's appraisal of Jack's potential short longevity on the job. "Of course Nigel; we always do."

He shook hands and sat down, lounging back in his seat and looking to Jack as if he was about to play a game of Mastermind. Nigel, holding a copy of his new apprentice's CV, opened up the interview. "Looking at this, I see you are not a chartered surveyor. I am of course. I gained my charter from the society as one of the youngest ever granted the honour of being one of the nation's elite. And I ..."

Jeremy interrupted him: "I have an honours and a master's degree in quantity surveying and contract management. Have you?"

"No when I gained my qualifications, and then my charter...of course which you don't have by the way.....degrees were only for people who did not understand the real work we do. They still are pretty worthless in real work I believe. I have carried out arbitrations and I..."

Jeremy interrupted him again. "That's what all the old dinosaurs in the industry think. Modern and intelligent QS's are now qualified to the highest extent. I have studied law and arbitrated upon ..."

Nigel stopped him in in full flow. "I see the only real law you have done is to win the Booker prize for law at your University. I once passed the examinations at my college for the much more relevant contract law qualification of the..."

Jack had had enough of this mutual self-appreciation and narcissism. His time was more precious and valuable. He stopped Nigel in mid-sentence. "Stop for ****'s sake. Just hire him, Nigel. I'm sure you both have enough brain power to sort this tiny piece of our Lord and Saviour's world out. Just go and sort it. Thanks Jeremy."

They both got up, Nigel throwing Jeremy's CV back at him across the desk in disgust but as the two of them left Nigel nodded towards Jack and said to Jeremy, "I was right about him though wasn't I?"

Jeremy gazed back at Jack curiously, nodding his head positively. "You may well be correct. Let's go and I'll show you how to run this business better than it clearly is now."

Yes quantity surveyors were Jack's nemesis - as it proved the next day when Nigel brought him yet another dose of "Do you want the good or the bad news?"

"So Nigel, what's the bad news?"

"This, Jack" and he showed Jack a letter. "It's the answer from Fothergills' QS.. They owe us a couple of hundred grand on the final account and won't pay it. My valuation is correct but their QS won't budge. In fact he's written back today to say we actually owe them money."

"And do we?" Jack asked innocently.

"Of course not! Any judge would agree with my masterful analysis. I've sent fifteen letters destroying his argument completely. He's written fifteen back and this is the latest. Should I write him again showing how wrong he is?"

"How long has this money been owed Nigel?" Jack asked innocently.

"Well, it's a technical and legal point which you will never understand of course, which only chartered surveyors can resolve but I pointed out in letter six, that pursuant to clause number six point three two in article two point seven and subject to interpretation of the specification in the subcontractor's separate contract..."

"Just stop Nigel. Give me an answer I can understand. How long has this dispute been going on and how long have we been waiting for this money?"

"Err...probably about 14 months now," Nigel concluded.

"For God's sake, man! While you two brains of the unknown plant Zog have been debating the rights and wrongs of contract articles and who has the biggest dick or best Booker prize for law, we've been struggling to pay the men, and Norway has being going ******* mental at me over the debtors and cash flow. Give me the file and I'll try to arrange a meeting with the owners and get this sorted between us."

"No you don't need to get involved Jack. It's beyond your experience. It needs a QS letter to go straight back," Nigel spluttered, clearly disturbed that Jack would even think about interfering.

"No it doesn't. Fix up a meeting and let's talk, surely there are some rational people in their place. What about the owner," Jack asked politely?

"Well, KT was sending Ernie's lads down to have a little chat. Two Bats went down with them with his favourite baseball bat in case it got naughty but I managed to persuade Ernie to tell KT that the guy had gone on holiday. So I went down instead and had a meeting with the QS. Sadly I took Jimmy, The Mule, down with me as he'd been in charge of the job at one time and it got a bit heated."

"Oh my God what did that lunatic do now? Garrotte the bastard?" Jack asked, really not wanting to know now. After the hanging episode anything was possible.

"No. Of course not! He just smashed the contract file over the QS's head. The metal rings just cut his nose a bit but he didn't press charges. I think the bastard actually liked the war wound as a battle scar. Mind you he does write a good letter. After this maybe I should ask him to join us?"

Jack sat back and stared at Nigel. Nothing seemed to faze this man. He was indeed flawless and intractable. A master at his trade, Jack was slowly coming to understand how it worked.

His next meeting was with Domino Dan, his company accountant. Dan was so called because his teeth matched a hand of double sixes in dominoes - mostly black with little bits of white. His dress was similar to his mouth, pretty disarranged most mornings. Once when the auditors were in, he had arrived late still hung over and wearing one brown shoe and one black one. Despite his propensity for several beers at lunchtime and many more at night he was a genius with figures according to Nigel. "He knows little about QS'ing or how to run the business like I do. No one could of course. But as you know little about this game and the business he may be of some use to you before KT moves you on. You might learn something from him."

Indeed Jack did learn something. He learnt that the business was what might be described on its last legs. KT had sold him on the fact it needed a breath of fresh air. What Domino Dan revealed was that it really needed the entire year's supply of oxygen from The British Oxygen Group just up the road in Birtley, Tyne and Wear.

This morning's meeting was to determine what lies Jack would report to Stavanger this month in a futile attempt to survive another month. Domino Dan took his comb out his hair, looking puzzled about why it was there, and put it in his back pocket. He leaned over to Jack with yet another spread sheet. Jack could smell the sweet odour of Cameron's Strong-arm beer and cigarettes. Domino Dan smoked about sixty a day it seemed and supped about ten bottles but was as thin as a rake and could knock out a Profit and Loss and Balance Sheet in the time it took him to stagger back from the pub. "Jack," he said, pointing at the red figures at the very bottom, "it looks bad mate but I have a few provisions I can release and the work in progress I'll just fiddle again. Don't tell Nigel, he likes his figures honest. I'm not sure what to do with the debtor days mind. If Nigel had let Two Bats break the biggest debtor's legs, I could have chopped them by half mate."

Jack pondered who Two Bats was and then quickly decided best not to know. He then panicked as he realised he probably worked for him and the nervous tick came back again.

Domino Dan continued his tale of woe, "The van that went missing was found after a ram-raid stuck into the window of an electronic shop in Sunderland. Well, I'm going to have to reduce the fixed assets yet again. The balance sheet will need propping up. But worry not Jack, I can fix that. Big Ed has 'acquired' a dozen welding sets. A mad Scots guy called 'The Big Yin' turned up threatening us with violence as he thinks we 'borrowed' them from a new site he's set up over the river. Ernie had a word, and he's gone away. I'll stick them on the register."

"So, you think we can show a profit then, Dan?" Jack asked with a deep sigh of relief.

"Hell no, Jack! Even I'm not that good mate. But I can reduce the loss to something that might keep you in a job till next month. Maybe you can win some work by then and we can get some cash in. That's your job mate. Mine is to con the auditors yet again and keep you alive another month." And he smiled slightly showing a really good domino hand of fives and threes glistening through his smile

Jack sat looking at his dishevelled financial genius. He wondered if he could persuade him to fiddle it just a little bit more. He shook his head. He'd done that the last two months, time to face the music. But first a beer. "Ok Dan thanks. Get the numbers crunched and give them to me and I'll knock up the monthly report. Fancy a beer?"

"I'll be at my usual place at the bar at twelve Jack. See you there for a few."

And they did.

The day after discussing what to do about the Fothergills' account and drinking himself into a coma with Domino Dan, Jack arrived at the site and the business complex at about 6 am. It had been an icy cold morning with sleet coming down heavily as he drove up the A19 from his haven of security and fresh air in the north Yorkshire moors. As he drove into his allocated parking space he saw KT's large Range Rover already there and a light on in his office in the cabin. He was normally first in so it was obvious that KT had keys to everywhere. He entered his office and KT greeted him with: "Where the **** have you been?"

"It's six o clock, KT. I get here every day about now," Jack answered a little annoyed.

KT hollered across Jack's desk, red in the face, "I've been here since four and walked your night shift. They are doing **** all and some of the lazy ******* clocked off early. And what a mess the place is. No wonder we are ****** and losing money. Get your boots on and follow me!"

And he walked out to site; Jack following behind like a lap dog.

At each work site Jack was shouted at for a messy this, untreated that, welding equipment broken, gas bottles lying half empty, generators still running but no one using them...you name it and it was his fault.

"What the **** have we got a crane on hire for here? No bastard is working here. Wait....let me check the serial number." And he took a material and equipment request form from his suit jacket. "For ****'s sake it's been on hire two months. You are just letting them piss away our money, you daft bastard."

He dragged Jack across miles of barren featureless Teesside desert, arms waving, hands gesticulating and language to frighten Eddy Murphy. Jack's men just observed, shaking their heads; they had seen it all before. Many new bosses had tried but many had fallen on their own, or KT's Viking battle axe and now were burning in Valhalla. They didn't expect this new one would last long.

Ernie arrived. KT shook his hand and Ernie quietly took the Viking aside and they started laughing about something. Jack speculated that maybe it was about another client or subcontractor who had been 'spoken to' when Nigel's millions of letters had failed.

KT shouted over to Jack and pointed at a man walking as slow as a tortoise. Each of his steps, were deliberate and pondering, heading slow and methodically towards his goal, with one small tube of scaffold over his shoulder. "Look at that lazy bastard. You could train a chimp to work faster than him. I'm sure I told you to fire that son of a bitch. Sort this lot out will you - before I do!"

Jack recognised the 'chimp' as Empty Heed. Ernie had told him who he was when he had himself noticed the man take thirty minutes to traverse two hundred yards in front of his office carrying nothing but a wrench. Ernie said they kept him on the books as he was good lad, could be relied on - absolutely no sense or skill but a 'good lad'. And like Big Ed, he had to go missing if and when KT arrived. Obviously this morning they had been caught unawares.

"Come on you. I'll show you where you lose our money," KT shouted across to Jack. In the breaking dawn he lead him over piles of old paint tins, mountains of shot blast grit, mounds of old hoses and dead clients and subcontractors until they reached a wire fence bordering the warm, flowing waters of the Tees. It was warm not because of the ambient temperature but due to chemically-induced exothermic reactions that occurred constantly as the morning effluent from the chemical plants poured into it. The Middlesbrough Gazette wrote that the new Brazilian and Italian football superstars would feel well at home at the new Riverside Stadium given the warmth of the surrounding bathing water in the Tees. Port Clarence was like the Copacabana those days. Mind you the press also said that Emerson and Juninho would be right at home in the local council housing areas of Brambles Farm and Southbank, home from home with the mayhem, drug gangs and rampant football violence they were so familiar with back home: Happy days indeed.

KT picked up an old hessian sack that was hidden in a bunch of weeds. Worryingly for Jack who had to live here, these weeds had been chemically mutated into plants looking suspiciously like Triffids. KT opened the sack and out poured six or seven scaffold fittings.

"See what I told you, pissing away the money!" shouted KT and he took another material request form out of his pocket and pointed to Jack's signature. "See! You ordered two hundred of these last week you son of a bitch. You can **** off. You can send the lads around the site and find me two hundred of these buried in this shite before I'll sign. Come on let's get back."

Jack trudged the lonely and torturous road back to his cabin, constantly berated for the progress, cost and cleanliness of the site. His lads were all looking at him in anticipation of what would happen once he was bent over the desk to be caned by his headmaster.

In fact once back, Jack made a couple of cups of coffee and they sat down to talk. Surprisingly after such a beating by his master, KT had calmed and was talking about life, his new wife and his new home he'd rented in Stavanger. It was quite pleasant but unsettling for Jack who'd expected the roasting to continue. This behaviour was bizarre.

At eight am Nicki arrived and came in with more coffee. KT greeted her warmly and smiled as she left. "You still not screwed her yet? I haven't seen anything on your expenses. There are rumours you might be gay."

"Nope KT, no shagging, and I'm not gay."

The great Viking shrugged his shoulders, got up, shook Jack's hand and said goodbye. Jack sat back and decided it was definitely time to change things.

6
DURHAM CATHEDRAL
THE MAN IN THE VAN

Sometime after many changes

KT was delighted, he turned to his finance director and said:

"I told you he'd come good. I was a bit worried I'd made the wrong decision when he wouldn't use the lads to sort that English subcontractor bastard out, but he's coming on well now. Pity about the figures, I'm sure that Domino Dan is fiddling them, but if Jack keeps firing people, maybe we'll break even."

His tortured and weary finance director just nodded. He knew the consequences of firing anyone who displeased the crazy Viking. Sadly, for KT, this wasn't ninth century Northumberland but a brave new world of peace and democracy, human rights and employment law. So Bjorn had to find the money to pay off the employees who were sacked at a moment's notice and save KT the horrors of being dragged before the employment tribunals. He had being doing that for years. KT never knew that he had a secret pot of money hidden in the depths of his off-balance sheet financing to pay off the victims of the Viking's wrath. But Bjorn had been using that lately mainly to pay off those dismissed by Jack, whose actions gave KT an orgasm every time he sacked one.

Jack had realised early in his tenure that things had to change. KT wanted the project and the new business to succeed and to expand his mega empire across the UK and the world. He needed new people, systems and businesses to do that. His initial run ins with the police, the mafia, the clients, the ambivalence to his leadership and his strange staff and KT's mania about scaffold fittings had made him determined to succeed. So he changed things.

When someone told him to slow down because he was working too hard and might have a heart attack - "Boss, if we have no work, then we have no worries." - he was gone in the morning. Another came perpetually late to his management meetings, eating while Jack was trying to explain the dire circumstances and when remonstrated with said, "Look at these hands, with these I'll never be out of work." The next day he was. Ernie's boss and half the management; all moved on. He even retired Red Tom after he had been found tied to a raft wrapped in bubble wrap floating down The Tees. Jack felt, with a whiff of humanity and compassion, that this was the only nice thing he'd done in months.

He started introducing accredited quality systems and employed people to do this. He recruited specialist managers for each discipline. And he slowly began to turn it all around. Recruitment was a problem though. Because the base they had was really an absolute shit hole and with Ernie and his charming lads and the internecine gang warfare, football violence and general assaults with deadly weapons raging all around the offices, it wasn't a great place to ask normal, career ambitious and sane people to come and work. And obviously he couldn't let them meet KT. So the only way he could recruit people was to interview them remotely and get them pissed, so that they couldn't remember what they had signed up for.

He brought in a proposals manager to help them expand. He recruited him from the competition by dreams of massive expansion, a great future in head office if he wanted in huge palaces in Stavanger and Oslo, massive bonuses if he succeeded and also the benefits of his own unique humanistic leadership. One day he told the victim he might well have shares in the company and become a millionaire. He even allowed his prey to ask questions. "Could I come and see the site and my new office?"

"Of course but not quite yet as we're in the process of relocating and buying other businesses with much better facilities. Just sign here and we'll get you on board as soon as possible. Can you manage another pint?" And a bit later…"I'd like a taxi to take this gentleman home now; he's feeling a bit tried and weary."

Yes. Jack used this same interview technique, his drinking prowess and his sales skills and wallet, to get on board some really good potential staff from the competition and also his clients. Most were shall we say surprised at what greeted them.

The proposal's manager looked around his office and the site and thought he'd been transported to the set of *Alien 3*. After one week of sitting in his porta cabin office he couldn't stand the smell anymore so he raised the courage to ask Jack could he change.

"Like **** you can. There's no smell man. It's just the Tees. Grow some balls and get on with it." Jack was learning a new style of 'demonic empowerment' leadership from KT.

Jack did go to Nigel who said he'd get Big Ed to have a look at what was causing the stench. Big Ed duly arrived and tore up the floor and the tiles in the ceiling and was so pleased when he dragged a putrid rat out of its place of concealment. "I've been looking for that for ages since it ran across Nicki's desk into your room, mate. It used to piss in the coffee jar we think. Just as well it's dead now then eh..."

The proposals man just sat at his desk and wondered what he'd done.

Jack entered, oblivious to the smashed ceiling and floor and Big Ed holding the decaying rat. "Pleased you're here Ed. What's that old caravan doing over the other end of the yard behind the blast sheds?"

"Oh, well Jack...you'd best ask Nigel," Ed said sheepishly, obviously hiding something.

"I'm asking you," Jack repeated.

"Oh, well, err...it's one of Ernie's. He has let one of Empty Heed's relatives live in it for a while because their lass has thrown him out."

"For ****'s sake. I hired that dodgy bugger from Hartlepool to try to get BS5750 approval and actually employed an HSE man for once and we set up a shanty town for the homeless reeking of bubonic plague in our bloody yard. Tell Ernie to move it off site." And as he remembered the next visit was due from his personal Beelzebub, " I want you to live in the bugger and go missing next Wednesday as KT's coming."

Big Ed ran out, rat dangling from his fat hand.

"Now then; how many tenders have you done this week and have we got any orders?" Jack asked his new proposals man.

"We've had no tenders in this week Jack and no orders. Sorry but seems it's a bit dead out there."

"Oh well, you better check with Stavanger. They're chasing a couple of big ones in Scotland and in Yarmouth. They want us to bid with them for a big ship in Holland too," Jack said and turning to the empty white board on the wall, took a marker pen and drew one line horizontally along it. "Leave the mark on the board please. It's a management technique I'm trying out. I think KT will love it," Jack left the stinking room smiling.

Nine weeks later the proposal's man sat head in hands. It was nearly Christmas and he was reflecting on his last months with Jack and his deranged team. He had survived both Jack and *The Boro* and he prayed and hoped his Christmas box in the form of a bid acceptance would come in the envelope he had just received from the client. His life depended on it. He looked up at his white board and moaned again. Each Friday Jack had come into his office and asked one question. "Had he won them any work?" at the negative answer, Jack had drawn another line on the board. It took him five weeks to realise what he was drawing and today he knew that Jack had only one more line to draw and he was history.

He opened the letter and jumped up in glee. He ran letter in hand through Nicki's room and into Jack's. "We've got the job Jack. We've got the bastard man; at last! Happy Christmas!"

"Well done son. Well done. Guess I can wipe that Hangman off the board now." Jack said smiling as he rubbed the board clean. "Let's go and start the party."

They joined the rest of the small management team in the porta cabin board room. Jack was introducing his latest recruit (hostage) that he hoped to give his version of a Teesside Stockholm syndrome to. He too had been captured by the same interview process that caught his proposals' manager. That was lies, statistics and gallons of beer. This victim had woken up one day later in his darling wife's arms with a signed contract of employment in his hands. He had left a great job with a client for Jack's tales of wonder and a golden future on the banks of the bonny Tees. Jack had asked him to come in today for his first visit to the horrors of the site, on Christmas Eve, before he joined officially in January. The man was visibly shaken.

He was introduced to The Bonny Lad; a middle aged large bodied man, who always dressed well. Even his overalls were ironed and creased and he was wearing an obvious blonde styled wig. He too had been lured away from a lucrative and important position as a respected operations manager by Jack. He was so impressed with dreams of riches beyond his ken that he brought his whole team with him, including his right-hand commercial man, The Wee Man. The Wee Man was exactly what he was named, Wee. A small compact muscular Northern Irishman with plenty of attitude; like a Jack Russell, you wouldn't mess with him. He drank Bushmills

Whiskey by the gallon which didn't help the Russell temper. Nigel's leg and huge ego had been bitten several times already.

The Bonny Lad was famous across the Industry as a hard man with great experience. He was also famous for a long memory. It seemed that, just as in *Fawlty Towers*, where *'you couldn't mention the war'*, around The Bonny Lad you couldn't mention his syrup. Anyone who did was fired or bitten to death later on by the Wee Man.

Even Ernie and his lads respected The Bonny Lad and despite ripping the piss out of anyone and anything, even they dared not mention the wig. Jack was told of guys who had mentioned it on past jobs starting work on a new site and when they realised that The Bonny Lad was the boss, they just packed their tool bags and left before he sacked them. The Bonny Lad's vengeance knew no boundaries and the Wee Man's bite was rabid but Jack was chuffed he had persuaded them to join him. Like all the other professionals he'd got both him and The Wee Man legless and sold on his plans. They were the best at their trade and good company at that.

The proposal's manager was gnawing on a leg of pheasant with a can of beer in his hand. He just looked at the menagerie around him. The new boy was talking to Nigel. He stood out like a spare male organ dressed immaculately in a three-piece suit and tie as no one had told him it was casual. The proposal manager could hear Nigel telling him 'Of course Jack thinks he runs this, but I'm the one who knows everything about the business. He'll move on soon. You and I will get on well once you report to me."

The Bonny Lad was talking to the new Quality Control man from Hartlepool, Dodgy Tom. "Why haven't we got BS5750 Tom?"

"Please don't tell anyone I'm here. KT doesn't know. Jack hasn't told him. KT hates accreditation companies. I have to hide with Big Ed in that queer old tramp's caravan behind the blast sheds every time the Norgie turns up. Jack is hoping we'll get the accreditation and KT won't even know"

The proposal man shook his head and shuddered as he remembered the caravan incident. It still gave him nightmares. He had reached the 'only one arm and two legs left' stage of his personal hangman motivation and had stayed behind late one evening to finish his last chance of survival and get out a tender price to the client by midnight. As he left to drive his weary way up home to his family and sanity, he saw a few of the lads congregating near the blast pens. Curious and thinking he'd impress Jack by his site leadership he walked over to investigate.

What he saw haunted him for life.

Empty Heed was trying to pull a body from the door of the caravan. The body was appeared to be jammed in the doorway. As he approached nearer he saw the backside was a woman's or looked like a woman's but it was massive and Empty Heed was pulling away at it with his foot jammed against the caravan wall. Everyone was howling with laughter. Then with a horrible slurping sound the woman's body came oozing out of the door onto the hard ground, swearing like a trooper at Empty Heed. She was indeed huge and with a face like a bulldog chewing a wasp.

Then at the door, the proposals man saw a hideous apparition. A scrawny thin looking body appeared; hair lank and covering his face and a huge dirty beard with old wood shavings or food in it, he couldn't tell. His hands were gesticulating and the shocked manager could see the finger nails were inches long and fifthly dirty. And mother of all horrors, he was naked except for his dirty grey white underpants.

The proposals man ran and ran back to his car. After a drive home that he couldn't remember, his wife gave him a large whisky and he vowed to resign in the morning. However once sober again his bank overdraft outweighed his fears and he got up and drove the twenty-five miles to work and sought out Big Ed to ask him what the hell was that dream he'd had last night.

Big Ed explained. "Oh that was The Man in the Van. Empty Heed's cousin. I couldn't turn him out like Jack said the other week man. Ernie would knack me. We have just kept Jack away from there every time he comes on site. And he's been out most days seeing the client or getting pissed with these new managers he's hiring. The lass you saw last night was another one of The Man in Van's girlfriends he brings in on a night. She was so fat she stuck in the door and The Man in the Van couldn't drag her in. She would have stayed there all night if Empty Heed hadn't been on nightshift. It seems The Man in the Van is some catch in Southbank."

"Jesus Christ almighty, a good catch! He's manky, man. He's bloody minging," shouted the proposal's manager, clearly shocked.

"Aye he is. But he's got a caravan and the lasses' like that. They think he has money. Don't tell Jack will you? He's okay man, does nobody any harm and he's one of Ernie's lads. You know what I mean?"

The proposal's manager just sat gnawing on his pheasant and remembering when life was so different back at his other company. Maybe Santa would bring him a P45. ....They were eating pheasant because The Bonny Lad had brought his fire-proofing manager with him. The Bonny Lad told Jack that this man was the best shot in the country and hunted day and night killing furry and feathered animals. So Jack had ordered some of his deceased animals for their Christmas Eve piss up. The Mule had knocked up a stainless-steel barbecue, from material he swore was scrap, and they had duly roasted pheasants, partridge, a whole leg of venison and what Jack believed, given the skinned size, was a dead badger.

Jack noticed a certain coldness about the relationship between The Mule and the Bonny Lad and asked his *paranoid android* about it. Nigel responded, "I knew you'd have to come to ask me about that. I know everything…"

"Yes, yes Nigel, just get on with it man,"

Nigel continued plainly miffed. "Well it seems they both were on the same platform offshore. The Mule had been suspended and had just got back on board after being not required back."

"Oh Christ! What did he do this time? Brain the offshore installation manager with a spanner?" Jack exclaimed rhetorically.

"No. He just tried to do what he does, make people laugh. He's one of the old school you know, one of the old boys. Not one of these graduates or business school know all's. Such people and me are much better…" Nigel was in his glory again.

"Just tell me the story without the angst man," Jack said getting frustrated.

"Well if you wish. The Mule just caused a bit of stir that's all. He opened the door to the radio room and told the radio operator that the OIM had said the radio operator was to contact his own family urgently. The anxious radio operator asked The Mule what the message was. The Mule just got both hands and drummed them on the table as if he was playing a set of bongos. Of course the radio operator went crazy and chased him all over the platform."

"Why?" Jack naively asked.

"Because he was African and black as the Ace of Spades," Nigel replied haughtily.

Jack immediately thought, *now a bloody racism law suit for Bjorn to find the money for!* He suddenly realised that he was beginning to stop panicking at the Mule's behaviour. It now worried him *that he may well be falling into the next Circle of Hell; just when he thought he'd paid The Ferryman to take his boat out of the last circle.* He decided to play the game. "Oh dear, I guess that didn't go down well. Anyway what about the Bonny Lad?"

"The Mule got a fishing rod and hook and line and waited on the deck above the Bonny Lad. When the Bonny Lad took his helmet off to wipe his brow The Mule lowered the fishing hook and then yanked of his syrup and wound it up to him. The Bonny Lad chased him all over the bloody platform to get it back. I don't think he'll forget it."

Jack shook his head. Yet another thing to worry about. Maybe he'd send The Mule to Norway; he'll get on well with KT and his lot.

The Mule interrupted Jack's nightmare shouting. "Come on let's all go and see Ernie and the boys in The Navigation. They've headed back over the border to have the piss up you paid for Jack; there's strippers on."

Foolishly Jack decided to go. His wife was picking him up for Durham Cathedral's Festival of Nine Lessons at 3 pm. They went every year on Christmas Eve with their kids. He'd only stop half an hour just to show his face and Ernie had been good these last couple of months. He foolishly thought he had made progress with the lads.

The Navigation was close to where most of his employees came from; a rough pub in an even rougher area but good beer. Normally the landlord and his psychotic clientele had been okay with Jack because he knew *the lads*.

As Jack pulled up outside, a couple of men were carried out and dumped on the street. He shook his head and turned to his brand-new victim, his commercial man in the three-piece suit, who looked seriously worried. "Don't worry son. They're just letting off hard earned steam. Wait till you join us in January, man. They'll all be back in the saddle and working hard. We're going to show them all how professional we are. The best in the country and you'll be there with us. Great eh?"

As another body was carried out his new manager's terror grew and he smiled insanely at Jack and nodded his head.

They entered and were greeted by Ernie at the door, overseeing the ejection of the bodies. Noticing the new boy's anxiety he pulled his gonads up with his left hand and shaking the poor man's hand with his right, clarified the surrounding mayhem. "It's just a bit of bother with the boys from our competition. They started to take the piss. Can't have that Jack can we?"

"Certainly not Ernie: We are the lads eh!" Jack put his arm around the huge man's shoulders. Nothing bothered him now; he'd seen it all he thought.

"Have you come to see the strippers Jack?"

"No, mate. Haven't got time. I'm off to the Cathedral with our lass and kids soon. Just come to buy you and the lads a Christmas drink."

"No you're not, Jack. The lads are real pleased you paid for all this. We haven't had this before and you've looked after us. We all know that mate. Come on, have a beer on us."

They walked to the bar. Pure mayhem and debauchery seemed to be coming from the singing end where the first stripper was already performing. Time to get out Jack thought; he loved a peaceful family Christmas Eve and this was not heading that way at all.

His new man just stared vacantly into the crowd.

They stood at the bar while Ernie bought the drinks. Well it was a free bar Jack knew, but what the hell, it was the thought that counted. Ernie kept introducing the lads to the new boy. The men came and all thanked Jack for what he'd done for them. Whether they did it off their own bat or under threat from Ernie mattered not at all, he was enjoying the moment.

"This is Two Bats," Ernie introduced the large hulk to the new manager. "He's called that because he jumped on a bus full of Newcastle supporters on his own armed with two baseball bats and battered most of them."

The new boy gulped and said hello.

"This is Mick the Merciless, "Ernie said again as another strange looking, man approached. "He'll take anybody on coz his heed is full of zinc metal. He actually likes the stuff when he sprays it, never bothers with a mask…..hah hah."

The new boy just grinned nervously at a twitching Mick the Merciless.

"This is my brother. He's top boy in The Frontline and runs most of the doors for me. He'll look after you mate, even if you are a Mackem….hah hah hah." Someone resembling Goliath, with a face you could chop sticks with, crushed the novice's hand and grunted: "******** mackems."

Jack was watching, chuckling at remembering how he had felt the same all those months ago; wondering which asylum he had been shipped too. Soon his new protégée would get used to it and then he'd have him under the same spell he'd fallen under and hopefully all his new team would too.

He looked at his watch and told Ernie his wife was arriving soon and he'd have to go. Ernie took his hand and shook it hard. Then handed over a Christmas card. "Here's a present from the lads for you and her."

"Oh Ernie: They didn't have to do that man," Jack said.

"Just take it or I'll batter you - you ****," shouted over Two Bats, playfully whacking the new man over the back with his baseball bat. Curious Jack thought, *he still carries one around, even on Christmas Eve*.

"OK, thanks lads," and waving the card in the air, he left the pub. The new manager helplessly watched him go, pleadingly as if he'd been abandoned in Sodom and Gomorrah: Which of course he was.

As they drove towards the sanctity of Durham, Jack sat in the passenger seat feeling satisfied that he was changing things for the good. And he loved a good carol service. He never went to church normally but liked the ambience of Christmas Eve at the Cathedral. He felt at peace; free from the purgatory of work; Christmas at last.

"Can I open your Christmas card daddy please?" his lovely innocent ten-year old daughter asked, full of the Christmas spirit and excitement that youth brings.

"Yes of course sugar," he answered turning around and handing her the card he'd placed on the dashboard.

"That was nice of your men to give you a card. I thought you said they were hard men," said his wife, driving past the multi coloured gasses emitted by Billingham ICI.

"They are. But I think I'm changing them. I think they might have bought a book token or something for me and maybe a gift voucher for you or something. "

"That's kind," she said, coughing, wondering where the green smoke crossing the A19 had come from.

"Daddy: what are these clear plastic packet things in the card? Oh! The powder's white in them. And Daddy, urgh….it doesn't taste like Sherbet."

Jack screeched.

7
ROTTERDAM
ABDUL THE TURK

Sometime after Christmas…

The unconscious man flew out of the cabin into the mud of the fabrication yard, quickly followed by a large body at the door shouting: "Get your ******* arse back to work. Don't you **** with Jack ever again."

The Dutch client looked down at the body and then the mud that the prostrate body had splashed all over his nice new Gucci suit and handmade, polished leather shoes. He stepped over the body and turned to Jack.

"I like that. Looks like your supervision have got a grip of the work on this site. I like a disciplined workforce." He nodded positively and smiled at Ernie who was standing in the doorway looking a bit shocked at nearly killing someone in front of his boss and someone obviously important at that.

Ernie grabbed his balls, bowed his head and apologised. "Sorry Jack. It's the metal sprayer who told you to **** off yesterday. He'll not do that again boss. I just gave him a little slap so he should wake up and be back to work in the spray pen soon."

Jack looked at Ernie, then at his client who seemed delighted. His initial reaction at the violence was anger and frustration that *here we go again; a client is sent by the crazy Norwegian to be impressed enough to give them a hundred-million-dollar contract and one of my lunatics knocks out someone on site and splashes his million-dollar suit.* But now seeing the client was pleased he felt a warm glow inside. Ernie had done that for him; he didn't have to do that, but he'd done it just for him. At last, he was getting respect, and his changes must be working.

And the client did like it; and awarded them a big contract.

KT was delighted and invited Jack to see the client in Rotterdam with him for a contract kick off and general piss up celebration. They headed off the next day to the dockyard where KT had an on-going large drilling rig repair job. As they drove from their company house in Hellevoetsluis, past the huge Pernis Dutch Shell refinery towards the yard KT was surprisingly talkative and positive to Jack who was beginning to feel wanted and needed at last.

The deranged Viking explained his dilemma in the dockyard. "Since you've been wasting my time on vacation the job has gone to rat shit. Ernie sent a lot of his lads from the North East over to fix the job. I fired the site manager and sent The Mule. If anyone could get it sorted it would be him."

Jesus wept, Jack thought. The Mule in Holland! They'd all end up in the International War Crimes Court in The Hague charged with genocide.

"Problem was the lads couldn't get on with the locals. The wacky baccy and booze every night didn't go down well and they all ended up either in the slammer or run off the yard by the Dutch for being pissed and beating up the client's supervisors. The Mule found them a nice place to stay away from normal people and the wacky baccy - in a holiday camp near the dam - and we shipped them in and out every day. It was going well."

"What's the problem then KT?" Jack asked as he looked out into the chemical wasteland of Rotterdam and felt homesick for Middlesbrough.

"The rig owner shipped in a team of American welders and The Mule, the daft twat, told them he'd found a great spot for them to lodge; our Holiday camp. Well, you know what happened, first time one of the Yanks piped up about being better welders than us and how great the US of A was; a mass battle broke out."

Jack was becoming wiser and asked what he thought was a sensible question. "So? Random extreme violence; that's normal for our lads and it wasn't on site, so what's it got to do with work?"

"Problem was the Yard owners had put the rig owners' families up in the holiday camp for a week's holiday. The main rig man's family were there. They were having dinner in the clubhouse when the fight kicked off. It might have been okay but when the wife tried to intervene she was hit over the head and bashed unconscious with a sunbed by The Mule. The kids are now in counselling in Amsterdam. For ****'s sake I told The Mule to watch the clock like his psychiatrist told him to after the last episode. He is supposed to sit back, deep breaths, and imagine a ticking clock before launching his temper." KT sat shaking his large head and whispering to an unknown person in his tortured mind. "Tick tock watch the clock...tick tock...watch the clock. Why didn't he just watch the clock? Just tick tock; that was all."

Jack felt as if he should give him a hug but coming to his senses realised Vikings don't do hugs. "I guess The Mule has been fired then and the lads sent home?"

"**** no! The Mule apologised. We sent his psychiatric report to the company and blamed it on too much work-related stress. You know the Dutch don't you? They love all that shit. Counselling, employee relations, European directives, free love, you name it those Dutch take to it. Hell, we are only working a thirty-hour week there to meet their caring employer mission. I priced the ******** job at sixty hours for the lads and now we are ********. That's why we are going down to meet someone who will give me lots of Turks to do the work. Seems the Turk we are meeting can supply as many as we want and he can sort the work hours laws out. We are meeting The Mule there…I've fired the men mind, sent them back to Ernie. He's using them as security now on the doors across Newcastle and Sunderland. I knew they'd come to good use. Should have used real welders I guess."

Jack should have been surprised and shocked at this and six months before he would have been, but sadly he thought, this is it; this is my life now.

They met The Mule in a café near the yard. He was sitting with a swarthy looking man, clearly of Middle Eastern background. The Mule was in great spirits, clearly comfortable in KT's company. Jack imagined them both leaping off Viking long boats onto Bamburgh Castle beach in Northumberland and KT cleaving the sunbathing holiday makers skulls open with his double-bladed axe while The Mule was braining them with their own sunbeds…he shook the vision from his head and spoke to the Turkish gentleman. "How many men can you source Abdul?"

"As many as you want, sir."

"That's good buddy," said The Mule, "I need about thirty to start on Friday; they'll have to work all weekend to catch up. Can you sort that?"

"Of course, sir."

"Magic: I'll take them out on the piss after work to get to know them. Where do they drink?"

The Byzantine body shop supplier looked shocked and hurt. He turned to KT, He looked first at KT then at Jack and finally back at

The Mule grimacing: "Sir; we are Muslim, followers of the one prophet. It is an insult to offer us drink."

The Mule's face changed from his beaming mischievous one to his, *'oh dear here we go again'* one and said through closed lips. "Well, I'll not ******** offer then. You Ayrab ****s can buy your own beer if that's what your prophet wants."

The Turk leapt up, his coffee spilling over the table, clearly at breaking point. "We are not Arabs and we do not drink. It is forbidden."

"You don't drink! For ****'s sake man everyone drinks…and don't shout at me, you son of a bitch."

KT intervened. He put his hand on The Mule's knee, holding him tight. He whispered into his ear. "My friend: Tick tock; remember…tick tock."

The Turk looked hurt and puzzled and enquired: "Tick tock? I don't understand…"

Jack butted in, trying to defuse the Mule induced bomb. "Abdul, neither do I. He lives in Middlesbrough. It's a difficult language to understand. Please sit down and let's finish our business shall we."

And they did.

They left The Mule and Abdul chatting and in the end apparently getting on like a house on fire, Abdul even asking The Mule to visit his house for a celebratory meal. In the car on the way to the airport Jack found himself hoping the Turk's wife didn't have a sunbed in their humble home.

8
ZURICH
GOLDFINGER

A bit later that day

They arrived at Amsterdam's massive Schiphol airport to meet KT's Dutch client, Rudi, in the KLM executive lounge. Their flight was delayed so they settled into drinking far too much of the free and gratis liquor with KT and Rudi enjoying reminiscing about their past exploits.

"Do you remember when we took Jani from Anotherstahn Oil to Switzerland skiing KT?" Rudi asked after one more large Scotch and water.

"Of course: what a week we had. I think I spent about ten grand on the dinner one night. Jan could drink and only the best. The Lafitte cost more than Jack's salary…hah hah."

KT howled with laughter along with his immensely rich client. Jack just sat and weakly smiled, looking down at his scuffed Marks and Spencer's shoes while the two millionaires talked about things he could only dream about.

Rudi, recalling a small stakes game poker continued, "I don't know how I lost the Ferrari. I think the Russian bastard cheated. Jani gave the car keys to one of his lackeys to take away. Any idea if he took it home or stayed there in Switzerland?"

KT said "I think he left it at the lodge. I took him skiing next winter and he arrived in a Ferrari. I don't think he'd drive all the way across the Caucasus and Steppes when he has a private jet. He flew me in it to Monaco one time all the way from Baku."

The Flying Dutchman added more unbelievable incidents to the mix. "I had to take him and the minister to bloody Phuket one week. Remember you lent us the yacht? No idea how many girls we shipped in from Bangkok. The minister preferred the boys though. Jani said it was because he was from Siberia. There is little else to do in the winter. Hah hah."

"Bit like Tromso then. It's reindeer up there they fancy. Hah hah" laughed KT.

Jack sat listening, unable to contribute much to their high roller chat. He reflected that they must trust him though to talk so openly.

Maybe he would like this job after all. The booze flowed, fuelling talk of mega deals, gold bars, luxury cars and political influence until they realised their flight had actually been cancelled.

"Oh shit," Rudi exclaimed when he was told by a pretty KLM waitress. "It looks like we will have to book in here in Amsterdam. I'm sick of this place mind you. I feel up for a change."

"It's a pity to end the party, Rudi. Can't we go somewhere fun?"

Rudi was staring at the departure screen and suddenly stood up and looked more closely. He swallowed yet another Scotch and turning to his fellow travellers said: "There's a flight in one hour. Let's go to Zurich. We can go see my gold."

And sure enough after a drunken night in the best hotel in Zurich they were standing outside a grey, unremarkable building in the financial district. The locked doors were of polished hard-wood and the brass plate on the wall had just the name of the establishment on it. The door opened and a small, very well dressed, elderly Swiss gentleman opened the door. He greeted Rudi with professional courtesy and invited them into the heart of the building. "It is so good to see you again sir. Will the gentleman be accompanying you to the vault? He spoke in German - Rudi was fluent in six languages.

"Yes, Her Schneider, they will. Can we use English as my two friends have little German?"

The banker took them through a security process and down to a side room near a large vault. "Please wait here sir. I will have your deposit brought in for you to view."

They sat down around a nice mahogany table and waited. A few minutes later Herr Schneider arrived through the door followed by a security guard pulling a small trolley. On the trolley were a pile of gold bars. He placed them in the middle of the room and left. Herr Schneider put his arms to his chest in a satisfied way and said, "Please take your time sir. If you need anything press the button. I will close the door now. Thank you."

Jack sat staring dumbfounded at the stack of gleaming gold bars. He had only seen anything like this in movies like *'Goldfinger'* after the evil villain had robbed Fort Knox of all of America's gold. At any moment he expected *Oddjob*, the Korean bodyguard with the killer steel bowler hat to run in.

Rudi and KT just smiled and looked at Rudi's millions.

It was Rudi who broke the silence. "Well that was all I wanted to see. Let's head back to Glasgow and Jack, you can tell me on the plane how you are going to build my ship."

9
TYNESIDE
MICK THE REINDEER SLAUGHTERER

Time has moved on…..

"He's boiling a reindeer's heed in the lad's Burco boiler, man."

The man facing Jack as he sat in his office on the River Tyne looked clearly stressed. Jack wasn't. He really didn't care anymore about little things like reindeer's heads in staff tea urns. This was just another day in his tortured life and one which was unlikely to give him as much grief as the last had three days in Middlesbrough had.

Nigel had entered his office and as usual he said: "Do you want the bad news?"

Jack, who had by now given up the will to live with Nigel just said, "Yes, please."

Nigel looking so pleased at being able to spoil his boss's day and explained, "Interpol and the local old bill have just arrested two of our lads on site. They are alleged to have killed someone in Amsterdam. Of course Ernie says they didn't. Oh and by the way, Ernie has had a bit of bother with one of our vans in Southbank on his way in to work this afternoon. Seems the guy who killed the head gangster in *The Boro*, thinks Ernie has been talking about him. He's just got out of Durham jail, saw the van parked up and bashed it with a hammer."

"Just another day in Southbank," said Jack gloomily. "What's so tragic about that? It's insured." And then panicking; "Isn't it?"

"Oh yes. I always insure everything at the same time. As you know I manage all of those day to day things you can't be bothered with but which are so important to actually keep…"

"Oh shut the **** up Nigel." Jack was long chewed with the self-adulation stuff. "What's the real bad news? A bashed van by a lunatic resident of this place, well that's trivial isn't it? A normal day in this Teesside Beirut. I've just lost two welders to the International terrorist squad so nothing much can harm us surely?"

"Well, after the van was bashed, Ernie came out of the shop he was in and saw him with the hammer and an almighty scrap took place. They say it was like the fight in *'The Quiet Man';* John Wayne versus Victor Mclaghan. They fought up and down the high street.

In the end Ernie had the better of him, but the baddie fell into the butcher's shop and grabbed a huge boning knife and really came after him. Luckily Ernie's brother had been in the shop with Ernie so he'd run to our van and got one of the baseball bats out of it...'

'As you would', Jack thought.

"...and threw it to Ernie. Well, a baseball bat versus knife? A bit like The Duke, the Yank, goodie - versus Irishman, boxer, baddie, in the movie: so the bat won."

Jack stared at his commercial manager. This was not the bad news. More like a normal day shopping in Southbank.

Nigel continued in his Eeyore manner. "Well Jack, the real problem is that our bad guy has told the world he's coming on site to kill Ernie."

"That's okay, man. He has to get past security and the lads can sort him surely?" Jack asked, feeling a bit happier in the knowledge that his site contained more than its fair share of psychotic madmen.

"Well; the problem is a large car has just pulled up outside Ernie's cabin. The security must know them or the men have paid security off. They've opened the boot and it's full of guns," said Nigel with more than a hint of satisfaction in his voice.

"Jesus Christ almighty! Why haven't you phoned the police?" howled Jack.

"It's okay Jack. Ernie is out now talking to them. It seems they're his mates and maybe his guns. Everything should be fine now."

"It should be fine? Okay? This is a construction site for ****'s sake not the Los Angeles Hood. Let me sort these bastards out!" and Jack ran out of the office.

Ernie was stood talking to his 'mates', one of whom was showing him a hand gun. Big Ed was there too and Jack assumed they'd dug them up from his poor wife's rose bed.

"Hi Jack. The lads just popped in to help out with the bit of bother I've had. No worries mate. We'll sort it." Ernie shouted as Jack came hurrying towards them, closely followed by his minder, Nigel.

"Ernie man! You can't let the lads come on here with weapons, man. I'll get locked up. And how the hell did they get on anyway?" Then thinking, *why worry about the security guards, that's the client's problem*, "Don't answer that. I don't want to know."

Ernie grabbed his scrotum, hunched his huge shoulders and bowed his head a bit. "Sorry boss. They'll go now. They just came in case. I didn't want anything to upset you here on site so I asked them to help make sure you weren't disturbed…or the job. We'd have sorted it behind the blast sheds, out of the way of the work." Turning to the two monsters with the open boot of guns he added "Cheers lads. Take these back to Big Ed's and bury them again. I think he'll get the message now from his spy mates here."

The boot was closed, hands were shaken and they left in a cloud of dust. Jack looked around and could see no client representatives or anyone who would shop him, so he decided best leave well alone. Interpol had just left for ****'s sake and he really didn't want another incident on the books. "Ernie man, please don't bring the feuds and vendettas onto site. I know it wasn't your fault but I can't have guns or the lads causing mayhem here. Do like you always do, do it in *the Boro* or '*over the water*'. Not on my site!"

"Alright boss. No worries, I'll sort it all out. You don't have to worry about a thing. I'd better get back to the boys on that stainless-steel vessel. They've finished the NDT now. See you tonight at the site piss up in the Bongo?"

"Err…okay, maybe. Yes, maybe when I've sorted out the report to Stavanger." He was still reeling with the madness of it all. He turned to go back the sanctuary of his office.

"I wouldn't go to Bongo tonight Jack," advised Nigel.

"Why not?"

"Well, after today everyone in *the Boro* will know there'll be a reckoning and where else but the Bongo for all the crazies to meet. They're in there most nights anyway."

Jack looked up across at his nemesis and said, "Thanks Nigel." *Maybe you are looking after my arse after all.* He would give the Club International Bongo a miss. He liked the Bongo. He'd been there a few times with the Bonny Lad and the Wee Man and always enjoyed it. And he had got to know the owner cum chief bouncer Abdillahi, the man with the hat and the stick, who had created his own inclusive nightclub after being barred from too many London clubs for being black. Indeed The Bongo was very inclusive, often containing the likes of Ernie and his lads from the other side of the river, and the lads '*over the border*' and all their arch enemies too.

Anyone who was anyone in *the Boro*, paid homage to the 'man with the stick and the hat'.

So Jack finally took Nigel's advice for once and now he was looking at a man upset over a boiled reindeer's head. Nothing at all compared to Interpol, grievous bodily harm and arms smuggling.

"I'm sure it was just a roe deer's head, Ralphie. You know Mick boils the flesh off to get the skull and horns for a trophy. They're fresh when he boils them so no worry about disease. There are no reindeer in Northumberland, mate, so don't worry about Santa's sleigh this year." As soon as he said it he realised he was now trapped in a matrix of madness, justifying a crazy man shooting furry critters and then bringing them to work, skinning them and boiling them in company equipment supplied to boil water for human consumption with absolutely no regard for workforce health and safety. And Jack justifies it as normal behaviour, treating an employee, who rightly blows the whistle on it with a David Attenborough lecture – yes, he'd finally made it…he was one of the lads.

And the man in front of his desk was one of his favourites. He'd recruited him to sort out the Tyneside work and he'd done a great job. Dedicated and keen but hard enough to keep control of the maniacs who worked for him.

Jack chuckled thinking about the reindeer. The week before he'd received a letter from the landlords up there on the Tyne that he'd been 'rearing peacocks in the offices', a breach of his lease and a health and safety issue from which he must desist. Forthwith. This was a direct result of Ralphie complaining that the reindeer slaughterer, Mick, had peacocks on his desk. Jack had had to point out to his outraged site manager that they weren't peacocks but pheasants, and didn't his last company allow their employees to butcher stuff in their offices?

Then there was last Monday morning when Ralphie was in front of him trying to explain why he'd been locked up all Saturday night in an Edinburgh prison cell. "I'm sorry Jack, I know you sent me up there to sort the lads out and keep them out of jail again but it just got a bit out of hand. All my fault: I shouldn't have done it and I've let you down, boss. You know I would never do that unless it was serious," pleaded the distraught man.

"I know, Ralphie. Big Dan told me the whole story, mate. But I sent you to make sure we got the job finished man, and now I'm facing a week's liquidated damages. You should have kept them out of jail this time. You know that."

"Ah kna that Jack. I'll go back up tonight and we'll get it done by Wednesday. I'll get the lads to work two shifts and I'll not sleep. I'll gan now."

"Ok mate. Get your arse up there and keep them daft Geordie bastards out on the job this time: And yourself!"

"Thanks Jack. I'll not let ya down, mate." And off he'd gone.

Jack chuckled again because he'd sent Ralphie up in the first place only because his workforce had caused mayhem in a pub outside the docks and battered half the local Scottish hoodlums to death. They'd spent two nights in the slammer and Big Dan, his operations manager, had had to bail them out with the petty cash. Jack had lost a weekend's progress and that was the real disaster so he bollocked Ralphie for his lads' misdemeanours, Ralphie had promised him so sincerely that he would personally go up to make sure the lads didn't cause any further bother and look what came of that. Sadly, they went back to the same pub, where the local hard men had congregated to take revenge and even the bouncers had taken sides against them. Ralphie had made all the lads promise on pain of death that they would cause no trouble and was standing at the bar when a bouncer came up and called him a '*black bastard*'. Now Ralphie was black, possibly the only black man in Sunderland, so he'd grown up hard and very handy with his fists to say the least and he duly knocked the bouncer out. When the next one came he got the same treatment. Cue a mass brawl with his lads jumping in to protect him and fight the battle of Flodden field all over again, jail the result for them all. But the worst thing for Jack, who had grown more like KT every day in his indifference to human slaughter and his focus on profit - the job didn't get done and he'd lost KT money again!

Compared to all that today's incident of liquidated reindeer was far less stressful than liquidated Scotsmen or liquidated damages.

After the lecture, Ralphie went off to watch '*Life of Mammals*' and Jack relaxed, watching the Tyne flow past his office window. The company had bought a few more businesses over his last year there and also moved into other overseas territories. KT had given Jack much more responsibility to run the resulting major projects adding the major bonus to his life of taking much more time away from the madness of Teesside.

What he should however have learned by now, was that Stavanger or Newcastle, Aberdeen or Humberside, Great Yarmouth or Rotterdam, Esbjerg or Baku, Doha, or Singapore, you name it and it had 'the lads' in it. He couldn't get away from them.

As the Tyne rolled inexorably on past him, he dreamed of days gone by when he was young, out of Hell and sane. Relatively speaking.

10

TEESIDE

BEANO TOM

Before KT…

Jack sat looking at the Tyne thinking how he'd got here. Once upon a time he had dreams; he believed he'd change the world. Now he was trying to pacify a man, telling him how reindeer's heeds and pheasants were just part of God's great plan, and not a reason to get over-excited. He managed people who gave him greetings cards full of cocaine and shoved people who upset them through the wheel abrader and shot blasted their legs. Interpol and the Serious Crime Squad now had him in their sights. He was probably a named criminal on the FBI most wanted list. And he was a man with more degrees than a thermometer who'd had a successful career until he decided to move back North. *How bad was that for a move?* He shivered. Dear God, why didn't he listen to the chief executive who told him once he'd gone back, he'd never be able to come to the expensive South again. He drifted back to the horror of that first day in his new job.

"Have you met Hugh yet? I don't think he knows you," said the stocky lad from Seaham Harbour after they had been introduced that first day in the chemical wonderland that was Imperial Chemical Industries.

"Err, no. Who is he? I was interviewed by most of the board in London and our boss Andy. I thought they'd all agreed?"

"No one lets Hugh out, man, to meet new people. No one would join."

"Who is he then?" Jack asked, a bit anxious.

"He's the boss here. He's the managing director. Mad as a ******** March hare but he knows his stuff and keeps the rest of the useless buggers here in check. Have they told you the business is about to go global?"

"Eh, yes. I researched the information on the product and the market," Jack said, feeling uncomfortable with this inquisition,

"They told me the same, man. Mine is *******. But I keep on trying. They sold you on yours didn't they? Have you met the patent man yet? He's got no legs, as angry as Attila the Hun and hates all us graduates. But he knows his stuff and your product has no strong patent. The legless man told me the Japs own the lot. The only time I've ever seen him laugh"

"But they told me it was unique," said Jack.

"Aye, they told me that about mine. I bet they told you they could make it?" asked the chunky, ginger-haired lad smiling with great satisfaction.

"Well, yes. I gather we have a pilot manufacturing plant in Italy."

"They tell everyone that. They told me we had one in Calais. Go and speak to Jimmy the mechanical engineering manager and Big Tom the production manager. They'll tell you the truth. It can't be made, man. It's impossible. And I bet they told you it's safe for human skin application?"

"Well as it's a sunscreen, yes," said Jack, looking very worried now.

"Son, you need to wise up. We make chemicals. No one here has any idea about toxicology. That's why they hired some daft twat like you."

Jack listened to this last doom-laden missive and took a swig of his coffee. Surely this guy was just disillusioned; his part of the business must have been stuck in the mire. Mine? It's a wonder product and they told me I'll soon be in charge of the biggest thing to ever hit the market. I can make this work. And just as he thought those cheering thoughts, a smartly dressed, middle-aged lady came into the canteen and said: "Are you the new International Business Manager?"

"Yes," said Jack.

"Great. Hugh wants to see you in his office. You had better come now. Follow me."

Jack finished his coffee and stood up. His fellow business manager laughed. "Well son, now you'll see what you've let yourself into. I'll see you at lunch...if you're still here."

Jack nodded and followed the secretary. She took him along the corridor stopping outside a closed and forbidding, solid dark wood door. The corridor itself was dark with only one luminescent light along its length. To render the atmosphere even more forbidding, above the door were two traffic lights.

"When Hugh wants to see you he'll press the button for green. It's red now because he's still sorting out the last guy. When you go in you better make sure you wait till he says you can before you sit down. He likes his managers to stand in front of his desk. And call him by his surname. He will fire anyone who uses his first name. But I guess you're new so he may be nice to you."

The secretary smiled and walked away.

Jack stood in the gloomy corridor looking at the traffic lights. He had just left an American high-tech business where the bosses had open doors and you called them by first names - Brad, Chuck, Wayne. They all loved you to just walk in and talk. Well, they did if you had great sales figures and if not; you were probably not there anyway because you'd already been fired. But he had performed well and been promoted several times. Before that he'd had the joy of trying to teach very strange children in Northumberland - a temporary job teaching to pay his debts off before real work and to pay for his marriage and the Head liked him so he started him the next day; teaching science and also the joy of sex, educationally speaking, to spotty teenagers.

As he stood now in the corridor, he could almost hear Wendy on the subject of her sex life. "How Sor, it's allreet if he pulls it out before he comes. We divn't need arl this stuff aboot condoms and things."

"Well no Wendy. How do you know if he will *pull it out*? The male penis controls the male mind, pet. Not the other way around." As soon as he'd said it, he'd remembered a friend of his who knew an Air France pilot and the pilot's world view on penises and their proclivity to go anywhere: *'An 'howel is an 'howel and a penis has no eyes.*

And then his fifteen-year old pupil stunned him with her own world view. "He always does pull it oot man."

Jack had looked around at the giggling teenagers. He suspected that only Wendy had a clue what they had been talking about. He knew his lesson was really worthless - no one had an idea what a penis or an 'howel was. Teaching was not for him.

The green light went on and a loud buzzer awoke Jack from reminiscing. He entered an office with a huge, hard wood, polished desk at one end and a comfy sofa and chairs around a coffee table at the other. At the desk sat a thin, bespectacled, middle-aged man, dressed well in suit and tie. He stood, shook Jack's hand and invited him to sit the sofa and then ordered coffee for them both from his secretary by telephone.

Jack's new boss had glasses which were slightly tinted so he could barely see the eyes and if they showed any emotion, but the man was polite and welcoming. The managing director apologised for not meeting him before but he'd been travelling when head office in London had appointed him. Jack detected the merest hint of displeasure at not being involved but that was all. The Seaham lad must have it all wrong. They chatted warmly for about fifteen minutes when the boss's phone rang. He apologised for the distraction and went back to his desk to take the call.

"Tell him to come in." He put down the phone and turned to Jack, "I'm sorry but I really do need to talk to the production manager. We had a little problem on the number two line on Saturday night. He is your colleague so it'll be good to meet anyway and you may well learn something from the conversation. Take the Financial Times and read while I have a nice chat with Tommy."

Behind his huge desk, his body half hidden, the Managing Director pressed his green traffic light button and a well-built, balding man entered wearing company overalls. He nodded nervously at Jack lurking behind the protection of the newspaper's pink pages and walked over to stand in front of the desk, his hands firmly behind his back, like a school boy about to be scolded.

The MD didn't bother introducing Tommy to Jack. His smile flipped in an instant and he began howling at the man in front of him. "What the **** did you let that ******* happen to the ethyl acetate control system; you ******** useless ****. I've lost one hundred and fifty grand of raw material. Where the **** was that hapless, ********, useless production engineer you employed. I will have both your arses for this. What 's your ******* excuse and don't tell me it was a Saturday night."

The object of his vitriol just stood there, towering over his diminutive boss behind his huge desk. Jack just tried to hide behind his paper, embarrassed for the big man.

"I'm sorry Mr Corby it was not the engineer's fault. The control valve was faulty. And I was on holiday as you know," stammered the victim.

Tommy's explanation was cut off by another screaming tirade. "I don't give **** about your holiday! It's your responsibility and you let me down. And that engineer; it's his job to check the equipment.

Put him on a final written warning or I'll do the same with you. I hope you've ordered a new valve you useless ****."

The production manager just looked at the wailing banshee and whispered: "I have Hugh; just done it."

"I'll ******* check you have," said his boss, and then, two seconds later and visibly calmer, "Okay Tommy, thanks for coming. I hope you enjoyed your holiday. I'll see you at eleven for the production meeting. Thanks and goodbye." The change in temper, mood and attitude was surreal.

Tommy slunk off, his hands still behind his back as if he protecting his backside from an inevitable caning. All Jack could think then was that school kids used to put their comics down their trousers to reduce the pain of a beating. Tommy from then on was 'Beano' Tom to him.

Hugh came back around his desk and re-joined Jack. No mention was made of the ritual slaying of Beano Tom. He just talked sanely and quietly about the business Jack was about to launch to a world market. He poured more coffee and they chatted for another pleasant ten or so minutes. Then the phone rang again and Hugh got up and took it. It was a complete reprise of the previous interruption.

"Send him in," he said to his secretary and to Jack "Just read the rest of the paper while I deal with this."

This time it was a tall, thin, curly-haired younger man. He wore a loose-fitting suit with his tie slightly askew and carried a file of green computer paper. He nodded at Jack and nervously took up an already familiar stance. Jack stared over the top of the newspaper and thought *surely not again*.

"Where the **** is that sales report? And why did we lose the Hamburg contract you useless ****."

It was the same schizophrenia. One moment calm as a Tibetan nun and the next Attila the Hun. Jack sat there for several long minutes as the poor commercial manger was tortured, torn apart and then put back together again.

"Well thanks for coming in. This is Jack; I'd like you to help him correct his report. I will expect on my desk by three pm. And check the sales ledger before we meet at twelve will you please; I'd like an update on the ninety-day debtors. It's good to see you looking better after your breakdown. Goodbye."

The commercial man sloped off in his turn with his hands behind his back.

When Hugh finished with Jack, he returned to his cell of an office. He sat down to write out his resignation when the man from Seaham popped his head around the door.

"I gather you've met Hugh. It doesn't get any better, mate. I hear you have to get your report marked yet and our resident deputy head is going to help you with Hugh's corrections. You had better get the book down the trousers for that meeting. He's alright once you get to know him. You're the third 'fool'…err well – sorry - 'incumbent' - he's tortured. The others disappeared and joined a normal company. See you in the canteen….if you last…hah hah."

Jack watched his doom-bringer partner in business development leave and stared at the white powder and green smoke passing his grubby window. He saw in his in tray the paper on the potential market for his wonder product he'd written before he joined the company. He leant over and picked it up. Scrawled on the front were the words…'*See Me*' and when he opened it was overwritten throughout with but corrections and underlining in red ink. He had never had a '*See Me*' since school. He threw it back in the in tray. No way was he standing in line waiting for the bloody green light and buzzer nor was the twat going to cane his arse metaphorically or otherwise. He was heading home, out of this first circle of hell and into purgatory.

Now he was looking at the River Tyne flow down to Tynemouth and the two Shields. He chuckled and felt satisfied that even if he was living in an asylum, it was a site better than standing getting his arse caned by a mad man. Contemplation was broken by the door opening to admit his lovely, protective office secretary. He smiled at her. By now he knew how she ticked. Normally she managed to keep all the crazies away from him until he'd calmed down after the early morning news on progress, cost overruns, police reports and KT's phone calls but now the look on her face carried a clear message; '*Oh dear, Jack, you'll never guess what's happened?*' His heart sank. "What now?"

"It's the Mule Jack. He's snapped the client's finger in two."

Oh shit, not a 'bloody' gain, he screamed inside his head. The messenger of doom had worse news. "Oh and KT rang. He wants you to call him immediately. He sounds full of hell again Jack."

So, just as he was remembering golden days long past when he didn't feel paranoid about devil bosses, the latest Beelzebub wanted to talk to him. He picked up the phone and rang. A familiar voice rapped out 'Hello' and then shouted across the North Sea, "It's KT. Get your ass over to Stavanger on tomorrow morning's flight. I'm probably going to sell your business."

Jack put the phone down.

The Ferryman pulled up on the company's dock on the Tyne. Jack looked down at the shadowy dark hooded figure. Charon looked up at Jack's window and beckoned him to come with a wave of his ghostly hand

Jack knew he was going to the next Circle of Hell.

BOOK TWO
KITTY'S INFERNO

CIRCLES OF HELL

1
LONDON
MORGAN THE DRUID

Long before the ship-building

"Trust is just a word in the dictionary. I don't trust anyone. That's what makes a good salesman. What makes you think you can be one?"

Kitty looked at her potential employer and wondered how to answer that? She thought honesty, empathy, understanding were all part of being a *'good person'* and being a good person would help her new career as a medical representative and hopefully successful business-woman. Then she thought about her last interview with a large American multinational pharmaceutical company where she had actually got through to the psychological assessment stage. She'd had to fill in a questionnaire after a morning of psychometric tests and then be interviewed by a panel of psychologists. She was hoping she'd do well and decided honesty was the best policy.

She looked at one question and wondered how on earth they could add that and what were they trying to find out about her. It read: *'If you could assassinate one person, who would it be?'*

She thought seriously for a few minutes. Maybe they really did want her inner thoughts, fears and desires, so she answered truthfully. She wrote; Mrs Thatcher.

She went through a raft of other questions and came to the final one which she initially thought was to test if *I'm ambitious and dynamic.* She studied the question;

'If you couldn't be a medical representative and sell drugs, what would you want to be?' She wrote down – A Water Bailiff.

Satisfied she'd given the 'true her' and they'd be impressed enough to give her her first job since graduating in Biochemistry at Imperial College, London, she sat back and waited for the results.

She was sent off to lunch where she enjoyed meeting some old University friends in The Old Bull bar near Paddington station.

After that she arrived back at the hotel and was called into a meeting with the panel of doctors. There were three of them facing her, all tall, smartly dressed in suits and ties and with severe faces. There was no small talk or introductions. She was asked to sit down.

They all looked more like the banker who had refused her last overdraft than friendly understanding mental scientists. One of them opened the inquisition in a deep Southern drawl. "You have passed with flying colours the aptitude, IQ and team alignment tests. Your two other interviews with the company have identified you as a very positive potential employee..."

Kitty felt pleased this was going really well. Obviously honesty does pay as her dear mother had always told her.

"...But we have a couple of questions where we do not understand your answers. Frankly my dear your answers disturb us."

Oh dear she thought *what were they?*

And the tall man on the right of the speaker broke in. "Goddam right! You answered that the person you'd like to assassinate is your Prime Minister. So you have a deep hatred of strong leadership then?"

Kitty looked shocked. She had only put it down as a talking point. She thought they'd understand it was British humour. It was just that Brits were as a rule unimpressed by politicians and since Thatcher was the most famous and infamous, she'd put her down. It seemed an American drug company understood nothing of British culture so she tried to explain.

The tall man just stared until she finished talking and the two others were writing furiously onto her file.

"So you can't take leadership seriously. If Mrs Thatcher asked you to leap into a burning plane full of Israeli hostages and shoot the goddam Aayrab terrorists would you follow the order?"

The other two put their pens down and stared at her Gorgon-like. She thought any moment she'd turn to stone. *Sod it* she thought, *I can't be bothered with this. The dole has to better than working for crazy people like this.*

She remembered what her boyfriend had told her about his first interview with a famous chocolate bar and food maker as a graduate entry manager. The company were famous for paying mega money but asking for mega commitment. As he sat looking at the four male American interviewers, one of them just flew across the table and grabbed him by the nice new tie he'd saved the last of his student overdraft for. The interviewer pulled him across the table and put his head into his face. Her boyfriend thought *I'm going to nut this bastard* (he was from West Ham) but as he was about to do it the interviewer threw him back into his seat. The inquisitors all nodded in appreciation and the original tie puller explained: "You did well. On the production line you'll meet aggressive, violent employees. They come from London. If you react violently to their aggression it's a sign of weakness in your leadership abilities. We don't tolerate that. Let's move on."

Her boyfriend decided there and then he was probably not cut out for making chocolate bars and biscuits. And Kitty was beginning to doubt she was cut out for selling drugs.

The man in the middle said, "The last answer we can't analyse yet as we have no idea what it means. What the God dammed hell is a water bailiff?"

Kitty perked up; maybe if she explained honestly then they'd really begin to understand her desires and motivations.

"Oh let me explain. I didn't realise you would be foreigners."

She noticed them frown and whisper to themselves. *Oops*, she mused. She was new to meeting anyone from overseas except the French she'd met back-packing with her boyfriend around the South of France that last summer. And again she remembered a lesson learnt there by her unfortunate boyfriend.

He had needed the bathroom and had entered a small Tabac bar in Antibes. He had gone straight to the bathroom without asking for permission.

As he left the barman was wiping glasses with his bar towel behind the bar. Two or three old Frenchmen were sitting around drinking coffee with demi glasses of rose wine. The barman shouted to him in French that polite etiquette for using a bar's toilet demanded one buy a small coffee or small beer. Her boyfriend didn't speak French and had no idea what he was being told but he could say one sentence in an accent like the policeman in *Allo Allo*. "Pardon: je ne compriss pass. Je suize English."

The barman just hurled his towel down and howled out: " L'Anglais! Merde! L'Anglais…" He got no farther before a huge mangy dog leapt up from behind the bar, growling and barking like hell. Her boyfriend ran as fast as his terrified legs could carry him out and down the main street, the hound of the Baskervilles hurtling after him.

She pondered if Americans were as sensitive but now she had to answer anyway. "A water bailiff is someone who looks after rivers.

She walks up and down every day, checking water temperatures, feeding the fish, helping keep the river clean and tidy. If she's on a small river she may have nice little punt which she can pole up and down in the sun, watching out for water voles, maybe otters and helping fishermen with their leisurely day. I've always fancied doing that."

She sat back satisfied she'd explained her true inner self.

The Yanks looked astounded. Their chiselled jaws dropped. They took counsel together whispering and gesticulating, always looking over at Kitty. Then finally they gave judgement. "You do realise what this job is, don't you? You are expected to work as hard as you have ever worked in your life. You will do what the company tells you. You will be expected to sell and meet your target each sales cycle. If you do not meet what the company expects you will be fired. Goddam you will not be looking after furry critters or lounging around sunbathing in small boats. Do you really want to sell drugs girl?"

Kitty looked at the men and decided that she'd keep on following her mother's advice and tell the truth. "No I guess I don't. All I want is a job. Who the hell would want to sell drugs anyway?"

That was two failed job applications and two months before and now as she looked at the sales manager who believed Trust didn't exist and could make the decision yes or no about her finally getting paid work, she thought perhaps she needed to be less truthful after all. She told the man what he wished to hear and pleased he sent her to meet the training manager.

"Morgan is the oldest member of the team, boyo. He's seen it all. He was here when we first set up. He knows everything you'll ever want to know about the Industry. He trained and managed me and look where I ended up. If he tells me you're okay then that will do it for me. We call him *the silver fox* mind. He can sniff out a bad rabbit anytime anyplace. Enjoy the chat."

She was taken downstairs from the Welsh sales manager's office to meet *the silver fox*. Morgan was a small, bald-headed, elderly gentleman who was puffing away at a pipe behind his desk. "Sit down my dear. How did you get on with Mervyn?"

She couldn't help but notice from his accent that Morgan was also Welsh. She had never met a Welshman before and now she had a tally of two in two hours. Curious that. "Okay I thought, thank you. He's a nice man and very astute. I guess he must be great to work for." She was learning about truth and dictionaries.

"Oh certainly. We're all one team here. It's a great company. One big happy family. Trust, respect, honesty: we honour those values. I take our drugs every day and have done for thirty years and look at me. They keep me fit and my mind is as sharp as ever. I'll give you some of our multi vitamins to take home with you. Now then, can you just copy out this piece of marketing literature for me? Two or three sentences will do."

Kitty was given a piece of the latest wonder drug literature and duly took the offered pen, wrote out three sentences and handed the paper back. Morgan put on his glasses, knocked his pipe into his ashtray and started to refill the bowl while reading what she had done. After what seemed like an eternity of silence to Kitty, he grunted, lit his pipe and put the paper and glasses down. He moved his chair nearer to the desk and leaning back a little looked Kitty carefully up and down.. He kept quiet for some time thinking deeply it seemed and then spoke quietly in his soft Welsh accent. "Do you know, Kitty that hand writing can tell you many things?"

'Oh no,' she thought. *He's some form of graphology expert. What the bloody hell has he seen in those few words?* She started to sweat. "No. I didn't know. Thought the police used it to catch criminals."

His face brightened and he nodded. "Indeed they do. And so do we," he said with a hint of glee.

Kitty panicked again.

"But we can also use it to tell if someone is honest or deceitful. Did you know your handwriting can say if you're a genius or deranged?"

"No I didn't," Kitty replied and with a stupid, nervous giggle which she regretted immediately, she asked, "What does mine show? Am I a genius or mad as a hatter."

He puffed at his pipe and lay back in his chair. "It actually shows you may be both." And he watched her intensely as she squirmed. After a minute of silence he folded her paper up, took a file out of his drawer and slipped it in before placing it on his empty desk in front her.

"I've enjoyed our little chat. I'll see you get a bottle of our vitamins to take home. They'll help you I believe. I'm sure Mervyn will be impatient to hear how we got on. He trusts me to be honest.

As I said, the company respects all its employees. If you join us I'm sure you'll become one of the family. I'll get my secretary to take you back to personnel."

As Kitty drove up the M3 to London she wondered which she was - genius or madwoman and which of her personalities the two Welsh maniacs wanted her to but the very next day she got a phone call from personnel offering her the position of medical representative and asking if she could make a training course starting in three weeks' time for the launch of a new wonder drug?

Soon she would learn if genius or madness was the route to future success.

2
SURREY
BUSTER KNUCKLE

Three weeks later

"We believe in looking after our employees. We're a caring, compassionate company. If you do well, we will reward you. If you stumble, we in Personnel have a commitment to support and counsel you until you can reach your top performance and then the sky's the limit. You can be sure that there will always be an open door if you have any personal problems to resolve. I look forward to seeing you all move up and onwards in this great company."

Kitty was impressed by her personnel director's lecture. And in the bar after her third day on the residential training course she found herself telling her fellow trainees so. The man who had talked about care and counselling had been an imposing, handsome and powerful speaker. He wore modern tinted spectacles, a smartly cut suit and tie and a confident, relaxed manner as he explained the company's compassionate culture in a soft American accent. Kitty was mildly attracted to him not least because he resembled a movie star she admired and fancied.

This was her first exposure to big business American style and she had been worried they would be ruthless hire and fire people as she'd always been told by those who thought her mad to join a US drug company when she could have a nice life culturing bugs for the NHS and finding out how many polysaccharides they made per hour. This polished business man had allayed much of her fear and she was excited to learn more and get her new career started.

"I thought he was marvellous really; so much more professional than the crazy managers we've had so far on this course. I worry about the Swiss German one yesterday with the scary eyes. He seemed to want us to think we'd all be fired if we don't sell as much as he wants us to do. I never knew personnel management was such a great thing in business companies. And he was American too. I've never met one in real life, really charming."

"Lass; you are young and daft. He comes from Bradford, man. I met him last week on the pension committee. And as for personnel, well let me tell you something. Personnel should fill't forms in when you join and fill't forms in when you leave. And they should do ****

79

all in between." The Man from Lancashire then took a large draw on his cigarette, took a drink of his beer, put his pint down and then pulled at his braces which kept his trousers on his perfectly round tummy.

Kitty was astonished and disappointed. Her all-American hero was from Yorkshire and not from San Francisco, Wyoming or Phoenix? She felt violated. She was more surprised still when Andy, the lovely Scotsman she had befriended over the last four days and nights butted in. "Aye; nivva trust anyone from personnel. They're all spies and only there to find out what you are up tae. Not that they'll find anything on me like."

The middle aged Lancastrian, deliberately twanged his braces, drew on his cigarette, and blew a huge puff of smoke out of the corner of his mouth. "Aye: You can't trust any of them and as for the sales managers I've seen up to now, they're all either paranoid or schizophrenic, I can't make out which. That crazy eyed one may be both. I studied Psychology at University and worked in hospitals for the deranged. So don't get me on about the two Welsh ones. The one who reads your writing and then throws runes on the desk and deciphers whether you'll live or die. He's a whole symposium for ****'s sake. Aye lass, you've got a lot to learn. Do you want a pint Andy?"

"Eh, no thanks mate. I don't drink much nowadays. I'm going to have an early dinner in my bedroom and study the data sheet for the antibiotic. See you all tomorrow."

Kitty watched Andy go, wondering at his hunched gait and pondering step. He was about the same age as The Man From Lancashire but looked and acted about 20 years older. He had sat next to her most of the week and she had instinctively liked him. He was respectful, had been in the business for years and had left his old job for the opportunity to launch the new wonder pill. He lived on the Isle of Bute, a long haul to darkest rural Surrey and the opulent country club they were staying at for the next four weeks of intense sales and medical training. He told her he'd run a pub there but financial difficulties pushed him back into selling pharmaceuticals a couple of years ago. Supposedly he'd been teetotal for years so she wondered how it was that every morning he looked as if he'd gone through three rounds with Mike Tyson, his bulging eyes weeping and red in his florid puffed face. It would be understandable if he stayed up like all the rest of them, getting pissed in the bar and residents lounge till the early hours, but he went to bed at seven every night. She concluded, compassionately, that he must study all night and since he was clearly an experienced salesman perhaps she ought to start doing the same.

The next morning, waiting in the training room for the first session to start, Kitty was standing next to the window with The Man from Lancashire. She looked out over the beautiful golf course and thought how lucky she was to be staying here. She had never stayed in a hotel before. Her family holidays were always camping or caravanning and she could never afford to stay in a hotel as a student. She was enjoying the experience now and took joy in watching a bumble bee buzzing around the window pane. The bee settled on the metal strut dividing the window and she moved to open the window and let it escape when a huge fist flew past her face and smashed violently into the metal bar, squashing the bee and doing itself some damage.

Scared, she turned around, to see one of her fellow trainees grinning and holding his extended arm out, blood dripping from his knuckle. He said, "That won't be pollinating any flowers now will it? Maybe we should give it some of Morgan's vitamins."

He stared at Kitty for a long moment with a twisted grin, his broken knuckle not apparently bothering him and looked annoyed when she said nothing to him.

The Lancastrian, who had seen it happen shrugged her shoulders and twisted his finger to his head in a *he's crackers* gesture. "How he got through the writing and the rune test with that crazy Welsh druid, I'll never know. He's as psychotic as all the rest lass. Last night he told me he worked as a bouncer while he was at University and was nearly been sent down when he threw his Chinese flat mate from the third floor window just for sitting on his chair. Tells me he likes hurting things. Used to treat similar in the Liverpool asylum where I worked. He's got a PhD as well it seems. We just call him Buster Knuckle. You can see why."

Kitty sat and waited for her Andy who was late as usual. Unusually Morgan was late too delaying the normal 8.30 am start of the morning's lectures. The Man from Lancashire had a theory about that. "I'd worry if I were you. He's probably got a goat slaughtered on the eighteenth tee and is examining its innards to see if you have any issues with his training course."

About fifteen minutes later, Morgan came in with the fake American personnel manager. They brought the fifteen trainees to order and Morgan kicked of the day's education. "Good morning, my friends. Before we start on the Microbiology module, Brad would like to talk to you all again. He seemed to go down well with you all yesterday so sure you'll be pleased by what he's come to say today."

Kitty was pleased. She had studied Microbiology in her second year at University and was much more interested in learning the skills of compassionate business.

"Howdy folks," Brad began. A beaming smile showed his pearly white teeth and dark shades obscured his eyes.

"Dear God, he's a ******** Yorkie and he thinks we're in The High Chaparral," said The Man from Lancashire, leaning forward to whisper into her ear. "Remember what I told you about personnel lass."

Kitty ignored the comment. She was busy falling back in love with the charm and great man's charm and looks.

"Sadly, I bring some bad news folks. As I speak Andy, our Scottish buddy, is in a taxi with Gunter on his way to Heathrow."

The Lancashire man tapped Kitty's shoulder. "That Gunter was the Swiss man with the scary eyes. That's Andy sleeping with the fishes. I've seen and heard it all before lass."

Kitty ignored him, worried about Andy.

Brad continued. "Unfortunately, Andy had some issues. Gunter had a chat with him about them but we couldn't in all fairness let him continue. It wouldn't have been good for his future well-being. As I said yesterday, we like to spend time understanding our employee's issues and concerns but in Andy's case they weren't resolvable and he's now on his way home. Gunter will make sure he gets his plane alright, so please don't be concerned. We always treat our past employees with respect and dignity."

"He's stopped being a cowboy. He's playing a funeral director now for God's sake," the Man From Lancashire man was whispering to her again. "I bet that Welsh druid knows where all the bodies are buried too."

Brad looked up and turned his face to Kitty. She couldn't see his eyes behind his shades but she was sure he'd heard and would be gunning for her now. She trembled.. *Oh dear, what if the old bugger behind me was right after all.*

Brad refocused on the task ahead and concluded his motivating speech on employee relations. "Anyway, Andy has gone to that Prairie where all the medical reps go and where there are no first calls, sales targets or even sales managers…..hah, hah, hah. We wish him well. So folks, I'll let Morgan get you started. I hear he has his morning joke ready. It's all about the pseudomonas and the petri dish…Hah, hah, hah. Enjoy. So long partners."

He bounded out with a spring in his step. Kitty sat back and didn't pay an iota of attention to Morgan's latest hilarious bug joke. She was too busy wondering about poor Andy and what on earth had prompted them to fire him, three days into the course. At morning coffee she looked around for the Lancastrian, curious to know what his thoughts were. He had been in the industry for years already and had left his last company over some ethical dispute with his boss. *He must know a hell of a lot about how this all works* she assumed. She found him with a small group and Buster Knuckle in close attendance, under a tree outside.

"He's been fired lass; that's the rub. Don't listen to bullshit about Prairie's and counselling. I told thee that Gunter was only here to sus us all out. If he's not ex- Wehrmacht or Broadmoor prison, then I'm a monkey's uncle. That Druid was probably reading the tea leaves left in Andy's cup every morning. Did you not see that Gunter's eyes when he met us all. They were like shit house rats, watching all and everyone. I told you to be careful. Thirty five years I've been in this business. Every training course is just another way of sorting out who they want and who they don't. But we never lost one after three days; this bunch take the biscuit lass," her Northern mentor explained.

They were joined by a huge man. He had the biggest head and hands Kitty had ever seen. 'Heed like a medicine ball and a sniper's dream,' Andy had said. He was a half-Russian called Vlad. He made Buster Knuckle look small, but despite that Buster had challenged him to an arm wrestling contest that first night after dinner and won.

Ivan said, "That was weird about Andy. I liked him and he didn't even drink, just worked hard. What the hell are they going to do to us if they sack him? I mean, I have no problems I'm great at this game. Top rep last company and I will piss on you two and a;; the rest. That Gunter likes me. Another coffee?"

"Eh, no thanks Ivan. See you later," garbled Kitty, desperate to remove herself the latest strange *team mate*.

After a nice buffet lunch they were introduced to yet another Welshman, the regional sales manager, Ivan's boss. He was to take them through their first session on PSS - Professional Selling Skills. They had been told that it had been developed by Xerox, the fax and photocopier giant, and by a host of psychologists and behavioural therapy gurus and was now what all good American pharmaceutical companies used to train their sales reps. Kitty was looking forward to it and sat down, this time next to her Lancashire mentor, still thinking about Andy and hoping he would be alright.

They were just kicking off when Ivan came in late. He sat down next to another man and opened his briefcase. The man jumped up exclaiming, "Good God, man. What the hell's that?"

Ivan said; "Sit down. It's my business."

"Is it hell your business. It's a bloody turd!".

"That's what I said, my business. If you don't sit down and shut up I'll thump you."

Buster Knuckle stood up. methodically cracking his broken knuckles, offering to help. "I'll batter the two of them if you want."

The sales manager looked perplexed. "That's all right Buster, just calm down boyo. Ivan what's the problem?" He walked over to see what had excited Ivan's seating partner, looked into the open briefcase and reeled back in shock. "What the hell have you got that in there for, you daft Russian idiot! Get it out now!"

Ivan ripped two pieces of paper from his notebook and was about to use them on the offending object but the Welshman went apoplectic. "Not that for God's sake man. Take your bloody briefcase out, and get rid of it. Why have you got it in there anyway? Who the **** carries a huge turd in their briefcase?"

"It was too big to flush down the toilet. And this place is posh and I was worried they'd tell you I'd blocked the drains and I'd get sacked like Andy,"

"Dear God. You won't get sacked, but you might if you don't get that out of here now, boyo. Just take it to the toilet, please boyo."

"Told you so didn't I. Should be sectioned. The whole bloody lot of them," her Lancashire friend said, just a bit too loudly, to Kitty.

3
LINCOLNSHIRE
TIM

After the training course

"Urgh…urgh…@##, Doctor Jones. ***** urgh, uh huh ****
off."

Kitty stood astonished as her new boss attempted to talk to her
and her colleague in The George Hotel at Stamford, an ancient
coaching inn. They had just been introduced after graduating from
their training course with flying colours. She was now a fully trained
medical representative with a brand new car and had moved up
from London with her partner to live in the rural loveliness of
Rutland Water since her sales territory covered part of the East
Midlands. She had spent the day with Geordie Barry, the rep who
covered Nottingham who had been given the task of helping train
her on the ground as she *carried the bag* around her own allocated
doctor's surgeries. The day had gone well and each of the three
doctors she had seen had been kind to her and Barry. So she was
feeling well satisfied with life.

Tim, the regional sales boss for the whole East Midlands had
arranged a meeting and dinner in Stamford that evening. When she
met him earlier that evening he was a perfect gentleman; a small,
thin, upright, middle-aged man from the West Country,
immaculately dressed and incredibly polite. Three hours later he had
turned into something resembling a gibbering idiot.

"Err, uh ….*****, grrr, sales..uh…mummm..m?

She thought he seemed to be asking Barry a question as he stood
swaying, glass of wine in one hand, the other tucked into his trouser
belt , head now cocked in Barry's face seemingly expecting a reply.
She had absolutely no idea what he was saying but assumed Barry
dis because he was nodding positively.

"Yes Tim I completely agree," Barry said confidently.

Well I'm pleased someone knows what he's saying she thought. *I am
definitely going to have to learn Cornish.*

Tim's face twisted in disgust and anger. He stuck his face nearer
to his salesman's and uttered a rebuke littered with four letter words.

" urgh ***, ###, rhg, sales….****..ugh, mmmm, reports uh huh?

Barry nodded again and answered both laconically and sarcastically in his Geordie slang. "Well, mebbies not then, Jim."

This seemed to please their boss, and he nodded in agreement and walked off to refill his glass.

Kitty was curious to know what he had been so upset about.

"*******'d if I kna pet. When he's pissed none of us understand the bastard. We just nod. He goes away eventually. Come on, let's sit down and eat, I'll introduce you to the others."

"Is he always like this on two glasses of wine?" asked Kitty as they walked to the round table where the rest of the region's reps were sitting.

"It usually takes about three or four and then he gets aggressive. Not physically but verbally. After a few more he'll just fall asleep. I then have to throw him over my shoulder and take him to bed. You'll get used to him. He's really good at his job and always perfect professional with the doctors but sadly when he's had a couple, he goes a bit wayward. But we like him and he's a sight better to have as your boss than those mad Welsh buggers. What did you think of that lot?"

"I was terrified of Gunter, the Swiss sales manager, Tim's boss. His eyes are scary and well, so is he. Did you hear they sacked a poor Scotsman after only three days? Gunter took him away and we never saw him again."

"Aye: we heard. There's always one they get on every course. Did you have to meet Morgan and endure the handwriting test? That's a beaut that one; always gets a few too. He's mad you know don't you? What about Mervyn, the National Sales manager? He normally wanders around conferences with a huge leek getting us all to sing 'Men of Harlech'/ Like Ivor Emmanuel in 'Zulu'. If you don't sing, Morgan takes you into his room, throws small bones on the desk and howls at the winter solstice. So, what happened with the Jock they fired? Anyone know?"

"Don't tell anyone, but he phoned me at home, the poor man. It seems he had a drink problem and he'd lost a couple of jobs. He's in a real mess now. All the time we thought he was just tired each morning, he'd been knocking back the vodka in his room. It seems Gunter sussed him first day. He told the poor man in the taxi on the way up that he had stalked him as he left to get a bottle every lunch time at the local off license. He also paid one of the hotel staff to check his mini bar and his room bills each day. You'd think they'd have a talk with him first before firing him. That personnel guy seemed such a lovely man. It seems Gunter had a pair of handcuffs to chain him to the taxi door handle but the poor man just took one look at the scary eyes and decided against doing a runner or tackling the guy, so he sat crying all the way with Gunter singing '*Sound of Music*' to himself. Barry, is it really like this? You've been here years, so it can't be all bad, can it?"

"No pet it's not. It's a great life, you'll love it man. Just hit your sales targets, keep your call rate up, keep your head down and don't get promoted. If you stay as a rep and we keep Tim as the boss, life is good. You'll soon learn how to make a bob or two outside the job as well, like the rest of us. We get on well this region. It's a great team."

Kitty felt much happier after this chat and enjoyed the evening. Tim got more and more tired and emotional as time wore on, slurring more and more as the wine went down.

A table of ladies was next to them in the dining room and Barry got talking to them. One said she was the Conservative MP for Lincolnshire and the others were from the Woman's Institute. When they found out Kitty's group were in medicine they were curious and Barry became decidedly mischievous. "Aye pet, we're all doctors at The General," he lied..

"Oh that's an interesting co-incidence; I'm going in on Monday for a hip operation. Mr Jones is the surgeon doing it, I haven't met him but I'm told he's the best. Do you know him?"

"Aye bonny lass I do. He's sitting over there." He pointed to Tim.

"Oh that's lovely. And Mrs Ponsonby has a terrible knee too don't you dear?" The lady, turned to the MP. She didn't wait an answer. "This nice Doctor tells me that the man over there is Mr Jones who's doing my hip on Monday. Maybe if you have a word he'll have a look at your knee for you next week?"

The MP got up from her table and walked the short distance to introduce herself to the nearly comatose sales manager. "Hello there. Mary Ponsonby, your MP here. I gather you're a surgeon at the hospital?"

Tim looked up moving his head in a rapid sequence of movements, stared intensely at her as if she were an alien and

mumbled through his curled up lip.   "**** off, hhhm, err, …****
off.. mmmm, slish, slish…bastard….!" His head dropped first onto
his chest and then into his soup. He was unconscious.

Even a Right Honourable MP who had seen a great deal of life
was understandably shocked and the lady hip replacement patient
fainted. As she came around, Barry shouted over to her.   "Divn't
worry pet. He always operates sober."

The ladies finished and left, clearly disturbed and on the way out
Mrs Ponsonby spoke to the manager who felt impelled to come
over and intervene in person.

'Lady and gentlemen; I'm sorry but we can't have guests asleep in
their soup: especially our doctors. I'm sure you know that isn't quite
right is it?"

"Sorry, we'll get him to his bed. He's had a hard day in theatre
today. Come on Kitty give us a hand," Barry said hauling his boss
off his seat. He wiped the soup from his face and threw him over
his shoulder. "Bring his jacket will you pet."

Kitty had never felt so embarrassed, walking past the posh diners,
aghast and horrified, in the wake of her new boss, slung over Barry's
shoulder, soup dribbling out of his mouth and briefly compos
mentis enough to shout at them all. "Mmmm,   ****
off…ggrrr..hhh..sshh…**** you…."

They took him to his room and Barry slung him onto the bed but
he bounced off and smashed into the wall. He lay there in a
crumpled heap, comatose again.

Barry laughed.   "He'll be arlreet in the morn, pet. Divn't
worry."

And sure enough next morning when Kitty entered the business
centre conference room there was Tim, standing at the front of a
table putting an acetate slide of sales figures on the overhead
projector, ready to start the meeting. He stood there proud and
confident, immaculate in his well-cut suit and tie, hair brushed
perfectly, not even a speck of soup on his new tie. Kitty was amazed
at the transformation and Barry whispered, "I told you, he's the best
of all of them."

Tim switched on the overhead. "Good morning team, let me
show you the Region's sales performance for March."

4
LEICESTER
BLIND PUNJABI

The day after the soup incident…

"Doctor, one tablet two times a day - ok?"

"Oh yes Barry. One two times a day. I give for all problems," said the elderly Asian doctor.

Barry put his detail aid right in the doctor's face again and pointed to the back page and repeated, much louder.

"That's right; one tablet, two times a day for all problems. Have you got that now?"

"Oh yes, Barry, I have got it. Powerlol; one tablet, two times a day, for everything."

Barry looked pleased and picked up his bag. He stood and shook the doctor's hand, clearly happy with his mornings work and invited the doctor to their regular lunch together.

"Good lad. I'll see you at the Punjabi next Thursday then"

As he left the room with Kitty, he turned and said, "Come on then Raj, tell my colleague, Kitty, what you have got to remember?"

"Oh goodness me Barry, I am not that bloody old, hah, hah, hah. One Powerlol: two times a day for everything. I write all time for you my friend. See you Thursday."

As they left the surgery Kitty noticed the whole waiting room was full of Asian patients except for one little old lady who was white. She had never been in such a place where the population was mostly of Asian extraction and the language she heard wasn't English. Her rural territory of Lincolnshire, Norfolk and rural Leicestershire and Northamptonshire was very different.

Also different were the ways of selling pharmaceuticals in the real world – very different to what had been taught on her training course. Barry had used none of the professional selling skills endlessly practiced with her colleagues in front of video cameras and her Welsh inquisitors. He had used none of the initial benefit statement, no probing or stating of benefits or trial closing she'd been taught. And he had made no use of any of the expensive marketing or medical literature, data sheets, clinical papers which all stayed in his bag except at the end when he pulled out the six page detail aid setting out all the features and benefits of the drug and even then he used the very last page. He was supposed to be training her on the job and this was very far removed from what she'd been taught.

Kitty watched Barry with the Asian receptionist making sure the Doctor had his lunch appointment in the diary. She was smiling, chatting and laughing about the pens Barry was giving her.

"Make sure the Doc uses these to write the prescription. Here give me the pad and I'll write a few to start. You just put them in front of him."

Dear me she thought. *He's writing out the prescriptions. No one told me you could that. And he never told the doctor what the drug was actually for. Just use it on everyone. Surely not? Doctors wouldn't just prescribe it for anything? It's supposed to be for Arthritis and joint pain.*

As they climbed into Barry's company car, a Ford Cortina, she had to raise her questions with him. "Barry, you never used the detail aid to sell the doc. You just stuck it in his face and told him the dose. Surely that's not right. I thought we had to respect the doctor."

"The old bugger is blind, man. He can't see a bat. There's no point showing him anything. He can't see it. You just have to tell him the dose time and time again and the name."

"Blind! How the hell does he treat his patients then?" Kitty was clearly shocked.

"By touch and listening I guess. They all seem to like him. As you might have noticed they're all Asian."

"But he's going to prescribe it for everything. I thought we only had a licence for arthritis and joint pain. Is that ethical?" said Kitty for whom a real moral dilemma was forming.

Barry, smiling at her naivety and youthful innocence, gave her more insight into her new world. "Listen pet, he's a doctor. They can do what they like. It's great for pain relief and everyone has some pain, so why not give it to them. He can't see what illness they've got anyway, so he'll just give them the drug and hope it solves their pain and they don't come back. And he prescribes it in bucket loads anyway. He's one of my best doctors. You'll soon learn, pet to take whatever you can get. It keeps Tim off your back and if he gets his sales targets it keeps the mad bugger Gunter off Tim's. And believe me you don't want Gunter on your back."

Kitty shuddered. She felt the hairs on the back of her neck bristling at the thought of the man with the staring eyes and the handcuffs, whistling Edelweiss.

Barry thought he'd scare her some more. "Did you hear about one of Gunter's reps that disappeared? That girl in Cornwall…"

"No. I didn't. What happened?" asked Kitty, worried.

"Well, when he was Regional Manager there, his region was the best sales in the country. This new girl didn't come up to his standards and he decided to find out what she was up to. So he called her all the time, turning up when she didn't expect him at her first doctor's appointment. He hired cars to park outside her house to see if she actually went out. He worked on her day after day and you know what that must have been like; his eyes on you all day and his rotten temper."

Kitty shuddered again, holding her legs tightly together. She thought she might wee herself at the mere idea of Gunter sitting outside her house all night waiting for her. Barry smiled as he saw her fear and continued; "Anyway, one day the girl was there, the next she'd disappeared. Her family called the police but it seems she took a ferry from Penzance to the Scilly Islands and is now living in a nunnery there. Gone and never to be seen again. He replaced her with a bloke from the Rhonda who sings *Climb Every Mountain* and Wesley hymns with him at conferences while Mervyn walks around with his leek. No, my dear, you don't need that. Keep Tim happy, and that's a doddle compared the crazy Swiss. Keep your call rate and sales up by wining and dining the Indians and getting them to prescribe our drug for anything and everything. Most of all keep your head down. Don't let them take you into head office for training, marketing or sales management; competing with Gunter and the rest for promotion – that's a recipe for instant oblivion and life in a mental institution. You take your chance, pet."

As Barry drove to his next call Kitty thought about what he'd said. *Surely it wasn't really like that?* No one told her on the training course. But then she remembered the evenings with The Man from Lancashire who had tried subtly to counsel her about life in business; especially he drug business. "You see, as soon as you reach your sales target they increase it for the next sales cycle. Okay, you get a bonus for reaching it but you're then penalised for good performance by increasing it again. Never ever exceed it by much.

As soon as they see you've hit one hundred and fifty per cent of your target they use that as the base plus another fifty per cent. So they do this constantly until it becomes impossible for you to reach the new targets. Then they send in Gunter," the laconic psychotherapist had explained while he drank his pint and tapped his unlit cigarette on the table.

Seeing her shocked and unbelieving face, he had continued to elucidate his theory on how to survive in the drug business. "Kitty, always try to just hit your target, or a little bit under. No one focuses on the average. The best and foolish ones always get higher targets and ultimately they're promoted to the hell of head office or are disappeared by the likes of Gunter when they ultimately fail because the targets become impossible without fiddling the figures. Mind you, in my thirty years in this business I haven't quite met any like this lot. We did study a case very like Gunter at University and I met a few in the hospital. I reckon its paranoid schizophrenia. Do you know what that is?"

"Err no, but I think you're going to tell me," Kitty had said, a bit bored now.

He had taken a long draw of his cigarette, exaggerating the slow flow of his hand from mouth up into the air and he had blown out the smoke before giving her more of his wisdom. "A paranoid person thinks someone is around the corner. A schizophrenic is the person around the corner. A paranoid schizophrenic is someone who looks around the corner and sees themselves there. That's Gunter."

Kitty had shaken her head. It had all been too much for her at this stage and she had wondered if her new found counsellor friend had been diagnosed with the same condition he believed everyone else had.

Now Kitty observed Barry driving through the Leicester streets all decked out with the lights for the festival of Deepavali. He seemed at peace with his lot. Maybe this wasn't going to be too awful after all. She would just have to stick with it and show them all that she could do it as well as them and maybe better.

They pulled up outside another surgery. Barry got his bag out and put a few drug sample bottles in it along with a detail aid. They entered and once again the Asian receptionist was very pleasant, unlike the fire breathing dragons she'd practised her sales training with on the course. She greeted them with a lovely smile and, "Yes the doctor would love to see you after his last patient, Barry. Take a seat with your friend."

Barry gave her a couple of pens and note pads as a thank you and they sat down.

"What's this doctor like, Barry? Does he prescribe for you?" asked Kitty.

"Aye, he's pretty new but I saw him first days he was here. The last one did a runner quickly back to India or Pakistan. Talk of a bit of hanky panky with his patients but no one's saying anything. I took this one to see the new movie *Ghandi* with about ten others and their wives and then on to *The Punjabi*. Dear Lord, when they started beating the crap out of the Indians with them sticks and that twat of an English general took a tank into the cricket stadium and shot and slaughtered all them men, women, and children I just looked at their stony faces and thought, *Here goes my budget this cycle - I'm knackered now."*

"I haven't seen it yet. Is it that bad for the Indians?" asked Kitty.

"Some more advice, pet. Divn't take Indians and Pakis to see it together. They hate each other worse than us. To be fair I'm not sure which of them this one next is? But he enjoyed his meal with the rest after the movie and he drank a gallon of beer and wine, so I guess he's Indian. He's a bit weird though so best be careful. He kept touching wor lass up under the table."

Kitty looked shocked again but just then a buzzer rang and the receptionist told them they could go in as the morning's last patient walked out.

A chubby Asian doctor stood up from behind his desk to greet them and asked them to sit down. After a bit of chat about the movie and the meal, Barry asked him if he'd prescribed the drug since.

"Oh many, many, many times; I use it on everyone," said the doctor wobbling his head in the by now familiar manner as he spoke.

"That's great Doc. Can you remember the dose?" asked Barry, smiling and then winking at Kitty.

"Oh, yes, wait, one, two, and three? Sorry Barry, my mind is busy today...I just prescribe, many, many, many times. Can you remind me please?

Barry got his detail aid out and told the Doctor the key facts and then after a minute of actual sales talk he took a stick down rubber egg cup put of his bag, emblazing with a logo *'Powerlol: one, two times a day'* and showed it to the doctor. Kitty had seen these cups being displayed by the product manager for Powerlol at the training course. They were giveaways for doctors to help them remember the drug. They were designed to make it easy for Arthritic patients with a poor grip to eat boiled eggs as they could stick the cup to the plate or table and then use both hands with their spoon. Barry had other uses for them. He showed it to the doctor, licked the bottom and leant over the desk to stick it firmly on the doctor's brow. "There now my friend, you can keep it to remind you of the dose."

The doctor laughed and left the egg stuck on his head. "Barry you are funny, funny man. I prescribe lots for him you know, my dear," said the beaming doctor to Kitty.

"That's nice, "she answered, still bemused by the lack of professionalism on display.

Barry interjected. "Doc, I see my sample is only the third on your shelf after the competition Powersyn and Powerfen. You can't really be prescribing a lot. I thought I was your number one friend?"

"Oh Barry, you are, you are. But my wife, she liked the Egon Ronay hotel restaurant on Rutland Water where we spent last weekend with the Powerfen rep. She loves lobster. She's a bit sick of *The Punjabi*. So I have to keep her happy and I prescribe a few scripts to help the rep for being kind to her. And the girl who comes for Powersyn...well have you seen her Barry? Oh my goodness, she takes me to the pub where I drink a few pints and she is very cuddly with me. I can't let my wife see her. She is lovely and says she'll take me to a conference in Barcelona. Oh my goodness, just the two of us. I have to help her, Barry. Maybe this young lady sat with you might come and see me on her own and I'll move your sample back to number one?"

Barry looked at Kitty, who by now was looking aghast, shrugged his shoulders and said, "I'll see what we can do, Doc. But first let me book you and your dear wife a trip up the Trent on the luxury river cruiser. They do a lovely Lobster Thermidor. Is next Friday night is okay?"

"Oh she'll be so pleased. Thank you Barry, I'll put it in diary," he said, smiling profusely and writing it down. He got up and moved

Barry's sample one place up past Powerfen. Kitty realised this was all a game and that he'd prescribe whatever depending on how many goodies he got. She decided there and then that she certainly wouldn't be going 'on the game' to get Barry past Powersyn on the shelf.

Barry interrupted her thoughts. "That's better, Doc. Now then I need you to prescribe more of our wonderful antibiotic for ear infection. Here is a sample for your shelf. Just one capsule a day for five days. That's it, Doc."

"Oh Barry I use this all the time for you. See I have no antibiotics on the shelf at the moment. You are my favourite. I use this for everything, especially for female problems, I give it to them for all their female troubles,' the doctor said excitedly. Too excitedly for Kitty who now felt very uncomfortable.

"Doc, it's for bloody ears, man. Not female problems."

"Oh, Barry it's an antibiotic. I always examine my patients for female problems even if they have ear infection. It's best to be safe. I treat them even if I see nothing when I look down there just in case it travels. I am good friend to you, yes?"

"Err…Yes, you are, Doc. Just keep the egg cup on your head and keep writing my friend and I'll see you on Friday."

Barry stood up to go and Kitty couldn't wait to get out of there. "Please, young lady. Barry has my personal number. Ring me and we will go to the pub and maybe a conference together," shouted the doctor to the back of Kitty's disappearing head.

They visited the nearest chemist next and she told them that the doctor had started writing loads of prescriptions for Powersyn, even for teenage acne, but he'd written nothing for Barry's Powerlol.

"You just take him to that cheap shit Indian restaurant don't you? Every time a rep takes him somewhere massively expensive he changes his scripts. Unless of course it's someone like the Powerfen rep. Bloody brazen hussy that one. I've no idea how she fits into that suit with those breasts. Is this new girl your answer to her?"

"No I'm bloody well not," exclaimed Kitty. "I'm the new rep for Lincolnshire and the South and I won't be doing anything of that sort so you'd better not say things like that."

"Keep your knickers on girl. You'll soon learn this business. He's a pervert for sure. The last one was too. I'll not give him long. People are already talking about his habits and I think he's already been reported to the police. I've had women in asking if they should have been examined '*down there*' for their depression. He'll probably do a runner back to his country long before they catch him. They all do."

As they got into the car Barry, looked sad and Kitty asked him why. His astonishing response was "That's my antibiotic sales target knackered if they bang him up; just my bloody luck."

Kitty just sat and stared at him as he drove on.

"I'll drop you off at your car now. I've got to get back to get the movie stuff in my car and arrange the catering for tonight's show," said Barry as he drove out of Little India.

Kitty checked the dashboard clock. "But it's only eleven fifty five Barry. Aren't we supposed to see three more doctors and three chemists and two hospital doctors to meet our call targets?"

"Haway man pet! My blind doc will write enough scripts to keep Tim off my back this month and the pervert will murder the antibiotic target on his own until they bang him up. No one gives a real monkeys about call rates if you hit your targets. Most of us have some other business to run anyway in the afternoons. I put on films in village halls, churches and schools and charge for the food and booze as well as the movie. The lad who does Liverpool just graduated as a doctor. He did his whole medical degree while working as a rep, man. Our Bradford man runs a whole chain of chemist shops. One of my mate's bosses from our main competitor has a chain of children's nurseries and the other one runs a physiotherapy clinic. You just go home and say nothing to Tim if he asks. Just say you had a busy day and enjoyed it. You'll learn lass, you'll learn."

And she did.

5
DUBLIN
MR O'HARA

Many months later

"The whoor is swimming the Irish sea as we drink."

The Irish doctor chuckled with his friend as they swallowed large slurps of well poured Guinness. Kitty smiled only from pure business survival. In truth she was aghast at what he had done but as a potential future source of prescriptions she could not afford to show her shock or to remonstrate with him. It was wiser to go with the flow and of course with 'the craic'.

They were at Jury's hotel in Dublin. She had flown to the Emerald Isle from East Midlands Airport to Shannon to take two important doctors pike fishing. After a fruitless couple of days throwing raw herrings into a huge loch and catching nothing but the odd boot, coping with a large quantity of Guinness and little sleep, she had seen off the fishless doctors and taken the hire car to Dublin to attend a medical conference.

Unimpressed by the first presentation she had sought out a coffee and was now sitting at the hotel bar at nine in the morning listening to two strangers banging on about their dog racing exploits. Only one of them was a doctor, and he had already suggested he could move vast quantities of her wonder antibiotic across the border from Northern Ireland to his own patients at great profit to them both.

"It's more of a food than a drink, my dear," he told Kitty in his soft accent when asked if he'd taken breakfast yet, "...And why would I eat when there's a pint of Guinness to hand."

The craic followed naturally from the drink and Kitty could hardly refuse trying the great black beer offered by her two new and generous companions. And as the Guinness flowed they got into increasingly bizarre conversations around why the Irishmen were actually there.

They had taken a greyhound across the Irish Sea on a ferry for a big race at the White City track in London. The dog was a ringer; it wasn't the dog it was supposed to be. They had dyed it the colour of its alter ego who'd been left sleeping back in its kennel in County

Claire. The ringer dog was many times faster than the substituted dog. A bit like switching Terry Wogan for Usain Bolt assuming they were both identical in colour and shape. The punters and bookies had the Irish dog on long odds and sure enough when trackside betting opened it was 6 to one to win so they placed a couple of thousand on it before the odds could drop. It romped in and the good doctor and his mate had made over ten thousand pounds. Very nice for a couple of days work.

Kitty tried to smile at the story. After all it was only the bookies who got hurt and she was receiving part of the proceeds of their ill-gotten gains in free Guinness. But she wondered where they kept the dog while staying overnight in the hotel and she didn't expect the answer she got. "What on earth do you mean?" she asked.

"Well darling, we got out of London quick and made Holyhead the next day. Before we got on the ferry I called my friend in London and he tipped me off that we were going to be investigated and when we arrived in Dublin, the Garda and the vets would be waiting to examine the dog. Bejesus I thought what would me father have done and the answer was simple; no dog, no vet examination. So she went for a long swim from the back of ferry. It'll do the hoor good; she was getting a bit too fat for a champion…hah hah."

Kitty realised her few days in Ireland had shown clearly that the people of this green land were indeed crazy, even if this behaviour from her doctor friend was just 'the craic'.

Her arrival at the pub near Shannon two days earlier should have forewarned her. The three rooms they'd booked existed all right but she'd confused matters by asking if the boat for loch fishing was reserved.

"To be sure my dear it is," said the landlord-owner.

"That's great, thank you very much," replied Kitty, pleased that something seemed to be going well.

"But the engine will be coming a bit late."

Kitty couldn't help her immediate sense of panic. She'd had a truly torturous time trying to get anything confirmed or agreed with her genial host in her past telephone conversations with him. "Why on earth, Mr Conroy, have you supplied a boat and no engine?" she asked, not of course expecting any clear answer.

"Now, the boat will be having an engine but not just yet. You all have to be having tea and a drop of whiskey with olwd Mister

O'Hara. It's his boat and engine and he always likes to be greeting our new guests. Now don't you be worrying over nothing. As I said the engine's a good one."

"How and where do we meet this Mister O'Hara," asked the older of Kitty's two guests.

"Now then, Big Paddy will be after taking you there in his van. He'll be here in a while. Take the keys and I'll be pulling you all a pint while you get sorted upstairs."

Two hours later and several pints of Guinness on the bill, Big Paddy turned up and threw them all into the back of an old transit van full of bits of engines, tractors and suspicious looking boxes. They drove about half a mile out of town to a little cottage and Paddy tugged open the van doors with his huge gnarled hands and showed them into the small house.

There they met a wizened old man, oddly dressed in suit and tie. He greeted them warmly enough. "Top of the morning to you all, you'll be taking a seat." He pointed to three wooden chairs lined up facing his own. Paddy none too gently shoved them in the direction of the chairs. Feeling slightly aggrieved they sat down.

"Now then you'll be taking some tea and Paddy will pour you a drop of our whiskey," the old man told them.

Without waiting for an answer Paddy poured three cups of tea from the teapot into the cups already sitting on the dresser. He then took a bottle from the dresser top and poured three tots for them and finally one for the old Irishman.

"Slàinte," the old man said and poured the whiskey straight down his throat leaving the others with little option but to follow suit, Kitty nearly gagging at the biting harshness of the alcohol.

The old Irishman from his armchair facing the three visitors to his home asked: "Now then tell me what you are doing in this fine country and be wanting with my engine?"

Kitty looked around as he spoke noticing he had framed pictures of himself placed on his old wooden furniture. Her eyes grew wide as she noticed one of him posing with the Pope and wider still at one of a much younger man shaking hands with John F. Kennedy. She realised that whoever he was, around here this old man was important.

They spoke for about twenty minutes, drinking their tea. The old man asked a few more questions about catching pike and what they all did over the water and then stood up. "I'll be letting you go now. You'll be getting a thirst for sure and Donal's bar will be filling up with the boys. Paddy here will see you home and he'll be bringing the engine to you. Enjoy your stay, for it's a terrible beautiful place for the fishing." He shook their hands and they left packed into the van once more.

Sitting in the bar they reflected on the weirdness of the meeting. They had all noticed the photographs and the consensus reached was that whatever or whoever Mr O'Hara was, they had been subtly interrogated and warned that fishing was all they had better be doing. Not that they had their engine as yet.

The night had drawn on. Curiously the bar didn't start to fill up until around ten but by then they were all tired and a bit drunk. Kitty went to the bar and asked about their engine. Two barmaids were busy pouring pint after pint of Guinness and leaving them to settle while Donal himself was having a drinks with three of his customers.

"Bejesus Miss, just be chilling out now. It's early yet. Paddy doesn't start drinking until now. He'll be along soon now. Just be having yourself another drink." Just as Dolan said that Paddy came in with a large outboard engine over his shoulder. He dumped it on the floor next to the two doctors

"Hey, here he is, the man himself," said Dolan. You'll be buying him a pint of course. Mary, be giving Paddy one of those pints and mark it down for this lovely English lady here to pay."

Without a word Paddy took the offered pint and drained it in one.

Kitty was delighted. At last they could get to bed. They had planned to get up at 5.30 in the morning for breakfast and straight off to the Loch. "Oh Mr Conroy, that's great. We've got an engine!" she said joyfully. "We'd like an early morning call if that's alright."

Donal Conroy stopped in his tracks, his glass frozen halfway to his lips. "Now then miss, what will an early morning call be then? Something you have over in England?".

"No, Mr Conroy. Every hotel or boarding house has them. We want a call to wake us up early tomorrow," explained Kitty.

"Oh, that'll be not a problem. And what time will youse be wanting to be called then?" Donal asked.

"Oh about five thirty if that's all right and we'll have breakfast at six." Kitty requested, pleased at last that they were getting things to work here as they wanted. She didn't notice the two bar girls chuckling.

"Bejesus! Five thirty in the ******* morning!" shouted the surprised landlord, his face twisting in pain. "We'll just be closing the bar at four lass. **** that! We don't do breakfast till nine. You'll have to be getting yourselves up. I'll be comatose." And he turned to his giggling staff and said, "Five thirty to get up, for fecks sake…and they say we're thick."

"But what about our breakfast?" Kitty shouted above the noise from the rapidly filling bar.

"Just do what any daft ******** does when they'll be wanting to get up before nine. Make it yourselves. I'll give you the keys to kitchen. Just take what you want out of the fridge and cook it." And turning to his amused customers: "******** English; five thirty in the morning, hah. They'll never be understanding Ireland."

And indeed Kitty didn't understand Ireland and only two days later in Dublin was still learning from her new doctor friend the ways of that wonderful bizarre island. She asked him what time did his morning surgery's started and he nearly keeled over the bar.

"Morning surgery! I only have one surgery man. From four thirty in the afternoon. The whoors are just too drunk or lazy to get up before that, girl. Thought you might be knowing that by now."

Kitty took a drink and realising she should have expected that. She was starting to like Ireland.

On her return home she was asked to come down to the head office in Surrey to be interviewed her for a promotion. She was delighted. She had really tried hard over the previous eighteen months. She had actually worked. Unlike so many of her colleagues she hadn't been diverted into cramming the work for which she was employed into an hour or two in the morning whilst setting up a multi -national business, studying for an MBA, running catering firms, a chain of pharmacies, children's nurseries or her own physiotherapy clinic, supplying movies to the country folk of rural Britain. She had instead actually worked hard. She had visited doctors and tried out her new found sales skills on them and surprisingly it had worked. She had climbed rapidly up the sales target ladder with massive increases in areas and cities long known as barren deserts for the company. Now it appeared she was going to be interviewed for a Regional Sales Manager position.

She would be sad to leave the regional team she had grown to love because even Tim had grown on her. He had continued to collapse into his soup, to need carrying to bed and to be incomprehensible to all normal human beings after a few glasses of wine but he was a good company man and had taught her well. She was reluctant to leave such a great bunch of people. Morgan however told her that change was necessary and during her interview he threw his runes across the table, looked closely for a couple of moments at them and said; "You must move on. Life is like that. Those you leave behind will soon not be there. You are destined to move on. You will soon forget them as we all do."

And he puffed at his pipe as she wrestled with what that statement really meant. She knew she liked and respected her colleagues and was quite happy in that life. She didn't want them disappeared by Gunter or to even think she might be able to forget them and leave them to rot.

As she had driven down the A1 towards the M 25 and her interview she had reflected on what The Man from Lancashire had told her about his own interview with Gunter for a regional sales manager's job. The interview was very short and started with a rhetorical question, "So Mein Herr, you are a psychologist then," Gunter had stated and then stared at him for what seemed an eternity.

"Yes, that's one of the degrees I studied for," The Man from Lancashire replied in his posh voice, precisely and firmly.

His potential new boss leaned back violently in his chair and posed another, sharper question. "Would you like to psychoanalyse me then?"

The Man from Lancashire looked across at the man whose eyes were running back and forth like shit house rats. He realised that this would not end well. "I'd rather not. You may not like the result," he answered truthfully.

His interviewer thrust himself forward, arms onto the desk between him and stared fiercely at the older man. After an eternity all he said was, "Interesting."

Gunter leant back in silence while his interviewee sweated. When he next spoke it was a quietly malevolent utterance. "How would you stake out and trap one of your reps you thought was not working as they should?"

The Man from Lancashire saw all too clearly that he was not on the same management page as his Swiss interviewer and gave up any hope he might have had of a promotion and a pay rise. He said, "I thought you wanted a manager not a policeman."

He was not offered the job.

Now Kitty would have to face the same ordeal. She shivered and turned up the volume of the car radio, listening to Terry Wogan ramble on about who had shot JR Ewing and wishing she was back in Ireland. Mr O'Hara and his IRA interrogation were far less unpleasant than what she would be facing.

….However Kitty was offered the opportunity denied to the Man from Lancashire.

And in the end she took the move.

6
MARBELLA
JOHN PAUL THE SECOND

One year after Ireland…

"When you are in the shite, I will be standing on your shoulders"

Kitty sat amid the massed ranks of her colleagues as her new sales manager motivated them all to higher things. She shook her head at the perverse statement from someone she was rapidly coming to see as a perverse person and was tapped on the arm by one of her reps who was sitting next to her. He was an ex nurse who, even though only in his twenties, looked and acted like he was fifty. He dressed in tweed suits, wore brogue shoes, smoked incessantly and would rather be fox hunting than sitting in a sales conference in Marbella taking in his bosses' curiously bizarre leadership.

"For ****'s sake I thought that mad Welsh bastard with the giant Leek was the last straw. This bugger is worse. Kitty, let's get out of here please. Don't let them get me please. I won't carry leeks around and I won't get up and sing or dance. I ******* hate this shit."

Kitty patted his hand gently to calm him. He was not meant for this world. She already knew that after only a few months working with him. He really couldn't take the endless sales meetings, conferences and bullshit from the stage, the flashing lights, the songs, and now the new Peter Drucker style of motivating the troops by grinding them into the dust. Curiously for a medical salesperson he also wasn't keen on either hard work or doctors. She realised in her compassion she'd have to encourage him to move onto safer ground – before Gunter fixed his Howitzer aim on him. Maybe she'd encourage him to buy himself a gun shop and kill small furry creatures; it was less harmful than working pharmaceutical sales.

All of this razzmatazz, glitter and bullshit that terrified and sickened her tortured rep was also hard for her but she was used to it by now and was moving upwards towards the day when she would be one of the lunatics running the asylum. If she ended up there she vowed to get rid of the giant leeks, druid worship and psychoanalysis.

She had actually flown through her interview with the Managing Director. Strangely Gunter, Morgan and Mervyn were not there although the charismatic SalesDirector was. The American was full of enthusiasm and drive and she liked him. He was always referred to as John Paul the Second.

"Call me JPS Kitty. That's what all my friends do. And I think we are going to be friends. I hear you are one of the ones to watch. And I like a good salesman."

John Paul Senior was one of the original super stars from the New York State-based company. His son was becoming a legend in turn. He had changed the company in the few months he'd been there, driving new products out into the market while creating new sales forces, new management systems and management development. He smoked huge cigars and seemed to spend money as if it grew on proverbial NHS trees. He put his company car in the garage and hired Porsches, Lamborghinis and the like. He took doctors on foreign conferences by private jet and his managers to exotic locations for training and motivation. In fact he was driving a medium-sized company with tired products towards market leadership by clever marketing and very aggressive sales. And it was working.

As Kitty endeavoured to calm her nervous and distraught rep she smiled at the recollection of JPS at other conferences sitting up all night drinking with his teams and leaving them only at 7 am to take a shower and get ready for the 8 am start where he launched the show in a blaze of lights and, as many would have it, a shower of absolute bullshit.

She chuckled as her gaze settled on the Northern Irishman at the front, stocky bald-headed and upright staring blankly at the flashing lights. At one sales conference just six months before JPS had come down from his gilded cage after the initial blast from the audio visual show and handed the Irishman a bottle of Bushmills' whiskey and clean glass to keep him going through the morning session. They had naturally only stopped drinking an hour before the glittering start while JPS, the ultimate professional actor, appeared all the innocent to any early to bed reps, looking for all the world as if he'd been to a health farm for the night.

She looked over at her old boss Tim, now only her equal in rank, sitting upright, wearing immaculate white slacks, shirt and tie even in the Spanish heat. Again the smile - she'd heard from Barry that they had thrown him into the bath at about eleven thirty the night before and left him there unconscious. *How the hell did he do it?*

As JPS got into his road show under way she remembered how much pain his super sales reputation had caused her. She had been tasked with getting their super- duper antibiotic into three hospitals because so many sales reps, marketing people and medical people had failed to convince the three microbiologists in charge of them. These three esteemed doctors had decided not to add this new product to what they thought was the perfectly capable armoury of high powered antibiotics already on their approved list. She as the new super sales person was the last chance.

Unlike other hospitals where Consultants could break the approved list control if they wished to prescribe and use a new drug, here it had never been possible. These three problematic men were in absolute control of the prescribing regime in their respective hospitals and the challenge to Kitty was to break them down.

She had decided to use feminine guile and charm and so asked a rather attractive young clinical research associate from the medical department to join her when she was finally granted an audience with the head guru who everyone told her was the hardest nut to crack.

"Good morning Doctor. I'm Kitty; here's my card. And this is my colleague Amy from our medical department. As you know we've launched our injectable antibiotic Maxicillisporin which has already become the drug of choice in most Teaching Hospitals across the UK. I was hoping we could discuss your thoughts on the drug and why you have yet to put it on the approved list."

The Doctor carefully examined their business cards. "Uhm," he mumbled under his breath. When he lifted his head at last he said,. "I see you are finally trying the sex thing on me. Two pretty girls following on the heels of a host of particularly ugly men who were not that clever. They all turned up unable to string a lucid argument together for me. And now I'm sent one who purports to be from the medical department but is really a disguised pretty salesman in a dress."

JPS had obviously lied when he had briefed Kitty that the man was ready to crack after being softened up with an all-expenses-paid trip to a microbiological conference in Florida and sponsorship money for his pet department.

"That's not true Doctor. I am a PhD and a CRA, I report to the medical director. I have no sales responsibility," said Amy, making her personal distress at this calumny obvious with her ample heaving bosom and flashing eyes.

"Uhm. I have read the clinical reports and papers you have in your bag. And indeed," the doctor paused to pull the relevant file out of his filing cabinet, "I have here all of them. Most are flawed as I suspect are any answers you might give me. I've met your medical director. At the time he was tipsy and driving a motorboat across a Florida Key at full speed with no concern for the manatees. Those are sea cows to you I guess. But let's move on from that." And he put the file on the table.

"Kitty, this sales director of yours…" He pulled his desk drawer open and shuffled through a fistful of business cards. Finding the one he was looking for, he threw it at Kitty. "Here, I'd forgotten his name. Some stupid American. How can you have someone the second? Just says it all, power mad; thinks he's a Pope or King. John Paul the Second, indeed. And you people want to convince me to use a second rate drug.

"This John Paul person introduced me to a foreigner, a German he said was his Field Sales Manager. I believed he was going to attack me there and then when I asked him how many 'fields' he had sold."

Kitty interrupted. "Actually there are a lot of your doctors here in the hospital who would like to use this drug. I have spoken to them and they all believe it to be a life- saving addition to the armoury you've selected."

The Microbiologist shook his head and continued in a most patronising and misogynist way. "Dear me, now another pretty girl tries. You should not be talking to the doctors here about any drug that is not on my approved list. If you do I will have you banned. And I do not have an armoury. This is not America and we have no need of weapons, just well researched and clinically tried and tested chemical entities. I appreciate it's your job to try to convince me with your big brown eyes but I have had all of you try everything and I really can't ever forget the vision of your John Paul person trying to get me to fly a two seated airplane with him over the

Florida Keys, big cigar in his large mouth, dollars oozing out of his pockets. He looked like a snake oil salesman in a cowboy movie. I'm sorry my dear but dollars, sea planes, pretty ladies, Germans selling fields and bullshit don't beat pure microbiological facts. So it was lovely to meet you but I have patients to see."

JPS had made an extreme and negative impression on him that not even Kitty could undermine. That was obvious. He might be a hugely successful extrovert in his world of profit and expenses - his monthly expenses could probably have bought Kitty a small house - but sadly in the face of pure science, neither he nor Kitty and Amy could hope to win.

As for poor Amy, Kitty knew full well that the medical department had its share of lunatics and Gunther equivalents too. One of the medical advisors she'd met at this latest conference, an extremely tiny man with small round glasses on secondment from a Belgium company had been traumatised by one the night before when he'd joined her sales region's dinner table. He rather resembled the famous pervert comedian but despite his Belgium ancestry he liked women and having fun as well. More to the point he had a fixation on one of Kitty's reps, Big Bad Betty which was why he'd joined their table.

Betty was known for her propensity for using her sexuality to shock. The night before she had pushed the little Belgian under her skirt and he'd popped out again wearing a huge grin. Now she enticed him to sit on her lap having eased her G string down her long legs onto her shoes. The medical man hopped up onto her chair and wriggled his bottom appreciatively on her lap, his eyes bulging and making guttural noises like Benny Hill. The nervous fox hunting rep Kitty was next to said loudly to nobody in particular, "Dear God, and he treats patients. It's a mad house again."

Big Bad Betty then lifted the tiny Flemish doctor up under his arms and held him up like a teddy bear for inspection by the drunken rabble around them. "Look he's managed to get a hard on."

"Put him down Betty," Kitty insisted.

Big Bad Betty gently placed the over-excited man back on the floor and he ran off embarrassed, or to relieve himself, no one really knew or cared which.. It was indeed a madhouse.

As JPS finished his introduction, he lit a huge cigar and sat down waving to the crowds. Her shivering rep just whispered, "For God's sake Kitty, can it get any worse? Don't put me into one of those focus groups please. Can we not just keep together as our region? I can't function if that Welsh maniac comes in to observe."

She tried to ease his anxiety with a few words of comfort. "It's okay. Once marketing has gone through the new cycle's promotion plan this morning, I think we have a team game planned for all of us."

"Oh God no! I can't do that again, no, no. That mad bastard had us blowing up plastic leeks to bash each other in the pool last time and building daffodils out of sticky backed plastic for ****'s sake. Kitty, can we not just go on the piss? I hate this team stuff. They watch everything you do and if they think you're shirking or not interested they ******* fire you. Gunter stands on the pool chair with Nazi Zeiss binoculars just staring at everyone, watching and staring and those scary eyes man. I'm going mad."

"Calm down man. You might end up like poor Angus," Kitty warned him.

"Kitty man, that's not funny, is it. Poor bastard; how the hell do you put up with it all?" he whispered, looking seriously worried and quite ill.

"No it wasn't really funny but it's black humour when you think about it. You couldn't make it up. One day it'll make a good episode for a book and then a comedy series, but no one would believe you man," she whispered back.

"**** me, anyone who had worked here would," her rep whispered back, looking years older than when he had woken up a few hours before.

Kitty reflected on Angus and his fate. He had been a manager and Gunter had been his boss. Obviously, Gunter's relentless search for perfection and sales took their toll on the man, as it did on all his subordinates. Some could handle it but most couldn't and sadly for Angus his behaviour got more and more peculiar as his paranoia grew. Then one Winter Solstice evening, after a supposedly motivational phone call from his scary boss, he was found howling at the full moon, bollock naked on Ben Lomond. The company as usual took care of him after the Duly Authorised Officer had completed his examination. Gunther meanwhile was promoted..

Kitty was made of sterner stuff and while she might well consider howling at the moon after Gunter's motivating sessions, she'd keep that to herself. Though, as she sat having a coffee with her Cambridgeshire rep, she did wonder why a ghostly hooded, dark figure appeared to be standing on the banks of the river Cam beckoning her to over to him. She kept the change from the coffee bill just in case she needed to pay the ferryman.

BOOK THREE

THE BIG YIN'S INFERNO

CIRCLES OF HELL

1
LIVERPOOL
THE BIG YIN

About the same time Jack and Kitty met the ferryman...

"He's lying dead on the pavement next to B site. One of your scaffolders has thrown something off the scaffold and hit him. This is a very serious matter. We may well throw you off the job and claim liquidated damages. And the police here to arrest you."

The police woman nodded in tune with the developer's Project Manager. The Big Yin sitting in his porta cabin wondered what on earth they could accuse him of next. Understandably his response was defensive.

"We don't have any scaffold on that part of the shopping centre. It can't be us. I want to see where this happened, now before the press or the public go ******* mad."

"Okay follow us," said the project manager and they led the Big Yin out of his office onto the bustling Liverpool Street next to the huge new Liverpool One Shopping Centre. A small crowd surrounded a few men in overalls and red hats who were putting safety rail tape around a body lying prostrate, face down, on the street.

As the Yin approached the body, a member of the public shouted "Here comes the coppers; late as usual and now the bloody boss. We hope they ********* crucify you. You greedy bastards"

Marvellous thought the Yin. *We try our best to keep them all safe and give them a brand new town and we get hung drawn and quartered.*

Lying next to the body was a small object. As the Yin got closer he could see that the thing was an old scaffold fitting. His were new. He looked up and around, but as he already knew, there was no scaffolding anywhere in the immediate vicinity. The nearest was about fifty metres away.

"It looks as if some one's thrown that at him from your scaffold fella. Youse are ******* mate," the petite policewoman stated. The Yin thought, *nothing like innocent until proven guilty.*

"Look hen; It would take a ******* Olympic javelin thrower to hit him from over there. And we have nae ********** men there this morning. It canna have been one of us." And turning to his site

115

manager he asked, with no compassion at all, "Is the bastard dead yet?"

"No boss, he's still breathing. He won't wake up though," said a large man in orange overalls.

"Where's the ambulance then?" asked the Yin.

"They called it ages ago. Should be here by now."

At that very moment the Yin heard the siren. The ambulance wasn't in sight yet though. All he could see was heaving crowds of shoppers and commuters going about their business in complete ignorance of the tragedy and certainly the impending doom to be inflicted on him and his company.

The Yin owned a large sub- contracting company from Glasgow. He had been at the site in Liverpool for some time now due to certain problems. The main one was that if the work didn't go faster and more cost effectively his client would bankrupt him and he'd lose his nice house on the banks of Loch Lomond, his yacht and his fleet of vintage Aston Martins. He was not amused at this latest horror story. From day one it had been one disaster to the next. The Yin was not known for his placid and forgiving nature and a series of his own site management casualties had flowed out of the huge shopping centre project on his increasingly frequent stays in the city. This latest incident was trying his very short patience.

He was called the Big Yin by all who knew him and he was a legend in the Industry. He had built up a large business from nothing, starting as a welder in John Brown's shipyard on Clydeside many moons ago. He should have supported Partick Thistle Football Club as he lived in Ben View a few yards from Fir Hill, their ground, but following his family's Irish roots he supported Celtic football. His got his name as he was the spitting image of Billy Connolly, the famous Glaswegian comedian, except he was bald. In all other respects he was Connolly's twin - the same, goatee beard, which he stroked just like Billy and the same height and build. Only the eyes gave him away; when they bulged, unlike Billy,: it wasn't going to be a funny punch line but a full-blooded punch, or a Glasgow kiss, the forehead brought down sharply on an opponent's nose.

Seeing an opportunity to make good money away from the daily grind in the yard, like many of his kind, he took the high road to Aberdeen to work offshore. Two weeks on the rig, and two weeks on the piss back home. He loved this life right up until someone told him there was more money to be made doing his own thing. The yards in Glasgow were now turning their hands to building the oil rigs and platforms needed for Offshore but they had few reliable sub- contractors who understood Oil company specifications and needs so he started a painting business with one container and one blast pot and spray gun. Fifteen years later he was the biggest sub-contractor in Scotland and moving into England and overseas. But today he was dangerously vexed.

"Ehh…out of the way you scallys, let us in there." The Yin heard the ambulance man shout at the few members of the public who had bothered with the allegedly dead shopper. Scousers had usually seen much worse than a body lying comatose and a single police woman. The Yin stayed in the famous St 'orges hotel (well it was really called the St Georges Hotel but as the management hadn't bothered replacing the missing 'Ge', to all of the unsuspecting customers who looked up at their place of haven from the madness around Lime Street, the hotel was the St 'orgies) and every night he watched fight after fight, drive by attacks by young scallys (hooligans, con men, you name it, a scally was it) and people lying battered in the road, so this was nothing new.

The two ambulance men parted the way with their stretcher and resuscitation equipment and reached the small circle surrounding the unconscious man. One paramedic kneeled and slowly turned the poor man's head towards him. He then abruptly dropped the head, stood and kicked the body in its side; much to the astonishment of the assembled witnesses. Turning to his partner and he let rip. "For ****'s sake not again. This is the third time this ******* week." And he kicked the man again shouting, "Jimmy get the **** up man. It's Billy and Jerry again. You can't ******* con us man. Get your ******** arse up now."

The object of the paramedic's wrath opened his eyes and looked up at astonished onlookers. Then in a burst of miraculous resurrection movement he slowly stood up.

One of the older onlookers shouted out: "Here mate. Take this," and he threw the Lazarus clone a half-drunk plastic bottle of water which the resurrected man promptly grabbed. The Scouse wag then shouted, "You'll need it. You must have used up all the

******** Holy water in the Metropolitan Cathedral, you lucky bastard."

They all laughed, even the policewoman. The Big Yin didn't. He was not enamoured with 'Scouse humour' or quaint con schemes to extract large amounts of compensation from his tight Scottish purse for faked injuries. "Take that **** awa afor I muedda the bastard,' he said menacingly.

"Eh, calm down, calm down now. It's only Jimmy man. He's tried this on every site in Liverpool. He alright now; he's just a scally. Come on Jimmy. Just **** off back your pub and leave us in peace will you now."

Liverpool was famous for its so-called 'scallys' - anyone who tried anything to make a bob or two but normally through petty criminal activity. The Big Yin was not amused when he had found his Aston Martin on bricks with all the wheels missing. He was less amused when someone told him that this was nothing as in Liverpool a Scouser would've put John Wayne's horse on bricks to steal its horse shoes for scrap! He didn't see the humour and promptly head butted the budding comedian.

The Big Yin walked back to his cabin shaking his huge head and cursing. His men seeing the grimace on his empurpled face feared another burst of sackings and mayhem at this latest attempt to screw him. The Yin was cursing under his breath. This was far from being a lone example of a *Scouse bit of fun*. Only the week before another such incident had nearly caused him apoplexy.

"He's done what?" the Yin had howled at his site manager Bill.

"He fell down a ladder on night shift and his mates took him home," Bill replied, looking constantly for somewhere to hide for he knew what was coming.

"How the **** did he do that the stupid Scouse twat."

Bill futilely tried to calm the Yin down. "No one knows boss. He says there wasn't any rail around the hole or barrier tape. But when big Alan went to look and take the incident report there was a barrier and tape still there. Al thinks he's trying to fake it all. His mates carried him out and they didn't call big Al until he was already on a stretcher being carted took off. I've just rang him and asked if he's staying off work and he says he is."

"We can't afford a lost time incident you bastard. Get him back in here. Tell him we'll stick him in a cabin all day and he can read his horse racing paper or summit. No ******* LTI's on this site. It'll ******** break me. The bastards will fine me and we'll get thrown off when those ****'s from the developer investigate. Get him back in on light duties. Tell him we'll pay him overtime."

Bill looked sheepishly at his irate leader and wondered if he should tell him it all now. He decided best get it over with. "Big man, I've already asked him. Said we'll come pick him up and all he has to do is sit in the cabin, smoke, drink and do **** all. He just said **** that I want my compensation. I sent big Al around to his place with the health and safety man to talk to him. He's got a collar on his neck and crutch and told us he's taking us for every penny he can."

"Can we have him topped?" the Yin asked calmly .

"Eh....well aye, of course you can but maybe it's best to let it run its course, eh boss?" Bill didn't fancy twenty years in the slammer.

The Yin was raging now. "The bastard! The ******* bastard! I pay these lazy bastards good money, pay millions for safety and good equipment and they just take the piss. I should have stayed in Scotland. Thieving Englishmen that's all you ******* lot are."

Bill stood still watching his master pacing up and down the cabin, steam coming off of his bald head while he constantly stroked his Connolly beard. So much for his English workforce and of course, his English manager standing there, Bill thought. But he was terrified to say it and the Yin broke the silence first. "Get back to work and kick those lazy bastards' arses. No more safety incidents or I'll sack the lot of them." The Big Yin had yet to read about let alone adopt behavioural safety motivation, the buddy principle and honesty with near misses.

Five days later the Yin was getting ready to drive back up to beloved Scotland and his lovely family and his sheep farm on the bonny, bonny banks of Loch Lomond. He was unamused to be handed a solicitor's letter asking for compensation or they'd sue him for the neck and back injury from the guy who had fallen. It fact he ripped it up in front of his site commercial QS and told him he'd fire him unless he could get the man topped. As the QS was also a magistrate and City Councillor in Liverpool, he was unlikely to comply with his boss's' demand. Instead he took a huge gamble with his tenure on site and asked if he could take the morning off as he had a court session as chairman of the bench.

The big man's the predictable reply: "**** that. I pay your wages not the ******* poliss."

The quantity surveyor, being a QS, naturally knew his rights, and told his boss that it was the law and that he had to let him off to do his public duty. The Yin howled and paced up and down stroking his beard but eventually saw reason and let his Perry Mason go. He had just made one of the best decisions he'd made in some time.

His QS came back from his morning's sentencing of local Liverpool villains and unusually for a dour and serious man (he was a quantity surveyor remember) he had a spring to his step and a huge grin as he entered his boss's torture chamber.

"What the **** are you deeing here? I thought yeah were working in the slammer or something?' the Yin greeted him morosely.

"No boss; finished sentencing half an hour ago. I came straight around to tell you the good news before you go."

"There's nae good news ya daft twat. The job's about ******** and you tak a day off tae play at being a ******** judge."

"Well, I've got some news. I was sat on the bench with my fellow magistrates reading the charge sheet and the next scally in was a man who'd been taking lorries without consent and selling scaffold from them. We sat waiting for the accused to arrive in the dock, when in strolls our injured scaffolder, as sprightly as a gazelle. He had no neck brace, crutch or bandages. We both stared at each other open mouthed for three seconds and he turned and ran back out, followed by Merseyside police. Let's see what his solicitor says about that then; a miracle cure it seems!"

And after his revelation the QS sat down smugly.

"Aye; And I bet the thieving bastard was selling my scaffold too. I told youse all we should have topped the bastard."

But as he left to drive up the M6 to his beloved wife and his mansion on the Loch and pat his four children on the head and feed his new born lambs, the Big Yin smiled for the first time that week.

2
ABERDEEN
WULLIE THE MAGICIAN

Sometime after the court incident…

"Boss the poliss are all ower the yard. They've got their doggies with them tae."

Wullie was looking out over the mobilisation yard full of containers bound for the oil platforms offshore. A group of uniformed policemen with sniffer dogs were rifling through his precious equipment and materials bound for use by the company's men on the cold forbidding North Sea. He was not amused. This yard was his territory, his kingdom, and no one messed with his kit.

'Bloody poliss," he said to no one but himself, *"why don't they just let us get on with making money for the big man. I'd better let the boss know they're here. Let's hope they don't find anything or heaven forbid find out for ****'s sake."*

He picked up the phone and rang the Big Yin, who didn't seem too worried and said so. "Whit's yeah problem, Wullie. We dinnae have any drugs in our stuff man. The doggies are only there to sniff oot the drugs man. Whit's ya woory ya daft lune ya.?"

"Big man, it's nae the drugs am worrying aboot with the doggies. Ah just hope the bastards canna coont!"

The big man at the end of the phone in Liverpool smiled for the first time in a while. He loved Wullie, a fellow Glaswegian and Celtic supporter who had been with him since the beginning. One of the very few he hadn't sacked in his furies over losing money and equipment. Wullie never lost a thing and he made him lots of money. "Aye Wullie: let's hope the doggies are as daft as the oil companies eh?" And he put the phone down.

Wullie took a swig of his tea and watched the dogs running between the containers. *Aye big man you are correct. They'll have to be smart to catch us.* Wullie was a master at magical tricks and his lads offshore were his lovely assistants. Wullie could make the client believe that each of his containers was full to the brim of material when in reality they were empty; a masterful illusion worthy of Houdini. Similarly he could make the client believe there were fifty men scaffolding his rig when in reality there were no more than ten.

This was the secret that the two men had been alluding to on the telephone. It would be a disaster if the police dogs could actually count, as they would find out that his precious containers heading offshore were actually empty. The illusion would be revealed and the money flow be cut off because the money flowed only because the client believed he was paying for full containers not empty ones. They wouldn't keep paying for thin air and this would make the Big Yin very unhappy indeed.

Wullie took another sup of his tea confident that the dogs were probably as thick as the crude oil the company extracted from the North Sea. After all he been performing this trick for years now and the audience was still in awe of his magic. He put his feet up and began to shudder a little as he remembered the only person who had ever seen through the illusion.

"Wullie, the new client's Operation's Director wants to come and see the site. He's a ******* nightmare so be careful." The Big Yin sat in his Glasgow main board room. Around him were his loyal and trusted directors and main managers. He liked to bring them together every now and then, into his own personal Circle of Hell where he could torture them and then, in the name of motivation, put them through heavy drinking and random violence in the bars and clubs of the dear green place that was Glasgow. He reserved one torment in particular for Peter, the only Englishman in the team. The Yin would wait until Peter was presenting some business school theory on engineering or the latest material management control system and then tilt his body and raise a leg up just as Peter used his modern laser pointer to show some intricate flow diagram on the screen. Everyone except Peter always knew what was coming. The Yin was now in proper farting position tilted perfectly to prevent any follow through and he'd smile back at everyone smiling and watching him. Then he'd let blaze with a resounding and often wet sounding fart.

"Oh for ****'s sake boss. Come on man. I've spent two weeks working on this presentation and you just fart yet again. It's not fair man," the poor victim would holler as everyone else laughed.

The Yin would more often than not follow up with a tirade such as, "Yeah should have been sorting out that ******* site I gave you to sort, nae writing ******* presentations. Pissing my money away you English twat. What's a process flow chart anyway and who the

**** cares. Sit down yeah precious bastard. Let's move on to who owes us money and how we can **** right intae them if they don't pay."

After these humiliations Peter would sit down and wonder which asylum he had joined. The poor man was intelligent and knowledgeable. He had actually started on the tools and learned the game the hard way but because he had also self-educated himself was always trying valiantly to introduce modern systems and heaven forbid, planning into the business he was a pariah. And he was English, which was his real handicap. But he survived because despite all indications to the contrary the Big Yin liked and respected him, but he had perennially to suffer the farting ritual to humour his less than enigmatic leader.

At this particular board meeting the Yin was exploring the consequences of one of their biggest clients changing its leadership team after an investigation into revealed that certain of them had acquired mansions in Spain, yachts, racing cars and several small African countries on salaries of around twenty five grand a year. Naturally the shareholders were disturbed by this revelation and decided it was time for a reorganisation.

"Even the procurement logistics manager had a seven series BMW, ten race horses and a villa in Andalusia." The Big Yin continued with a huge grin: "Diz anyone of yeah kna how his dog begs? Before they could answer, he stood up in a familiar canine begging pose with two hands raised up to his chest and fingers turned downwards. "It disnae beg like this." Then he put one of his hands behind his back, upturning it in mimicry of *getting a backhander*, "It begs like this."

They all laughed loudly most of them knowing the score in the business all too well.

"Anyway this new guy is a twat. I've tried to sort him but he doesn't drink fae ****'s sake. He's ******** huge and all he eats is Chinese. He has eaten me oota hoose and haem. He eats ten meals when I tak him tae the restaurant. Seems he's here to clean out all the company and the sites. On his last job he told me he closed ten companies and put the board of directors in jail. I thought, fae ****'s sake we canna let him near oor site but the bastard is coming up to see his yard in the Orkneys. Wullie son, that's your job wee man. You better mak sure he disna mak it haem if he finds oot wrong son."

Wullie just nodded and the next day flew north to the wettest place on God's earth.

The huge client's tour of sub –contractors duly reached Wullie who showed him round the large yard and the surrounding facilities. In accordance with the contract Wullie was charging the client and being reimbursed for everybody he had on site. Time- sheets and man hours totals were submitted each week but the client's QSs couldn't count. Well they couldn't count bodies so all they could add up were the man-hours to be multiplied by the hourly rate. The trouble was that in all Wullie the magician was charging for two hundred and fifty men, six days a week, ten hours a day plus overtime but he actually had only one hundred and fifty on site. The other hundred were ghosts whose fabricated time sheets were duly signed by the client's site supervisor who was Wullie's long-lost cousin from the Gorbals. Wullie and the team had been doing this for many years.

The client consulted the manpower chart and asked Wullie if this large onsite presence was necessary. Wullie confirmed that of course it was if he wanted his already late project out before the next ice age descended on Western Scotland. The client scowled and followed Wullie on a tour of each area in turn.

Wullie had prepared for this eventuality by instructing his ten supervisors to run from one site to another moving men between the various workplaces once the client had visited. If he counted he would see a total workforce of two hundred and fifty men in action.

The walkabout concluded, the client was grinning and responded with warmth to the offer of coffee. *Great* Wullie thought, *he's not as bad as the Yin said. He's happy; another sucker fooled by the magic.* They sat and supped their coffees but the massive client said nothing to the wee Glaswegian which began to grate on Wullie's nerves. *Why wasn't he talking.* Then the client threw a piece of white chalk onto the desk and asked Wullie, "What's that?"

"A've nay idea bonny lad. It looks like chalk tae me. Whit is it fae?" Wullie answered, very puzzled.

"It's what is going to **** you my Scottish friend and your company," the giant said, still staring at Wullie.

"Ah dinnae ken whit yeah talking about man," Willie replied, starting to get a really bad feeling about this."

"Let me explain; how do you say it up here - 'wee man'? I did not come up here on a banana boat. I'm paid an enormous amount of money to sort out people like you. I think you owe us a large amount of compensation. I started to sus you out when I noticed your big supervisor, the lad with the razor scar, at the first module. Then we walk five hundred yards further and there he is again, this time wearing a white worker's helmet instead of his green one. So, I did what I did when I put four thousand Indians out of work in Bombay. I started shaking hands, hugging and touching each worker your supervisors introduced to me and sticking a chalk mark on the back of their overalls. And of course the same men kept turning up at every site, all with a chalk mark on their backs, even in the offsite pipe shops. Now then Wullie: care to explain that?"

Now, some years later, Wullie was looking at the sniffer dogs jumping back into the police vans unable to count what wasn't there at all and he said out loud to himself: "What a twat."

It had cost the Big Yin one hell of a lot to repay the extra money claimed by the ghosts. The client decided arbitrarily how many ghosts he had paid for and took it off the final account. Wullie and his team were allowed to stay because it was too risky for the client to change sub-contractor when the job was so in the shit but the hit man replaced all his own supervision and QSs with new, teetotal, honest ones.

This was the only time Wullie had been caught and cost his great friend money. But even then it hadn't really been such a disaster. The Yin still made a million as the big English bastard never worked out the *disappearing stainless steel trick. He wasn't so ****** clever after all. The English will never beat us.*

3
LIVERPOOL
VIAGRA JIMMY

The 4th Circle…

"Big Man we have a problem."

"For ****'s sake I've just arrived Wullie. Whit's wrang the noo?"

The Big Yin had just arrived on site after a long rain-drenched early Monday morning drive from his loch side retreat to the Liverpool torture chamber that was his problematic construction site. He had replaced the last construction manager with his trusted Wullie just before Christmas.

"They had the docs and nurses here first thing man and drug tested everyone," Wullie informed his boss.

"Surely the lads were okay? asked the big man.

"Well, ergh, kna big man…forty two of them tested positive. Thirty cocaine, five dope and anither five of them both," answered Wullie, moving a bit further away from his boss's reach, just in case.

"Holy Mary and all the ******** saints! Whit next in this hell hole, not again after that young Jimmy thing. Whit have yeah done with them?"

"I've sacked them boss. I had tae, the client is ganning mental. He wants to see yeah noo. After Friday's episode they're thinking of throwing us off ah think."

The Big Yin sat down at his desk. This bloody place would be the death of him. *Drug and alcohol testing? Dear God, in the old days you would be sacked if you weren't pissed.* Even he'd been tested the week before. He knew with the beer and whiskey needed to get to sleep in the St Orges' zoo he was knackered. His alcohol level wouldn't pass and the last thing he could afford as the main man was to be thrown off site for being pissed. He thought quickly and by the time he met the nice lady doctor, he'd formulated a plan. After a few pleasantries she gave him a sample jar and asked him to go into the toilet and pee into it in. The Yin duly peed into the jar but in washing his hands he put the jar under the running cold tap. *'That'll dilute the alcohol to almost zero,'* he chuckled.

With a smile he gave the doctor the jar. She got up from her desk and went to a table where she kept her test equipment. She then took a thermometer and placed it in the jar. After a minute, she examined the result and said, "Uhm." She came back to sit opposite a worried Yin, looked him straight in his eyes and said: "It appears you should be either dead or about to die. Unless you have been shipwrecked and floating in the Arctic sea on a life raft for days, you have a serious medical condition because your urine temperature is way below that needed to support life."

"Is it that serious Doc? Maybe you made a mistake eh? " the Yin asked with a nervous smile and a raise of his eyebrows as if trying to suggest, maybe they should start again.

The doctor smiled back. Obviously she had seen it all before. "I'll have to recalibrate the thermometer. Never did like these electronic ones. It'll take some time. Maybe you should come back in the morning?"

"Aye thanks hen; that seems a good idea. I'll try to stay warm tonight. Tuck mesel up in mah beed a bit earlier; dae yah think that'll help tae?"

"I'd say that would be wise, medically speaking. Think you'd better get back to work now."

Now, she was a decent doc, not like the bastards this morning, He had to wonder what the client would do now. He shuddered and wished he was back in Glasgow with like-minded people. He put his boots and hat on and walked the short distance to the client's office where he found the client in full angry mode.

"Well you'll have to get replacements in by Friday or we'll send a notice to terminate your contract. We're sick of your indiscipline and downright incompetence. How many more of your lads are drug addicts? This is the second time in a month!"

"That's nae correct. Ah told yeah Jimmy was a mistake man. The other four, yes, they were positive but Jimmy was only scared. Dinnae exaggerate. We're all not drug addicts. Piss heads maybe, but nae all addicts' man," answered the Yin, getting annoyed.

"Oh yes Jimmy. Tell me again what happened with Jimmy," his client asked and turning to his stern-faced, commercial hit man from London added, "This is a good one. You need to hear this." He folded his arms, sat back and listened to the Yin reprise the circumstances of Jimmy's fall from grace.

Jimmy had turned up at site a few weeks before and spotted the nurses waiting to take his urine sample. He just turned and did a runner. Wullie had sacked the other four who tested positive and sacked Jimmy in his absence. Jimmy came back in the next day to plead for his job back. As he was one of the better young lads and a hard worker Wullie took pity and went to the Yin to him tell what Jimmy had told him in mitigation and plead for his reinstatement.

"Aye gan on then Wullie," the Yin said in a rare moment of compassion.

"Well it seems when Jimmy saw the nurses he was embarrassed; he disnae tak the drugs big man. It seems he had a huge hard on. He'd taken that new pill, eh, ah think it's called Viagra, the neet afor and it was still working. He was just shy."

"Dis the Scouse bastard think we're all awl Geordies - Scotsmen with brains bashed in. Sack the bastard. A ******** hard on for ten hours! Dear me what will the scouse twats think of next. And Wullie, ah think yeah are ganning soft in the heed man. Fire the bastard. Now what about last night's progress? - it was shite...."

And so Wullie had to say goodbye to Jimmy.

That next weekend the Big Yin had returned home and on Saturday went to his pub before the match. There he met his two young nephews and bought them a few beers. They looked knackered and he told them so. The reason he learned was that they had been screwing all night using this new wonder drug called Viagra.

"Where's yaehs get that and why the **** wid young lads want that, man?"

"We get it frae Wee Willy the bar owner. Yeah kna he can supply anything, cigarettes, baccy, booze, guns, yeah name it he's got it. And he's got a huge tub of these new blue pills man. Five poond a go: dae yaeh want some?"

"Like **** ah dee; I dinnae need that man and nay should yaehs. Why dee ya use it, man?" the Yin said.

"It lets yeah shag alneet. Problem with it is ah went to mah work last Monday and ah couldn't stop the lads laughing at me," answered his youngest nephew.

"Why would they laugh at yeah?" asked a puzzled and naïve Yin.

"Coz I still had a hard on man. Yeah canna get rid of it when yeah use this stuff."

The Big Yin stood at the bar and took a long pull at his beer and grimaced at the thought of poor Jimmy being sacked for nothing.

He thought *Maybe I should tell Wullie to give the lad another chance.* Then he remembered all the other trouble he'd had in Liverpool, finished off his pint and whispered under his breath to no one but himself: " **** him."

And he paid him no further mind.

But now the client had brought him back to mind but in the context of much more serious consequences. It wasn't going to be a good morning.

"Yes. How do you explain an armed thug coming on site and threatening my staff," the client asked quietly, surprisingly calm.

"Dinnae exaggerate man. He wasn't after your staff - he was after me," clarified the frustrated Yin.

The client was unimpressed. "I don't care if he was after Don Corleone himself. I can't have armed gangsters running riot, not on my site. Do you understand that? My colleague here from head office will be writing to you for a full report and explanation and you'll be getting default letters for this, the drugs and the progress. We've had enough of your incompetence and lies."

The Scotsman's eyebrows raised and his bald head glowed. He pulled violently on his beard and then exploded. "Dinnae talk to me like that yeah English bastard. Ah'll sort the gunman oot in mah own way and ah'll sort yeah and that stuck up bastard sitting with yeah the ******* same way if yeah dinnae show some respect. Ah can buy and sell you and your company and ah might just dee that. Ah'll buy ya company and I'll fire the lot of yeah. I'm ******** off back noo. Send ya ******** letters."

And he went back to his cabin to calm down, trying to work out what to do about the gun man.

The man had arrived on site fifteen minutes after he'd left to go back up to Glasgow. He'd stormed into the cabin, pulled a sawn off shotgun from under his Crombie and asked the commercial magistrate where the Big Yin was. He didn't believe the QS telling him he wasn't there, had kicked in the Yin's door. The gunman was not amused by the empty office and pointed the gun at the frightened QS gave him a message for the Yin; like Arnie Schwarzenegger, "I'll be back."

"Bloody unions," the Yin said to himself. The gun man was the direct result of a meeting with the union site rep he'd fired and his district boss. The district boss had sent the site rep out of the Yin's office as the angry man kept threatening strike action, disruption and violence and the Yin was threating worse in response if the man wanted it. In an attempt to defuse the situation the district man told the Yin that he'd accept that forty-five of his members had been sacked if the Yin would keep his rep on site.

The Yin had exploded. "Mah fayther would turn in his grave at what yeah propose.. He was Union and Labour through and through and you want to sacrifice yeah members' fae one lazy, trouble causing Scouse tossa like him. Ah dinna give two ****'s for unions, hate the bastards, but ah dinnae like being told whit to dee. Get the **** oota mah office afor I nut yeah."

"Okay, calm down, calm down. I'll go but you'd better be prepared for trouble here. You're not in Scotland now."

Sure on Friday the hit man had arrived.

As he sat in his office that Monday morning the Yin decided he could always call in Big Tam. Even if they only wanted to frighten him and show the site lads that they were strong enough to sort out anyone they wanted. Well what the hell….he'd just ride it out and if it escalated - he'd ring Big Tam.

4
GLASGOW
BIG TAM

One year on

The Big Yin was enjoying himself away from Liverpool and his own Purgatory. Back in his favourite place in Glasgow he was having fun at a board meeting. It was just after nine in the morning and he had just blown off a huge fart as his English brain-box tried to demonstrate the benefits of Primavera planning systems. The directors howled with laughter. The English engineer gave up, defeated by both the smell and the indignity of it all, and slunk back to his to office to contemplate a lawsuit for racial and physical harassment.

Now the leader of the motley crew was being interrupted in mid-flow by his amiable and very posh Scottish Sales Director who informed the meeting he needed to take a very important call from Norway. "Sorry mate but I have to take it. We're close to winning the Dutch ship contract on Clydeside. I've been wining and dining KT for months and it's about to pay off. Is it okay if I go, boss?" The handsome salesman threw his flowing blond hair back with his hand to emphasise the importance of the call.

"Aye, yeah may as well **** off. This is boring as shite," said the Yin, and slightly lifting his leg, he let off another loud fart just as the Englishman re-entered the room. "But yeah better bring me good news when yeah get back, ya bastard."

The immaculately dressed director strode purposely to the door and turned to face them all. With gusto and positivity he said; "Big contract this, guys. This will take us into the major league. KT has promised if we do well he'll use us on his next big one in Russia. I'll do my best guys, for the team." And he left.

The Yin giggled, stood and beckoned them all to follow him, miming them to do it quietly. He knew his sales director. He was the best in the business, iconic and a true professional but although a perfect gentleman in business, like most of his clan, the Yin knew full well he liked a dram or two.

They sneaked out past the Yin's lovely PA towards the kitchen. She looked surprised but before she could say anything the boss put his finger to his mouth and whispered, "Ssh." Chuckling he made them all peer around the partly open kitchen door. There they observed the super salesman filling a half pint glass three quarters full of vodka and then adding a small drop of orange juice. He mixed it and drank it all down in one go.

Chuckling, the Yin lead them all back to the board room without a word about what they'd just witnessed.

Fifteen minutes later the smiling sales wizard opened the board room door with a flourish, a spring in his step and a florid face even redder than normal. "Sorry folks; took a bit longer than I thought. It's looking great though boss. We should get the letter of intent next Friday. Had a great conversation and what a guy he is."

"Aye; he better come up with the job after all the ******* money you've spent on the bastard. You're looking better. The phone call must have picked yeah up." The Yin winked at all the rest of the vodka voyeurs. "Sit down and let's get back to money and how you are all pissing it arl away frae me on boozing with mah clients."

There was no other mention of the *morning pick up* again. The Englishman was the only one there who didn't see all the fridges in the kitchen stocked to the gunnels with as much booze as Al Capone shipped across the Canadian border as a perfectly normal facet of corporate life.

However, the Englishman was still there nine months later when they were facing disaster on the ship contract his fellow director had won for them with another brilliant sales pitch and competitive bit of pricing. At the time it had seemed carping to be so critical of it all. The guy had done marvellously at pulling so much business into the company, and *maybe a few drams of whiskey was really all it took*. The aristocratic Scotsman had also been close to securing an iconic bridge repair contract at the time having put the American client's tender team into an Inverness hospital with alcoholic poisoning after taking them on a distillery and golf tour. He had driven back the next day leaving the Americans in a stupor, whistling *'Speed bonny boat over the sea to Skye'* with a letter of intent in his back pocket. A sales genius and the best Glenmorangie drinker in the Highlands it appeared.

Now as the Englishman drove towards Clydebank and the ship the job seemed unreal, almost dreamlike. His instructions issued a week ago by the Big Yin one week ago were to meet KT and Jack, the client's English company's boss to solve the current union problem at the shipyard. Despite local and national negotiations the deadlock over a demanded pay rise continued as did the stubborn refusal to work. This was killing the job for both contractor and client with the latter threatening liquidated damages claims and all other manner of legal actions. The Englishman's mercurial boss was still stuck down in Liverpool waging war Glaswegian style on the developer with that job running a year late and also threatening their existence. The Yin had told him to sort the ship and unions out now, or he'd be up to sort them all. No one wanted that. And now the Big Yin said that he had to unleash *The Kraken. Dear God, how did I get into this* he thought as he pulled into the shipyard?

The Big Yin had howled at him the night before during his nightly stint of phone torture. "Yaeh'll tell that soft English bastard client I've had enough of his and your ******** efforts with those union bastards. I'm sending in Big Tam. Tell that useless twat Jack to take a step back, I don't want him getting hurt mind by Big Tam. It'll **** up my chance of pulling a final deal with KT. The daft Norwegian bastard likes him."

The Englishman met Jack in the site offices and discovered he liked him too. He seemed a bit like himself - persecuted, humiliated and mentally drained but basically sane. "The big man wants you to meet Big Tam tonight in the Yoker Ferry pub. He's having Big Tam sort out the job tomorrow on site," he told Jack.

"Who the hell is Big Tam?" asked Jack.

"Well, he's the guy the boss uses when things are going a bit hairy on sites or if a client is threatening legal action or non- payment. He's sort of the nuclear option."

Jack gulped. He'd brought a letter up from Nigel, threatening legal action and non -payment if the Big Yin's company didn't resolve the dispute. *How the hell did he know he had it? Or did he know? Who was the spy?* The usual paranoia reigned. Jack sweated again and his nervous tic started up. "We really can't have that on our site. We won't allow threatening behaviour or intimidation," Jack said, feeling a bit hypocritical given Ernie and his mates' proclivity for using the treat of mass slaughter in the wheel abraders to solve minor disputes but he had to put his foot down. He was the boss.

"Oh it's okay Jack. Everybody on site will know Big Tam. He's one of them. All he'll do is have a walk around and chat to a few people. You'll find it'll all be fine. Don't worry. I'm like you mate, always was a professional till I met the Big Yin. We can solve this without any of that hanky panky. Just meet Tam tonight and have a drink with him. I'm sure you'll get on with him. He says he'll be there about seven.."

Jack looked at his sub contractor's engineering director and wondered what they were really up to. He had had a tortuous time so far with KT's gold bullion owning mate, Goldfinger. KT had never been off the phone and had visited several times to drag him across the site, the ballast tanks, the bilges, the cargo pumps, each time crucifying him for late delivery, poor workmanship and, worst of all, for losing money. Now he had the strike.

When The Mule had snapped the paint inspector's finger for repeatedly poking him in the chest, the man having foolishly and tragically taken no notice of The Mule warning him to stop, Jack had known this was going to be a tough one to resolve. He'd sent the Bonny Lad and the Wee Man up to help sort it after things went a bit wrong with the crazy Glaswegian sub-contractor KT had selected mainly because their boss, the Big Yin, was just too like KT. They were both extremely successful businessmen and filthy rich and as Jack was struggling to survive in this world of madness, he had tried to adopt their style of leadership and management. That is until his wife noticed him staring wildly into the mirror and waking screaming at night at the curtains. She'd threatened him with the Duly Authorised Officer and he just gave up, deciding he probably didn't have it in him. And now he had to meet Big Tam.

"Oh shit Jack. You can't allow him on site man. He's a bloody hit man," hollered the Bonny Lad.

The Wee man butted in. "Aye Jack. Word is he was once one of the button men for Arthur Thompson. He's a bit of legend around here mate. Maybe wise not to stir up old Glasgow vendettas. The Big Yin has employed him for years as an operations manager. Well, that's what he gets paid as but he's always the one they send in to *review* how sites are being run. He reports back to no one but the big man and things always change after he visits."

Jack just sat back and shook his head. They were in the site office when he told the small site management team what the subcontractor wanted to do and that the man he was meeting might well have started the Glasgow's *ice cream wars*. Or ended them. What he never told them was that KT had already spoken to the Big Yin and agreed this was the best way forward, so Jack might huff and puff but couldn't stop the man coming on site. What KT wanted would happen, so he might as well meet the guy.

He was duly there at the pub at 7 pm holding a pint of beer and waiting for Big Tam to arrive. Two huge men with shaven heads, one heavily scarred, arrived. He half stood to greet them but they walked straight past him to join two other two men sitting in a corner, jabbering in the usual incomprehensible Glasgow accent. He sat down again.

A few minutes later in walked a slightly built man, wearing dark sunglasses, a smart double buttoned blazer and grey slacks, an outfit completed by highly-polished, patent leather shoes. Jack ignored him, presuming him to be some sort of sales rep or someone looking for a quaint Scottish pub with a quiz or Caileigh or somesuch entertainment. The small man walked up to the bar and asked in deep guttural Glaswegian if there was an Englishman called Jack in the bar.

The barman said, "There's awnly wan English bastard in here. Over there." And he pointed him out..

Jack stared unbelievingly. The man coming towards him looked more yachtsman than hardened gangster.

"Hallo. I'm Tam. The Big Yin said you need to talk tae me big man."

Jack sat through an entire evening of revelation about life in Glasgow in the fast lane. Tam relaxed as they chatted. He never drank alcohol, just orange juice. He was lucid, intelligent and funny. He looked and acted like a Church of Scotland minister rather than the alleged hit man for Glasgow's infamous mob. He explained how he had been recruited at fourteen into *the family* and of his first jobs at that tender age. Jack began to feel sufficiently at ease to ask about the man's nickname of him and who had had the temerity to give it to him. He was informed bluntly but calmly that the main man himself had called him Big Tam because he just did whatever he was asked to do without fear or remorse. To his employer he was *the big man*. Despite episodes of severe anxiety about the man he was sitting with, Jack actually enjoyed the evening and they arranged to meet again after Tam's *walk around* the site in the morning.

The next day Tam simply told Jack and his team, "Ah think the lads are happy now. Yaeh'll nay have any more bother. We'll pay them the first offer we put on the table and yaeh'll see the job start to fly now, big man. The Unions will nae be back, I can guarantee that. Ah've talked to the Big Yin. Told him I liked yeah and I sorted the lads out. He's happy with that. I'd give KT a call too, Jack. Good lad is KT. We go back some years."

Jack started getting paranoid again. *Thank God he liked me. What would The Big Yin have done if he hadn't? So Big Tam knows KT too?* Dear me; what a tangled web he'd got stuck in. But hey-ho what the shit, the lads were back to work; he still had his job and thankfully his legs, and one day he might even get that million-dollar bonus KT had promised him.

He should have known better. A dark hooded figure beckoned him from across the banks of the Clyde to join him on his ferry.

BOOK FOUR

JACK AND KITTY'S PURGATORY

THE SEVEN CIRCLES OF SIN

1
PARIS
BERNARD L'ESTRANGE

...Time has moved on...

"Look yourself in the mirror and then fire the bastard."

Jack smiled across at Kitty. She smiled back and made a circling movement with her finger adjacent to her temple, indicating *He's crackers*. The very important American management consultant didn't see the gesture as he was too busy parading up and down the hotel conference room in his bowling jacket and shoes, gesticulating with his arms and pronouncing pearls of wisdom on the subject of leadership and management to the small group of people selected by their companies to benefit from his world class consultancy knowledge and exalted skills for five solid days.

Jack knew from KT that they were closer than ever to selling off Jack's company so some world class training might come in handy when new owners were deciding whether to keep him on or sack him although Jack still hoped KT would let him stay in the original company, albeit in the cold and damp misery of Stavanger. This was in large part because posh he might be but the potential buyer's chairman, in the course of undertaking due diligence, was demonstrating even less knowledge than jack had about the business or the sectors they operated in. Still perhaps the management course would help him bond better with the man and so he'd agreed to come to Paris to be tutored by Bernard L'Estrange's The only other Brit on the course was Kitty and from dinner on the first night they naturally stuck together.

Kitty had moved on from her nightly sessions of telephone torment from Gunter with a promotion into the madhouse of head office and its marketing wing. Here her boss, the relatively new marketing manager, spent most of his day staring at the telephone on his desk. On her first day she entered his office to a doleful welcome: "When the line is cut off, I'll know I'm history. The computer went last week. It's only a matter of time," he said miserably. He picked up and pointed the telephone earpiece to Kitty. "Oh well it's still live. I've got one more day."

No one had told her when they asked her to relocate that the product she was to launch with the new super duper marketing manager they had hired from a competitor to move them into a completely new area had been discontinued before it even started by the big bosses in America. It seems the product was not the sort of thing the Chairman and Chief Executive thought the company should be selling. Why it took a year of market research, product development, manufacturing and field force recruitment before, mere weeks away from launch, the two elderly gentlemen from Zurich with the ultimate veto were consulted, no one seemed to able to tell her. Especially the man specifically recruited to head it all up.

Kitty agreed to being sent for the L'Estrange experience hopeful that it would ensure they found her another spot in head office in place of the one she thought she was getting.

Over a few beers Jack had explained to her that, like him, she had probably been sent away while the company decided what to do with her and that their investment in such expensive training might make the company look better in the eyes of the Chairman of any eventual Industrial tribunal. Kitty was still less cynical than Jack but her time in medical sales had rendered her rather more paranoid. Both decided to try to enjoy the time away from the respective insanities of their own businesses.

"If you're in a lifeboat with your colleagues and one of them starts rocking the boat, what do you do?"

"Restrain them?" a lady from Italy replied to Bernard L'Estrange's question.

"No Ma'am. That is not what you should do. Anyone one else?"

"Talk to them and try to calm them down?" Jack shouted across the room from. He didn't really think that. He knew from his experience with his own crazies that it would be better to take one of the guns buried in Big Ed's wife's rose bed and just shoot the bugger. But he was getting wise to the ways of humanistic, directional leadership that was the in thing these days and that words like empathy, counselling and empowerment seemed to bear more weight at job interviews than "shoot the bastard."

"No sir. Yet again you are missing the point." said the flamboyant guru of leadership. "You all seem to be in the same mode here. I will give you the correct answer. You should throw the bastard out of the lifeboat."

Jack looked across to Kitty and mouthed the name, "Gunter?"

Kitty nodded and whispered back. "KT?"

Jack nodded.

Bernard came to his conclusion. "You see the company pays you as leaders to lead and manage according to whatever rules they set. I am dressed as a bowler. If I decide to use my bowling ball as a baseball then I am not a bowler anymore and I am rocking the boat. I am not professional. A professional does the same thing every time they go on stage or the field of play. Their employers pay them to do exactly that. They have a behavioural rental agreement with the company. The company pays them to do exactly what it tells them their behaviour should be. If they don't then they must be fired. It's your job to make sure your people do what they are told. If not, you fire the bastards. Throw them out of the life boat."

"Oh I see. If we have a person whose personality is causing the boat to rock. We have to change their personality or fire them?" interjected the German managing Director of a car component firm.

"Do you know what a change of personality is, sir?" asked the consultant, leaping across the room in his bowling shoes.

"Ja, I think so. It is when you change someone you don't like into someone you do, nein?"

"Nein, my Teutonic friend is incorrect. It is not that. A change of personality is a sign of mental illness. I assume you are not a doctor, so don't go around trying to treat your people with mental illness. You will fail and probably be sued for malpractice." Bernard arms windmilled, dismissing yet another of his trainees to the rubbish dump of psychological incompetence. "Behaviour is what you are there to change. The things a person must do to get the job done you are paying them to do. If they smile, cry, hide in a cupboard with a small rodent after work, it matters not. You rent the behaviour every day at work that you are paying them for. If you try and try to change that behaviour, and the person refuses or can't change, you look yourself in the mirror because you have failed, and then you fire the bastard. Now let's move on to motivation."

Dear God Kitty thought, *American management, you can keep it. Maybe it's time to move on.* The phone on her desk would probably be cut off anyway by the time she got back. She looked over to Jack who was deep in thought.

Jack was considering what the great consultant had said and trying to reconcile his own management style with that. Some of what he said he had already tried anyway, and much of it would never work with the people he worked with because of their intractability. Maybe it was time to move on and try something different. He might well have no choice anyway if the take-over happened.

Both of them had shared their experiences openly in the bar and they had a lot in common. Kitty was increasingly of the view that her dreams of saving the world with wonder drugs and becoming a true leader in her Industry were a bit wide of the mark. As she had grown and been promoted in the business there was much which troubled her. There was the issue of profit and price: as she moved into marketing she was becoming much more aware of that. The fact that some drugs were manufactured in third world countries at very low cost and then shipped to the UK, packaged up and massively re-priced to be sold to the National Health Service disturbed her more and more. The NHS allowed companies to make a certain agreed amount of profit on their drugs and the annual price rises and marketing spend they could use to sell them were geared to that profit margin but obviously they were getting round that by manufacturing for peanuts in places like the Caribbean or Africa and selling on to the same company or a subsidiary in the UK for mega bucks and it was that already inflated base price which was used as their cost of manufacture for the NHS, not the actual cost in Puerto Rico or Bangladesh or wherever. She understood the need for profit with the cost of research and development running into the billions of dollars for most products but even so....

And there was the warehouse in Holland. She recalled the day she first found out about its existence when she confronted an owner of a pharmacy in Norfolk.

"Yes, Tony does very well with the doctors here. He's a great rep," said Mr Button the pharmacist.

"But there aren't any sales in this area, Mr Button. Tony's in danger of being sacked for that," Kitty replied.

"I buy fifty packs of Powerlol a month. Before Tony came I bought none. He's the best you've had here. All the doctors prescribe your product now."

"So why are there no recorded sales from our distributer then?"

"Because I buy them from you in Holland for half the price you supply them here. It's EEC law. You ship them there, and we ship them back. It's simple business sense."

Kitty was amazed and furious. She felt cheated because only the week before she had been hauled into head office for a meeting on her reps poor performance. In attendance were the Four Horsemen of the Apocalypse; Mervyn, Morgan, Gunter and Brad, the personnel manager, who she hadn't seen since he ran Andy off in handcuffs all those years ago. She thought he had moved on to Wyoming or Laramie or somewhere. And now here he was on his pale horse, *And death followed with him.*

"You've had enough time to change Tony. He isn't performing. Just look at his market share. It's dropped each month for six months in a row. Enough is enough. Give him a final written warning and if he doesn't hit target next month, Brad will fire him," Mervyn told her from behind his big desk, turning the pages of his dictionary, in search of the word *Trust.*

Morgan puffed at his pipe shuffling his Tarot cards while Gunter stared at her, his eyes moving from one side to another, whistling the Horst Wessel SS marching song under his breath. Brad shuffled his files and just nodded in agreement. He was still wearing his sunglasses even though it was a grey December day.

"But I know he's good. I've trained him and I've been with him on at least twenty sales details. He's one of my best, I tell you," pleaded Kitty, not really expecting much sympathy.

Gunter stopped whistling and rose half out of his chair, eyes fixed and glowing. He spoke quietly through clenched teeth. "But have you staked him at his house. How many first calls have you done on the bastard? I told you to do the same as we did to Big Bad Betty when we staked out her house all night and all morning and caught her in bed shagging her lover boy. You didn't even fire her like I told you. Bloody second chance you gave her. I believe you've gone soft."

"Betty has done great since. She had a few personal problems and we've resolved that. Her market share has grown nicely. And Tony is better than Betty, I know. They are my reps and I know something's not right with the sales. I heard we're parallel importing Powerlol from the continent and there may well be a warehouse we've set up in Holland we have set up."

Morgan looked up from what had seemed a nice morning nap. He looked at Mervyn who in turn looked about at his other apocalyptic assassins. This took some time until Morgan broke the silence. "And where did you hear that my dear?" he said gently, shuffling his cards once more.

Kitty realised she couldn't tell them that it was from a friend she'd made on her first training course who was now one of them in head office and as controller of the IT systems monitored all movements of product through the factories and warehouses. He was the one who had set her thinking about profit margins when one day when was visiting the head office and the adjacent antibiotic manufacturing facility, she had asked, "What's that awful smell, Andy?" and he had replied, "Oh, that's just the smell of unspeakable profit."

She shivered as she formulated her answer to the Welsh inquisitor. "Oh, it's a real rumour in the field. Other reps have said their companies are doing the same, "lied Kitty.

Morgan dealt a card. . Kitty noticed it was The Hangman. He smiled and continued, "Of course we sell products overseas my dear. You know that. We don't have a specific warehouse though just to sell them straight back into the UK. That would not be good would it? How would we know if our reps are performing if the chemists buy from us in Holland? Of course not: It's just not good business sense. We can't dictate what our partner countries sell at though. We are bound by the NHS price. If Holland or Germany wish to sell product at low prices and the chemists in the UK want to ship that in, well, you know my dear, that's the EEC for you."

Mervyn butted in. "Thanks, Morgan. Morgan's always the man who knows everything. That should put your mind at rest, Kitty. You need to discipline this man now. After Big Bad Betty, I've been watching you a lot. I am sure I told you that trust is just a word you find in the dictionary. Never ever trust a rep. You're a good manager Kitty. We are all behind you in this but you need to listen to experience. And another word of advice; when you can learn fake sincerity, then you've got it made."

Kitty sat back in her chair, stunned at the perversity and irony of Mervyn's advice

Gunther brought them back onto their agenda. "So we'll get him sorted then. Now what are you going to do about Zack?"

Kitty realised that Tony's fate was decided. Zack was another matter.

"Well I staked him out in the car I stole, bugged his house and phones and paid a Russian whore spy to sleep with him," she said sarcastically, regretting it immediately she saw the glowering faces opposite her.

"Well, maybe not," she quickly added. "I first called him last Thursday. He never turned up, so I waited until his weekly call report came in and he'd listed that doctor as seen. So we have him on falsifying reports. But as you know Gunter we're more worried about the cross-territory movement of drugs, so I turned up at one of his lunch meetings yesterday and asked him to open his car boot up. He was reluctant but when I insisted he did. The boot was full of packs of other company's products. It appears he's been selling these outside his patch to chains of Asian chemists. As we guessed he's in business with dispensing doctors who order massive quantities of drugs from us and other companies because they get a pack for every one they buy. I knew it was impossible for a country doctor to use ten times what a city doctor does with only half the patients. It seems Zack takes the excess and sells them on for the doctors to Asians who then sell them on to their family or friend's pharmacies. I believe I have him, as you what you might say, bang to rights."

Mervyn looked anxiously to Morgan who looked at Brad who was frowning. Gunter's stare for once was accompanied by a smile. He seemed happy that another one was about to bite the dust. But Mervyn shocked them both. "How do you know he wasn't just trying to help the doctors? We encourage our reps to get involved at their surgeries with anything that encourages the doctors to trust them and prescribe more products. He is entitled to carry products around you know?"

"But he had over two hundred packs of two other company's' top brands in his boot. He tried to persuade me that all he was doing was taking them to a wholesaler to return them as a favour for the doctors." An altered sense of reality was setting in for Kitty; all might not be as she had concluded.

"You see my dear..." interjected Morgan, nodding in sync with Mervyn and Brad, and puffing his pipe, "...sometimes all is not what it seems. Zack is one of our best sales people. I've been out with him many times and his doctors love him."

"Of course they bloody do because he's making them millionaires. He also spends five times what anyone else does on booze and dinners. Most of which I am certain now goes through his brother's restaurant." Kitty raised her voice for the first time, clearly getting distressed. "I never understand how you can send out so much bonus product to dispensing doctors without confirming they were actually using it on their patients. Of course I understand the *once it leaves our warehouse it's not our problem* argument. But it is my problem because when Zack gets massive sales in that area, the drugs are moved across into Tony's and Big Bad Betty's chemists and aren't being recorded as sales for them. On top of that we're shipping drugs to Holland at half price and chemists are buying them there and bringing them back. Hence the reason we're about to sack Tony. It's just wrong."

She sat back and waited for her P45. As she watched them she recalled The Man from Lancashire's laconic, doom-laden words when he had told her not so very long ago: "We once had a regional manager who came to work in a Rolls Royce. He had a dispensing doctor who the company were giving a hundred free packs for every fifty he bought. He had a single practice in the middle of Birmingham. Tell me..." as he tapped his cigarette filter tip on the bar several times, "...how many cows and sheep there are in ******** Aston. The company is always in on these things Kitty. They don't give a monkey's about individual reps only what moves out of their warehouse."

The she couldn't actually believe that her bosses could be anything but normal managers, obsessed with sales figures and paranoid about their peers and other corporate raiding genocidal maniacs. Now she was getting a sinking feeling that, some reps might well be more equal than others. She'd heard rumoured Buster Knuckle was about to be promoted. Now she could see it might even be true.

"If we can see that Zack is taking a personal financial interest in all this then of course we will fire him but I fear that won't be possible just on your evidence and the inferences you've drawn," Brad said quietly and firmly. "Maybe Gunter should go and talk to the doctors in question and see if they confirm his story that he was only doing them a favour."

Gunter perked up astonishingly breaking into another smile. "Yes that's a good idea. Kitty, you and I will meet with Zack. I'll put the fear of God into him and maybe he'll break and you can fire the bastard. We can stalk him for a few weeks and maybe the doctors too. I know an ex MI5 man who lives up there who could pose as an Indian chemist..."

He was interrupted by Mervyn. "No Gunter. We just want you to have a chat with the doctors and say that by accident we've found products we sent to them being used in Birmingham. Have they an explanation? We don't need you to deploy *your particular skills.*" He turned to face Kitty and placed The Hangman card face up in front of him on his desk. Kitty gulped and he continued, "Well, maybe not yet."

Kitty shivered again. She thought, *Good God, this is Liam Neilson in disguise. They'll find and kill me'.* Then she thought again, the sweat rolling down her temple. *Don't be bloody silly. You have known these for five years now and they have promoted you and nurtured you. Plainly mad as mad hares, but surely not some shadowy, secret society of maniacal assassins who protect the secret of a parallel importing and dispensing doctor bonus fuelled Asian pharmacist take-over of the known world.*

She awoke from her hallucination and saw they were smiling at her. Morgan puffing his pipe and dealing his cards as he said gently and kindly, "My dear you are one of the best I've psycho-analysed. Keep up the good work and you'll be in head office soon. We'll have to get you out of the field where I can watch you more carefully and help you. You remind me of myself when I was your age. Here take another bottle of our vitamins. Look what they've done for me."

Morgan agreed. "Yes Kitty, I believe it's time to take you away from the field force. Sometimes it can wear you down and you see things which aren't real out there. Remember what I told you, Trust is a word you find in the dictionary. Trust us and we'll find you a place where your outstanding talents can grow and so can you."

Gunter just grunted and got up out of his seat. "I'd better phone Buster Knuckle. He'll make an excellent replacement as Regional Sales Manager."

Kitty's brain stepped into paranoid mode yet again. Yes, she had obviously turned over the wrong stone. Time to move upwards and out of the real world of sales and Rolls Royces into that of marketing in head office where they can watch her twenty-four hours a day and soon the phone will be cut off...

"Come on Kitty lets mosey on to my corral and I'll help you draft the written warning for Tony. Should we make it a final one? Goddam; ah look mah self in the mirror every time and say, Brad, you failed with this one. But, what the hell, we'll fire the bastard anyway."

2
BELFAST
DEVLIN

Time moves fast towards the end...

"We're reluctant to leave you with a minority shareholding."

The Big Yin was feeling threatened by KT and Jack thought *this might well not end up good.* "If yaeh's dinnae, then I'm out," said the big Scotsman and pulled his large frame from his comfy chair.

"Please sit down. We're only negotiating the percentage," said a panicky Bjorn, the finance director.

"There is no ******** negotiation. I retain 35%. You pay me ten million and tak the debt. That's the ******** deal, tak it or leave it," said the Scotsman.

And they did meet the Big Yin's demands. KT, Bjorn and the fellow directors and lawyers finally agreed to buy the Yin's company after the successful ship conversion contract carried out for KT in Glasgow and added it to the growing list of companies they had acquired in the UK and Jack was given the task of putting them all together and simultaneously running the huge projects already underway.

Then there was the fateful day after the reindeer heed's incident that KT told Jack about an offer to buy all businesses Jack was managing. The sting in the tail was that they quickly needed to become larger and more profitable for the potential buyer, a man KT referred to as Chairman Meow.

So now Jack was arriving by plane in Belfast with the Yin to negotiate a huge cruise ship conversion project which the Yin's posh Scotsman sales and marketing director had been instrumental in securing for them after sharing several bottles of Glenmorangie single malt whisky with the UK Minister of Energy and the Norwegian President of the Cruise company; both of whom were still in rehab.

"Aye, he drank the bastards under the table and did the deal there and then. He's the best in the business drunk or sober," the Yin told Jack, proud of his fellow Scot. "Ah canna be ******* with all that politics, press, media and shite. He's the man for that. Yaeh'll need to use him more in the business if KT lets yeah. He's better than

149

those lazy Norwegian ******** yaeh've got. He can out drink the bastards tae."

They were heading to see the yard where the job would be carried out. The timing was seasonally opportune and they had been invited to the Christmas party. They arrived to be met by a large, stocky man who said he was their driver. The lift had been arranged by Devlin, the sparkling and gregarious owner of the Liverpool based company KT had bought a year ago. The man had his tentacles in many places. He had relatives across the Emerald Isle and in Belfast in particular. He also knew everyone worth knowing in Liverpool and the Yin had been introduced to his favourite drinking haunt, Ma Boyle's, when he was on the shopping centre project for which Devlin's company had done all the shop-fitting. The Yin grew to enjoy his periods away from the hell of the project, getting drunk with Devlin alongside the cornucopia of life's characters that frequented Ma Boyle's in those days.

"The coffins' are a great place to get rid of paint inspectors or awkward quantity surveyors," said the dark-suited gentleman chuckling over his pint in the lower bar. He took a drink of his Guinness and continued. "You should think about starting a funeral business in Glasgow, big man."

"Ah have nay need big man. Big Tam sorts any of that shite out; without the coffin. The Clyde is ******* deep in parts," replied the Yin, shrugging his shoulders as if this was a perfectly normal conversation to have over a beer.

It transpired that the funeral director, one of two O'Brien brothers, was a man of many parts. He also owned a contracting business and was explaining in a polite way that their territory was out of bounds to the Big Yin. Hence the periodic reminder about coffins being a good place to dispose of the bodies of anyone who trespassed on their patch.

On the bar itself lay two abandoned barrister's wigs. Their owners were tucking away a bottle of vintage port but were still compos mentis enough to spot a business opportunity when it presented itself. One of them interrupted the Yin and his friend.

"If you will be interested in any legal representation - and clearly from the sound of it, you may need it - then we'll be pleased to help. Any friend of Devlin's is a friend of ours. Isn't that so Judge?" and he raised his glass to the lady sitting across the room sharing a bottle of Chateau Lafitte with a lanky gentleman.

The lady judge shouted back across the bar: "Any friend of Devlin's is Not Guilty: Prima Facie!" laughed and turned back to her Claret, her friend and their lunch.

Devlin grinned. He was lord of the manor in this place. Everyone knew him and everyone did some sort of business with him.

Devlin was laughing with the Yin when the O'Brien brothers asked them to move down the bar so they could be introduced to one of their Scouse friends.

"Devlin, this is Mick. He's got some great craic about his daughter's wedding on Saturday. Tell him, Mick. You'll love this."

The small wizened man in the baggy worn suit shook hands with them and retold the story. "We had a good day. I'd booked the hotel near Scotland Road for the reception. The church and mass went great and we arrived to get drunk. My daughter was chuffed with it all. I looked in to the room before heading to the bar and the dining room was set up nice like. I felt proud as hell. The cake was made by our lass's mother and took weeks to decorate by her auntie. It looked great on the top table. It was boiling hot in there so I told them to open the window so the cake wouldn't melt and we started on the boozing. When we came in to eat, everyone sat down, I was on the top table ready with my speech. With the drink in the morning and then in the bar most were feeling half cut. So we just sat down to get hurled into the prawn cocktail"

He took a long swallow from his pint and continued. "Then my daughter grabbed my arm and said: 'Dad, where's my cake?' "I looked up and it had disappeared. *What the ****! Where's the bloody cake?* I shouted out."

He took another drink. "My daughter burst into tears. Our lass fainted and I stood up looking all over for the ******** cake. The manager came running over and he shouted to a waiter, *Oh shite, not again. Get out of the window and look you lazy bastard*. The man ran to the window behind us and climbed out onto the pavement. He popped his head back in and in his hand was the toy husband and wife that had been on top of the cake and he says *Sorry boss, he's nicked it again*." Mick laughed, put his pint down and concluded. "Some bastard had climbed in through the window and pinched the bloody thing!"

151

Everyone howled at the story. No one seemed concerned about the misery of his daughter or surprised at the theft. This was Belfast.

"We got pissed anyway. What a night. I woke up in the morning with my clothes all crumpled up in one corner of the room."

"That's not unusual Mick. Mine always are after a night in here," said Devlin.

"Aye for sure; but I was still in them!" said Mick, to hoots of laughter all around the bar.

The bar owner grabbed Devlin's arm and whispered, "Devlin, don't tell Mick, but I bought a wedding cake off some punter in here on Saturday night. I sold it to the judge over there for her niece's wedding this Saturday. Sold her a couple of those new suits you sold me last Wednesday too. It was a good night's business"

Devlin laughed and said he'd best not tell Mick. He raised his glass to the judge and shouted across to her, "Have a wonderful wedding my dear. If you need any Champagne let me know."

The judge raised her glass. "Of course I will Devlin. I'll call you tomorrow."

Ma Boyle's was some place and the Yin loved it.

"Anyway," Devlin said. "I know someone who could be very helpful to you. He's one of the senior Royal Ulster Constabulary people and a great friend and he's over to Liverpool every second fortnight to watch his beloved football team."

The Yin was surprised. Devlin was a staunch Catholic from good Irish roots. "How come you're in with the RUC?" asked the Yin..

"I'm not political mate. The man's Liverpool FC through and through even if he is a prod, but it doesn't bother me. I've got mates on both sides who support Liverpool. And if I can do business with them, why let politics get in the way?"

"Aye; Ah suppose yaeh're reet. But I canna bide them Rangers, Hun. Dinna expect me tae talk with them," the Yin blustered out.

"Just be careful mate, over in the Yard. There are not many of us there mate; all Hun mainly. My mate will look after you and of course that daft fella Jack. Just tread lightly with the boys there," Devlin advised.

They travelled through Short's aeroplane manufacturer's yard in the back of an armoured limousine with the stocky man driving them and Devlin's RUC friend in the front passenger seat. Jack was surprised at the reception and the route. He had been in Belfast before and had always taken a taxi and gone the long way around on normal roads. This time they had been allowed to drive through an MOD protected site to reach the shipyard by the shortest possible route. Jack feared this would not go unnoticed by in that troubled city. He had always been advised to be incognito in Belfast. *Don't bring notice to yourself as being English, a potential policeman, spy or soldier. Don't pronounce any form of religious bias, wear any religious insignia and definitely don't sit in armoured limousines, travelling on prohibited roads with senior RUC men.* This wasn't being incognito. It was putting a target on him with the words *shoot here* writ large. Maybe Devlin had another agenda? *Oh no* he screamed in his head, *stop it, this paranoia has to stop or I'll just go crazy.*

Jack's paranoia quickly proved to have some foundation. On site they were greeted by a large, grizzled general manger who straightaway observed "You must have connections. I thought you were just contractors. Only important people come through that gate and that car is carrying so much armour, it can hardly get over our sleeping policeman. You're with friends here though. No need for all that with us. No IRA in here."

And so it seemed as they sat on the top table at the Christmas party. The general manager was in the middle like the bride, next to him a huge man who they were told ran all the yards in Glasgow, *a true Prod* they were told. The Yin winced but kept his cool, which was wise in this company. The Yin sat next to the general manager with Jack on his other side. Earlier everyone had eaten exactly the same meal; meat, potatoes and carrots washed down with Bushmills whiskey. It had taken less than twenty minutes to be served and eaten by over two hundred men. There were no women. And now they were waiting for the show to begin.

People kept coming up to the head man and placing bottles in front of him as gifts. He shook hands with them and Jack noticed some even tried to kiss his fingers, Godfather like. In front of the man was a glass jar in which were his gallstones. They already knew he had signed himself out of hospital that very morning so he could attend the party. He was a hard man, self-described. While taking them on the tour of the yard, he told them that he had lost his wife and daughter in an attempted assassination when the IRA tried to ram his car. Allegedly he was targeted as a leader of the Protestant paramilitaries a position he denied holding. He also shocked both

Jack and the Yin when he told them how a man had been shot in the tanks of a ship some earlier. It was alleged he was Catholic and possibly a paramilitary. It was enough to get him killed.

Jack listened carefully and he kept reminding himself that this was indeed a dangerous place. *Don't do or say anything to upset anybody.*

Then the party started. A drag artist dressed as a transvestite Pope came on to a host of cheers and bad language. He leapt onto a table and began telling jokes, all anti-Catholic and homophobic. As he stripped off a riot began with people throwing bottles and anything else they could find at him. Then the singing started. As neither Jack nor the Big Yin could comprehend any of the words and didn't recognise the tunes, they sat saying nothing, Jack grinning inanely and the Yin scowling, clearly unhappy. This worried Jack and he told the Yin he should at least look as if he was enjoying himself.

"I'll nae bow down to these ******** bigoted Huns. They'll be marching with their ******* sashes and drums soon. I want to ********* gae oot o here afor I nut one of them."

"For God's sake no big man. We can't do that man. We have to show respect. Just try and sit still. Have another whiskey. Look, I think it's nearly over."

The drag artist was now being dragged by his g -string across the floor while the crowd hurled anti papist chants at him.

"Thank **** for that. I'm outta here," the Yin stated, getting up and saying goodnight to the head Godfather. Jack followed after giving profuse apologies to the effect that they had to get back as they had an early flight back. They jumped into the Devlin's limo and were driven back to their hotel where the Yin insisted Jack take a nightcap in the bar with him.

"Ah have to get the taste of that mob out of mah gob. Here let's have a wee dram of proper Scotch whisky."

All Jack wanted to do was get to bed and feel safe again. He took his drink and as soon as he could slipped away. He opened his room door, noticing contentedly that it had several bolts he could throw across on the inside. He threw himself on the bed and relaxed lying on his back, breathing slowly and looking up at the ceiling light. Finally he turned to set the alarm clock. Reaching over he froze at the sight of a small object placed precisely in the centre of the other pillow.

It was single round with a copper casing, tipped with grey lead.

3
LONDON
MICK THE MERCILESS

Nearer the end…

"What shape of balls do you play with?"

Jack stared at the tall, good-looking young man standing behind Jack's desk and wondered yet again, *What the **** is happening now? And what the hell are you doing sat at my desk?* The question the man posed about his gonads seemed irrelevant in the madhouse in which he now seemed to permanently live.

He had walked into his London office one Monday morning to find that true to his promise KT had sold off Jack's businesses and Jack now had a permanent position in at corporate headquarters after the merger with Chairman Meow's European business and then the subsequent complete take-over of the two merged companies by the Chairman. He had now been based in the capital about three months but had been constantly on the road trying to sort out problems all over the place. With the exception of Belfast where since the bullet incident he was not allowed to go.

On his return from Ulster, he had been sent to Central Scotland to talk to the police and attend the court hearings of his employees caught stealing several miles of copper cable from the oil refinery there. He bowed his head when the police told him they'd been caught only because they had got greedy. Each night two men had driven up to the isolated perimeter fence in a Ford transit van and their partners in crime had pushed a section of large diameter insulated copper cable through a hole cut in the chain link fence. The two men had then sawed lengths off the cable and stowed them in the van to drive away to their storage garages. They were caught because they had decided to speed up the nightly process and sawed off over a ton of cable. Sadly for them, when they drove past a police car sitting in the town waiting to catch drunk drivers, the police noticed the back end was trailing on the floor and the front end approaching vertical. There was no defence.

Theft of company equipment was also a growing issue on Teeside so Jack was sent there next. He confronted Ernie and told him that as he was now the manager there it was his responsibility to get to the bottom of it and stop it or face the consequences which would likely be demotion back to the tools.

It didn't help that they were also involved in another labour dispute about working conditions and one union man had sneaked onto site as an employee as a precursor to full scale unionisation. He had stirred up enough trouble that Jack had little choice but to intervene, especially given Ernie's suggestion. "I'll ask The Mule to talk to the man Jack. He's been sat in his office since he had to leave California quickly for the Greenpeace and ABC news incidents. He just watches that bloody clock all day... '*Tick Tock watch the clock*'....He'll sort it out for you mate."

"For God's sake no! Not The Mule. I've still got to attend the last disciplinary meeting with those personnel lasses from London over those misunderstandings in the States. And how the Sales Director got him off those criminal charges I don't want to ask but I can guess. The police chief saw us off on the plane in his own private limo with several empty bottles of Glenmorangie in the back, so I guess him and our wonder salesman must have got on well together. I can't risk another maiming with a deadly weapon charge Ernie. You'll just have to take care of it yourself."

Ernie lifted his balls up, put his hard hat back on and poured his huge body out through Jack's door. As he left Jack drummed his fingers on the desk and took a gulp of the coffee that the lovely Nicki had brought him. He shivered. Why? He really didn't know, but he had a foreboding that asking Ernie to sort things was probably not much better than asking The Mule. He looked at the large black clock on the wall and for no particular reason except losing his mind, he started to count as the second hand went around and around...*Tick Tock; watch the clock* ...*Tick Tock; watch the clock*.

The next day a large van drove onto site and Empty Heed, Two Bats and the lads started offloading equipment. Jack asked Nigel, "What's that van was doing there?"

"Oh, didn't you ask Ernie to sort out the missing equipment? Nigel replied, haughtily.

In a strange reversal of first impressions, Jack had grown to quite like and depend on his commercial paranoid android who he realised did actually keep a lot of things ticking and many balls in the air. More importantly for the tortured man, Nigel was adept at keeping Jack's balls intact with KT and all the crazy people around him. Nigel, he knew, still believed in his superiority over mere mortals but Jack had learned to live with that. All QSs were the same; it wasn't personal.

Jack said, "Yes I did. Looks like he's has kept his word and done it."

"Oh, so you haven't heard the news this morning then?"

Jack forebodings reached new heights. "Oh God! What now? Nigel, please don't bother me with the good news man, just the bad!"

"Well, Radio Teesside reported that a man rang the doorbell of a house in Grangetown and when the lady answered walked through into the dining room where her husband and three kids were having tea. The assailant grabbed the husband and attempted to drown him in his bowl of broth with the terrified children and wife screaming. When he allowed the husband to surface he marched him out to the garage where he helped himself to a load of machinery and electrical equipment and stuck it into a large van with the help of another man carrying two baseball bats. Police say they believe it was some local gang problem but the assaulted man won't press charges."

"Oh dear God Nigel! Is that the van outside?" Jack asked, head in hands.

"I couldn't say; for legal reasons of course: but co-incidentally the stolen gear is apparently back. I've told the police it was no one here that could have done that but as you know I can sort most of the things you've messed up and…"

"Yes, Yes, Nigel…I know you're the man. Well done then. Are you sure the police are off the case? No Interpol? Serious Crime raids to look forward to?"

"Well, hopefully not. Oh… unless the man in the accident last night reports it to the police. The ambulance took the guy straight to the General and I haven't spoken to him yet, but Ernie has and he says he won't cause any more bother. I've noted it in the Accident book."

"What ******** accident? No one told me," Jack shouted above the noise of the equipment van screeching away across the tarmac.

Nigel explained slowly and deliberately. "Well, it seems the union man you spoke to Ernie about accidently slipped and tripped up and put his feet in the wheel abrader. It's ok though; they were just shot blasted a bit. He's out of hospital already. He has resigned mind.

Two Bats and Mick the Merciless have had a chat and he won't be bringing anything against us for his own mistake."

Jack knew you had to lift steel three feet off the ground with an overhead crane and place it on the roller conveyor to move it through the wheel abrader. It would be extremely difficult to trip over a three foot wall. Instead of anger, guilt or fear, he felt proud of his team and of Nigel. He then realised in a flash of light that he had been broken. Like a wild horse or stubborn child they had tamed him and he was finally part of the pack. Sadly he now accepted that this was the way of things and his *team* could solve any problem he put in front of them. How and with what? He cared not anymore.

"I guess the union problem is fixed then?"

"Yes, Jack. It seems your chat with Ernie and my intervention has solved yet another crisis. I still wish you'd let me handle things before you put your big foot in it you know. I..."

"Yes, Yes, Nigel, I know I'm shite mate. Just happy you're here to keep me right. Put a small bonus in Ernie and the lads' pay packets this week. They did well. I'm heading back down to London now and I'll tell the new boss that I guess you can handle things from now on."

Nigel's smile of lasting satisfaction and pure joy was a wondrous thing to behold. He had won at last.

. And now Jack, on his return to his corporate office, was faced with the young man sitting at his desk. He had walked in early as usual and said "Hello" to the staff sitting in the open plan area around his corner overlooking The Embankment but opening his office door he was greeted by a this young man sitting on Jack's executive chair, using his phone. The man waved at Jack and put his hand over the receiver; "Hi Jack. Just take a seat a while I finish off with Jeremy."

Jack sat down. Astonished. He couldn't believe what was happening.

The young man continued talking into the phone: "Well I think Michael will win the by-election and when he does, we'll all be in clover...ha. Who would have thought he'd join our fathers in Government eh? It's a long time since we were all doing prep with Flogger Phillips watching over us holding his cane. A good whipping and rogering never harmed us, did it Jeremy?

Ha…ha…I'd better go. I've one of my chaps here to see me. See you at Twickenham on Saturday. Toodle-pip."

Jack sat with a blank look on his face, his mind running through the possible scenarios. He was stunned into attention by the young man's next words. The man levered himself out of Jack's chair, pulled his suit trousers up to his waist by his belt and then offered his hand. "Hello, I'm James. You look like a big guy and fit…what shape balls do you play with?"

Jack stood and shook the guy's hand. He was stuck for words and babbled, "Aren't everyone's the same shape?"

James looked puzzled by Jack's answer and frowned. Then he perked up. "Ha ha, a joke I see. I meant are you a rugger or a soccer man?" Then he frowned again and said, "I assume you play physical sport?"

Jack dropped the hand thinking, *Oh dear another public schoolboy and not the old adage that rugby is a sport for hooligans played by gentlemen, while soccer is a gentleman's game played by hooligans.* He replied with little enthusiasm for macho male bonding. "Not much now. I'm too busy working and bringing up a family. Well I thought I was? Can I ask what're you doing in my office?"

James walked around the desk and put his arm across Jack's shoulder.

"Let's sit down Jack. Here take a seat. The chairman wants me to explain to you what our plans are."

He was about a foot taller and a good ten years younger. Jack couldn't help feel that this man had some presence and confidence for his young years. Maybe the playing fields of Eton did grow leaders of men. *Or,* he thought *I may be being lead into the trenches and battle by a donkey and this lion is definitely not going to be drafted into it without a fight.*

Sadly, Jack didn't put up too much of fight; he was just cannon fodder it seemed. James explained that he had taken over Jack's position. There was no discussion about it. James said that after having dinner with his father in his London club, the chairman had called to say he was moving from running the French business to the new UK one. It seemed they had all gone to school together and most to Cambridge before spells at either Fontainebleau or Harvard business school. James had served in the Coldstream Guards and spent a year at Chase Manhattan bank in New York before

Chairman Meow made him boss of the whole of France. Now at twenty-five he was in charge of Jack's old businesses.

"Jack. We'd like you to work for me for a while and settle me in. After that the chairman thinks you may be interested in an opening running Iraq and Iran for us. The war's causing us a few problems with the factory and distribution but he thinks you and your family will love it there. And, if for some reason you don't want to move to Baghdad, it seems KT and the Big Yin would welcome you back to run a new business they've acquired. KT will call you after this chat. If you wish to move back over with them then come and see me and I'll get our personnel girls to sort the nasty paperwork and monies for you. It's been great to talk, Jack. I'm looking forward to you taking me up to meet some of the chaps up North. Do they play Rugger up there? I might bring my boots…show you soft Northerners how it's done eh? Hah hah."

He opened the door and beckoned. Jack's PA had arrived and James asked her. "Can you show Jack his new office please and get KT on the phone for me." He shook Jack's hand again and closed the door with Jack on the outside.

Jack pondered this new calamity carefully. He was certain James, as a gentleman who had attended Marlborough school, would have no real life experience of the crazy folk that inhabited the company's barren Northern areas. They didn't play rugger up there but indulged in other playful pursuits like ram raiding, gang warfare, arson and forms of baseball without the ball. It could all go badly wrong for Jack if say The Mule broke James's neck in a playful, Stephen Segal twist ploy or Ernie just knocked him out because he spoke impolitely to Jack. And heaven forbid he met Mick the Merciless. But Jack felt mischievous now he knew his days were numbered, fated either to be blown up by weapons of mass destruction in Iraq or have his head carved off by a bread knife by insurgents in Iran. A move back with KT and The Big Yin seemed similarly risky. So he decided to show his new Chief Executive the bad lands of the North East in person; the buried guns, the dead furry animals, the packets of white powder and all the psychopaths galore if that's what he wanted.

His new office door opened and in came the two personnel assistants from what was now being called Human Resources. He still liked the description of HR that that Kitty had passed on to him courtesy of The Man From Lancashire; *They should fill forms in when you join, and fill forms in when you leave – and do **** all in between.*'

However, these lovely girls were here to interfere with his imaginative plans to bury his new boss in Big Ed's wife's rose garden in the barren featureless desert which was Teesside, or in the burnt out stolen car dumps comprising the massive council housing estates of Sunderland or North Shields or his clever plan to push him along the dock where The Mule hung the client in Hartlepool, dressed in fancy dress as a French onion seller and watch while the residents of that fine town hung the bastard.

"We're to come with you to the disciplinary meeting with The Mule. James feels that as you will be *leaving us soon* we should make sure it goes accordingly to company HR policy not your usual ad hoc ways." Jack thought, *So even the two bloody lasses from ******** HR know I'm history and that posh twat is to taking over.* **** it; he'd have fun anyway. "That's fine. You sort the time and place out. Oh, and make sure you inform him that he has the right to bring a representative along," Jack quietly said.

"Oh, will he bring his solicitor?" one of the young women asked.

"I doubt it. He won't want witnesses. He'll probably bring Mick the Merciless, his mate from Walker in *The Toon*, Jack said smiling mischievously.

"The Toon? Where's that?" the older of the two asked.

"It's what the local's up there call Newcastle." Jack answered truthfully.

"Who is Mick the Merciless? Is he a union man or something?" the younger one asked.

"No. they don't like Unions. The last one we had ended up with few toes less after a very unfortunate accident with a wheel abrader. Mick was with The Mule in Nam or Iraq or somewhere when they were both killing people for their governments. Now Mick just kills opposing football supporters…or head office staff who upset him. He has little mercy in him, no one is spared, even non-combatants, women, children - it matters not - so he's named The Merciless."

The HR girls looked shocked and one began to twitch.

Jack continued: "Aye: Anything could happen. You and James will need to make no sudden moves or say anything that insults their country, their town or football team. I'd recommend James doesn't ask them about playing with their balls or Mick may just hand his back to him. That reminds me; you will have to search them first for weapons. I am not doing that - just in case."

"Jack. You are a laugh sometimes," the older HR person said, smiling nervously.

"Ay: For sure; it's just a laugh. You get in touch with The Mule and sort it out. I'll make sure it all works out safely for you all." And Jack got up and walked out to ask Nicki to get his own employment lawyer on the phone.

Two weeks later they were all sitting in an office in Newcastle waiting for The Mule's hearing to begin. Jack sat smiling to himself. He had taken James on a whistle stop tour of the businesses and at Jack's specific request the red-faced, iconic sales director had made sure James ended up in the Southern General in Glasgow with alcoholic poisoning.

The Big Yin just refused to meet him. "Ah canna stand them posh English bastards. I have nae interest in ya ******** business the noo and I certainly have nae ******* interest in posh twats. I'll give yeah two bits of advice Jack. Nivva work fae ******* Englishmen and nivva drive a Lada car. Both're shite. Ah need to talk tae ya aboot mah new business. Come and see me when you've been sacked. Ah've maybe got a job fae yeah.".

Now they were waiting for The Mule to arrive.

"Jack is he bringing Mick the Menace with him?" the young HR lass asked.

"He's called Mick the Merciless. You'd better get his name correct or I can't protect you. And I have no idea. The lads say it may be Big Tam coming with him."

Actually Jack knew exactly what was happening because he had met The Mule for beer in Wallsend Social Club the day before. He had agreed with The Mule that as long as he didn't lose it too much and caused no more than a small amount of distress to the HR girls and the new boss, he'd make sure he only got a verbal warning. He asked him to have Mick the Merciless with him for "A little fun."

"Who is Big Tam Jack? If he's that big, does he play in the back row or front row?" asked James, still in Rugby mode.

Jack thought he'd explain the real world to him. "Nah: He's seriously dangerous man who used to kill for a living. Unlike The Mule who did it for a constitutional government; he did it for a crazed psychopath. Or maybe the two are just the same, government or gangsters; anyway, apart from a propensity to maim, they reckon he's a good advocate."

Jack suggested they go through to the meeting room. Once there the HR girls started moving the white board to the middle of the room, whilst Jack moved several small tables in front of the four chairs they had chosen to sit on.

"Why are you putting those tables there? They're creating a barrier between us and them Jack. We should appear open and welcoming to ensure an even-handed discussion, surely?" asked the youngest girl as Jack picked up the white board and carried it behind the tables. "And why move the white board to our territory. I put it there so that we all can make notes in the spirit of shared learning about 'the incident.'

Jack put them straight with a twisted grin; "The tables are there to stop any one of them leaping at our throats. Both have *special skills*; and the white board? Well it has sharp edges, and we don't want anything with sharp edges in the room. The Mule is lethal with a sunbed or a lampshade. I'll search them beforehand…unless of course James wants to do the searching? It'll help you get to know them and start the bonding for when you've got rid of me."

James pulled his trouser belt taut and hunched his shoulders. "Err.. maybe best that I don't stand in this meeting Jack. I won't be too operational once you're gone…Oh sorry…once you make your mind up, and it really is an HR matter. I have every confidence the ladies can handle it. Isn't that so girls? I'll just go and make a call to the Chairman and my father. I believe they are lunching together today."

The women from HR looked at each other and at the *Rorke's Drift* barricade Jack had built. He guessed they felt a bit like every one of the one hundred and fifty British soldiers manning it against six thousand Zulus charging them brandishing lethal Assegai blades; except they didn't have Martini Henry rifles to stop them, just non-permanent marker pens.

Jack began to whistle, *Men of Harlech,* Ivor Emmanuel style. The girls decided that discretion was the better part of valour and asked Jack if they could take a break to make a conference call to head office about a more pressing matter.

That largely took care of matters.

Jack smiled as The Mule and Mick the Merciless left the meeting room. They had arranged to meet up for beers afterwards to celebrate the slap on the wrist Jack had been given for the maiming of the camera man and the Greenpeace activists. Mick dragged his knuckles across the floor outside Jack's open office door just to show HR that he could and The Mule shouted through the door at Mark in his best American accent: "Heh buddy, looking forward to meeting you on a real football field. Bring your helmet and shoulder pads; I'll bring the doubled-edged Gook knife. Y'all have a good day mind."

4
CORSICA
BERNARDU

Some months on...

"If you pay one hundred thousand francs I will release Kitty unharmed and put her on a plane to Nice. If you don't...well the Corsican Mountains tell no secrets. You have three days to make up your mind and deposit the money in my Swiss account."

Jack put down the phone in his Bergen office. He shivered, not with the intense cold, but with fear. How the hell had he got Kitty and himself into this mess? This was bloody serious stuff and he had no experience of dealing with Corsican gangsters - Glaswegians, Middlesbrough nutters, Scousers and even the IRA but never the Union Corse. What the hell was he going to do? Poor girl didn't deserve this. He looked out of the rain spattered windows into the dark skies of Bergen and his mind drifted back three months before.

Jack had finally been moved on out of his Inferno of Hell and was now circling around the Mountain of Purgatory, still seeking his own Garden of Eden at the summit. Strangely his wife didn't seem keen on moving to the killing fields of Iraq or Iran, suggesting staying in Middlesbrough might be a whole lot safer, with the additional advantage that you could buy Petch's pork pies, Suggitt's ice cream and Chicken Parmos there. So she told Jack moving was a no goer. He had hoped that Chairman Meow may show some compassion and allow him to stay in the UK, or send him to some nice place like Thailand or Bermuda but not a chance. He knew he must have finally lost his marbles to even hope this as, by now, he was fully aware of Chairman Meow's reputation and that he certainly wasn't a pussy cat. Indeed a supplier who had once been a manager in his new chairman's company told him early on that Meow had a reputation as a right bastard. The rep had once been detailed by to take over a manufacturing facility in Saudi Arabia and when he told the chairman that his wife wouldn't like living in a country where women were treated as second class citizens, his boss's answer, delivered whilst pushing his glasses firmly up his aristocratic nose, was, "Divorce her. I did." When the man didn't do as suggested and divorce his wife he found himself sacked and tramping the streets trying to sell valves.

The rep was full of similar tales. Another story concerned the company's car transport manager asked to deliver Meow's new Mercedes all the way to his Mayfair home. It was mid- winter, sleeting and raining and ten o'clock at night when he rang the bell on the large oak door, rapidly becoming soaking wet and with no idea where to stay or how to get back out of London. Chairman Meow opened the door, looked at the desperately bedraggled man handing him his keys and all the great man said was, "Ah! My new car: Thank you Bob," before slamming the door shut in his face.

The sales rep's own demise had come after promotion to being in charge of all the European businesses. Every year the Chief Executive for each country was required to attend a mass meeting to present their budget personally to the chairman and his group finance director who sat on a raised stage to receive the reports. After each CEO in turn had given a fifteen minutes audio-visual presentation of their business plan each found themselves destroyed by the not so *pussy cat* chairman, using no more than a single sheet of key financial data on it for each business, the budgets and business plans for which tended to run to four or more thick volumes and which had taken months to prepare Each found himself (in almost all cases the unfortunate CEO was male) sent back to revise the return on capital employed, the manpower allocations, the debtor ratios and the like.

When it came to the Italian company's slot, poor Luigi got no further than his first slide before Chairman Meow stopped him in his tracks and asked a biting question of the European boss, the poor rep sitting next Jack, who once had dreams of a glittering career at the top. "I see you are projecting a negative return on investment this year again. That's the third time in three years isn't it?"

The rep answered quickly. "But chairman, we're showing a sales growth of twenty five per cent on the last financial year and we've reduced the loss from a negative of thirty five per cent to two per cent. Year two we expect as you can see to make a 2% return on investment and the year after ten per cent."

Chairman Meow pushed his glasses up his nose and stared at the rep who had moved to stand in solidarity with Luigi. "That is in unacceptable," he said and turned to his finance director. "John, I expect you to give me the exit costs for Italy by nine o'clock tonight." He faced round to the rep and Luigi, who was now trembling. "Thank you Luigi. And goodbye:"

Luigi collapsed.

"He closed three factories and fired two hundred employees. Luigi is selling ice cream and me valves. So if I were you Jack, I'd watch my arse son."

As Jack didn't *'divorce her'* as per Chairman Meow's instructions, just like the valve seller he was moved on. After the final trip to the North East and the HR debacle with The Mule, he knew for certain he couldn't work for a man who played with funny shaped balls nor for a dictatorial Chairman who wanted him to wear a dinner jacket for his pie and chips at the Navigation pub with Ernie and who wouldn't give a second's thought to firing anyone who displeased him, even those with a disability, or seven kids, or a Northern accent or who liked their wives more than instant death at the hands of Arabs armed with carving knives.

So he decided to take up KT and the Big Yin's offer to run their new venture for them.

It turned out to be a specialty chemical and coatings business for the Aquaculture market. Based north of Bergen on the west coast of Norway, it had once been KT's uncle's family firm. KT had persuaded the Big Yin to put in some of his money from the business sale to Chairman Meow and make it a jointly owned enterprise. They both thought Jack could grow the business globally and they needed someone they trusted and also someone they could torture without legal complications getting in the way. And if they needed to get rid of him, well, there was always Big Tam.

He hadn't spent that much time in the company before Jack realised that he needed some marketing and sales expertise and new blood to freshen up his Norwegian colleagues. The pace of life in Norway was hardly hectic. Despite it being as dark as hell and as cold as a witch's bosom the Norwegians still liked a nap in the afternoon and finished work to eat, sleep and play with the family not long after midday. This drove him to drink; rather it drove him to more drink, but as drink cost more than Donald Trump's hair preparations per pint he started to detox and began to see things clearly like he once did in the old days before meeting KT, The

Mule, Ernie, The Big Yin and their cohorts In particular he saw clearly that he must change the operation or die.

So he phoned Kitty.

Kitty seemed to him to possess both ambition and go. She also knew about bugs and things.

She was also ideally placed to market the new wonder product his Norwegian scientists had discovered, a product they were now calling Bug-clean. He had changed the name from some incomprehensible Norwegian name which to his ears sounded like *Ubby dubby gooby*. It was supposed to act like *Domestos* and *kill all living things* but in the shape of a non-stick substance from which deceased bugs just fell off. In particular it purported to stop all known underwater bugs sticking to fishing nets, not to mention aquaculture tanks or even ship's bottoms. The company had trialled it in the laboratories and their own small fish farm in the fjord north of Bergen. If it worked it would be a wonder product for fish and shellfish farmers. The toxic substance they had been using for many years had been discovered to have an unfortunate side-effect; it produced male penises in female dog whelks. The regulators and, Jack guessed, Thai lady boys, were so worried that constant exposure might start giving every female in the animal kingdom a penis, they banned it.

This caused mayhem. Nets coated with the toxic stuff didn't become fouled up with bugs and weed. Uncoated the fouling worsened, making them heavier and heavier until fresh water didn't flow through the nets for the salmon and other fish being farmed. Eventually they could snap off their moorings completely. The only way now to keep them clean was to wash them every month or so causing major trauma to the fish and to the farmers. The fish cages in the North Sea and fjords were large and taking them out of the water required cranes and massive washing machines and techniques nobody had so far perfected. In comparison if Jack could coat the nets with this new wonder product he would make millions for KT and The Big Yin, the reason they had bought the business in the first place. They promised Jack a share if he could make it happen. It sounded great – until the Corsican problem arose.

Jack looked at the bleak skies and pondered how he got Kitty into this mess in not much more than a couple of months since first calling her.

His proposal had sounded straightforward enough. "Why don't you join me in this new venture, Kitty? I need someone with a bioscience and sales and marketing background. It's got be a step up for you. I'll make you Marketing Director. Norway's a smashing place as well. You can hide from Gunter there too; even Buster Knuckle won't find you. There are thousands of miles of nothing but water and snow."

"Well, I've been considering moving on. Since we met they've moved me from Marketing into Business Development. I told you about the poor man they recruited to sell the new wonder product didn't I?"

"Yes you did. They put him in an office and cut him off from the known world."

"Exactly. Well, when I returned from Belgium, I popped my head in to see if there had been any progress. He told me to close the door and picked up his phone. "Listen..." he said to me, "...it's dead as a door nail. Not long now Kitty." And sure enough while I was talking to him, along came Morgan puffing his pipe and asked the poor man to come with him to talk about the handwritten note he'd given to his secretary to order his lunch. He told the hapless man he'd read it and had some interesting comments to make on it. I never saw him again. He just disappeared. Just like Andy."

"Dear God," was all Jack could think to say.

"I don't believe they worship that God, Jack. The Sun or the Moon; maybe - and talking about the moon. The poor Scots regional manager who was found howling at the moon, bollock naked? Well, he was moved to head office as Assistant Training Manager. Oh yes, I nearly forgot. Gunter has been promoted to run our intellectual property and security division. He's got Buster Knuckle working with him. Since both of them started investigating security leaks, we've had several accidents in the secret research labs. One person accidently fell into a high speed centrifuge and one of the smoking beagles allegedly savaged a pharmacologist found with severe injuries in his office. Buster Knuckle reckoned the pharmacologist was the one who leaked to the press and that the dog must have sniffed him out as a traitor and turned rabid. Gunter had it shot."

"So nothing much has changed then?" Jack asked, rhetorically.

"No Jack...Oh, The Man from Lancashire; he's moved on to become a monk. Reckons he'll be safe in the monastery. And sadly Tim died. It was at the last sales conference in Sicily. He was found drowned in his bath. His team said they were sure it was empty when they threw him in but they were all pissed, so, as I learned all those years ago, *mebbies not*. The police wanted to investigate fully until John Paul the second had a word with them. His dad and it seems our Sicilian company, have contacts there and in New York. Accidental death was the verdict. His funeral was nice."

"Things certainly move fast in the pharma business, Kitty. How about my offer? Do you fancy joining me?"

"I'll think about it Jack. I'd email you but my computer seems to be off line..." And the phone went suddenly dead.

It was two days later that Kitty phoned from home to say that she, like her marketing boss had taken the long walk to Morgan and Brad's offices to be given a bottle of vitamins and a P45. Brad had offered her a good old fashioned American goodbye. "Well Kitty. We are mighty sorry to say it's time to say farewell. Thanks but I need your car keys. We've booked you a train to your little old home on your prairie. Y'all have a nice day mind." So Kitty stood up, smiled and said: "**** you! You Yorkshire bastard."

And she walked out. She knew The Man from Lancashire would be proud of her, even in his monastic penitent solitude. She too, like Jack, had passed through her own Inferno and her Circles of Hell. Purgatorio was not pleasant either as she pondered the various Seven Deadly Sins she'd been exposed to during her career to date. Maybe, just maybe, she could would get to see the summit of Mount Purgatory and that Garden of Eden with this new career. She could only hope that love would conquer all...but she wasn't that naïve anymore!

Kitty spent a few weeks in Bergen getting up to speed with the business and the products. She quickly found she actually loved Bergen and working with the Norwegians. She thought that Jack, however, seemed too pre-occupied with his own paranoia to enjoy a life of fjords, fishing and fornication. She made a mental note to try getting him to visit The Man from Lancashire in his monastery. If the Franciscan order would let him talk, he was good at diagnosing paranoia. Maybe Jack would benefit from time away from KT and his like and in a monastery where Big Tam couldn't find him.

She sometimes fell back into her own demons though - when she noticed a car parked outside her apartment in Bergen with a German number plate, or heard a tick or snap on the phone when she picked it up. She tingled when she saw a squashed wasp on her window pane. And she could never play cards with the staff at the thirty minute sandwich break they traditionally took at eleven o clock. The thought of Morgan's tarot cards was still too painful. And of course she kept taking the vitamins.

She soon realised why Jack was frustrated by the working culture though. It was so different to what they had both learnt elsewhere. She learnt more when she was taken by Ludwig, the brilliant scientist who had discovered Bug-clean, to visit fish farms up the Norwegian West coast. She found him to be a lovely intelligent man but one who struggled with Jack's new culture of lots of work, no sleep and little play, He needed to kip at about 4 pm every day while Kitty just wanted to keep on working and told him so.

"It is not the Norwegian way Kitty. We work early morning and take a small break and we finish mid- afternoon for a sleep and then family dinner and then the fjords for yachting or fishing or skiing. In winter we ski while it's light. You'll learn as you work with us. Now I must go and sleep."

A few weeks of this had Kitty falling into their culture. Also the drinking. After the afternoon sleep if the Norwegians weren't with their families they were drinking. Not expensive hotel or bar drinks but home brewed beer from ingredients bought from Boots the Chemist on trips over to Newcastle upon Tyne by ferry from Bergen. Or spirits and hooch distilled at home. Kitty enjoyed the stuff and told Ludwig about the time when she'd met a lovely old lady in the bar of the Irish hotel she was staying in who'd once been a nun. She liked the drink and they had a good old craic. She also liked potcheen and used to bring bottles back in her suitcase on the ferry to England for her sister. A customs official spotted the bottle of clear liquid and asked her what it was. *It'll be being Holy water, young man*, she answered, with a white lie, crossing herself. The customs man took the bottle, opened it, sniffed it and reeled back. *Holy water you say?* And putting it to his mouth he took a sip. He coughed and spluttered. *Bloody hell, that's strong water.* And he passed it across to the nun. *You taste that and tell me that's Holy water.*" The nun took the bottle and sniffed it. She looked at the man with a puzzled look and took a small drink. Then with surprise, and glee and shouted out *Bejesus, it's a miracle!* "

Ludwig chuckled at the story and offered another shot of his own miracle hooch before telling Kitty his own story.

"Do you know the Swedes and the Norwegians don't like each other. We call each other stupid. Bit like the English and Irish or American and Polish jokes. Well one day I was in a bar and a Swede was in and he was boasting about how good they were; how Sweden had the best girls, jobs, football teams - you name it, they were cleverer and better. So I went up to him and said, *If you are so clever then I bet you fifty kroner that I can piss in your pocket and you won't feel it.* He said, *You will piss in my pocket and I won't feel it? Hah, another stupid Norwegian, you prove my point. That is impossible I will feel the wetness.*" *Okay then I said, put your fifty Kroner on the bar.* He did and so did I. So then I took out my penis and I put it in his pocket and pissed out all the evening's beer I had drank. It covered his trousers and down into his shoes." Ludwig chuckled and took another drink of his miracle. "The Swede was so pissed off. He jumped back and tried to wipe the piss from his trousers and slipped off his shoe, the piss pouring out of his sole. And he shouted out to the bar. *See you thick Norwegians. I can feel it. The piss is everywhere. I win.* And he turned to the barman who was holding the hundred Kroner. *Give me the money.* The barman asked me, *Ludwig, does he win?* I looked at the Swede up and down, still trying to wring the piss out of his trousers and socks. I said, *Give him the money. He wins!*" Ludwig howled with laughter. "And we are supposed the thick ones. Only fifty Kroner and I get to piss in his pocket...ha...hah."

Kitty laughed and thought she'd try one that she had heard from Jack when she had first arrived. The drink was taking its toll. "Heh Ludwig. There were three guys in a bar. One English: One French: and one Norwegian. The Englishman says, *My wife is as pretty as an English Rose so before I go to work in the morning we make love for twenty minutes and then take breakfast on our beautiful lawn and when I come back in the evening we make love again under the Oak tree.* The Frenchman butts in: *Well my wife is so sexy that when we wake up in the morning I make the passionate love with her for one hour and then we ride our horses around the chateau grounds. When I return in the evening she is dressed in the finest Parisian gown and I ravish her on the table before dinner.* The Norwegian looks puzzled but he pipes up: "*When we get up in the morning we make love and I have breakfast of smoked fish. As I leave to go to work, I always smack her naked backside. When I return her backside is still wobbling. This isn't because she has a fat ass, it's because we work such short hours."*

Kitty laughed. Ludwig didn't. *Oh dear, a cultural boo boo*, she thought. *But what the hell*: "Let's have another drink Ludwig. We have to get up early tomorrow to get to the farm in Sandefjord."

Ludwig just put his head in his hands. *The English never learn.*

Jack had noticed there was an Aquaculture conference in Bordeaux so he sent Kitty over to listen to the papers, to network at the exhibition and to try to drum up some trials for the product. The conference was in Arcachon, home to rather a lot of oyster and other shellfish farms.

A few weeks later, Kitty met a charming sophisticated Frenchman at his exhibition stand at the Arcachon conference. He had a small family owned fish farm in Corsica but had been a senior executive in a Pharmaceutical company in Paris and they found so much to talk about that he invited her to his company's dinner that evening. Bernardu was the epitome of the sophisticated and sexy Frenchman and she enjoyed his company. Always a hint of sexuality but with a degree of restraint he charmed her over a dinner of fresh Arcachon Oysters followed by Coquilles Saint Jacques with an entre of Sole Meunière and Tarte Limon to finish. All washed down by a fine selection of Bordeaux wines.

Bernadu was twenty years her senior and had retired early to buy a fish farm and a new lifestyle in Corsica which was where he had been born and raised. Kitty felt herself falling for his Gallic charm as the wine flowed and the talk moved away from molluscs with one foot and a mouth and the dog whelk penis to more exotic things like Corsican mountains, the maquis (the dense fragrant heather that covers most of the island) and the warm beautiful waters of the Mediterranean. Bernardu's business was now plagued with the new EEC directives on fish cage net cleaners so he was fascinated in equal measures with Kitty's new product and her vivacious looks. He decided to road test the latter first, as any sane Frenchman would.

Kitty felt on a high the next morning. Bernardu had left her hotel room early to fly back to Nice and then over to Corsica. She had enjoyed her night of romance. The first man she had slept with since leaving her last partner nine months previously. She also had an order to sell him two hundred gallons of Bug-clean, the first ever sales order. The problem was that no one had ever coated these sizes of nets before and, more worrying, no one knew if it would work. But she was very pleased with herself and delighted that Bernardu had indicated a desire to carry on his affair with her in a more serious manner once she returned with the product and a method for coating his nets.

After some trials and many failures Kitty managed to develop a method utilising the type of industrial washing machines already in use at the Bernardu family aquaculture business. They sealed the ends and then washed the nets in Bug-clean to coat them. Everything seemed to work, at least under lab conditions.

This success put her on a plane from Nice airport flying to Bastia with a colleague from the French supplier of the main chemical constituent of Bug-Clean. Serge was nothing like Bernardu. He was pot- bellied with a large bushy beard and dark framed glasses. He was a Parisian now living in the South and a geek when it came to weird chemicals and bugs. Conversation with Serge could never be described as romantic. Talk of chemical monomers and coefficients of friction did not excite Kitty anywhere near as much as Bernardu's whisperings of love, affection and sweet scented heather. She couldn't wait to be reunited with her new customer …and lover.

That reunion had to wait. At Bastia Airport they were picked up by two men in dark suits they had already noticed talking to a man whose head was wrapped in a bandage and who was surrounded by other dark-suited acolytes whose main function appeared to be warding off photographers. She asked Serge what was going on.

"Mon Dieu Kitty. C'est La Bête. The beast. He was shot a few days ago in some gang battle. It was in the national press. He still has the bullet in his head and he is off to Nice hospital to have it removed. Why our drivers were with him I don't know but it's not good. This is Corsica, anything can happen. I never wanted to come but the boss said I had to. Merde!" The nervous man had turned from Einstein to Eeyore in minutes of landing. He looked terrified and stayed in that state throughout their journey. They were driven in a limo many kilometres, right down to the South West of the island, passing through many small villages and towns which appeared deserted. Serge was mumbling in French and playing with what Kitty were Rosary beads.

"What's the matter, Serge?"

"We are in Corsica Kitty. The people here do not like strangers. We could be police, customs, tax... And they don't like Frenchmen. I am from Paris. They especially hate us. This gives me un mal penseé."

The limo approached a large gate with security cameras and a guard post containing an armed man. He came out as the car approached and spoke into an intercom. The gates slowly opened and they drove down to a bungalow facing the sea or rather a cove full of fish cages. It was a much smaller operation than she had imagined from her discussions with Bernardu. But the early evening warmth was beautiful and the sea shimmered. She was at peace. Unlike the shivering Serge.

Bernardu greeted them in person and showed them first to their rooms and then around the site. He was it seemed a single man with no family living with him although he still described it as a family business albeit one from which he felt sure one day he'd make money from. Kitty noticed that everywhere they walked a man followed just ten steps behind, carrying an automatic rifle. Serge just shivered even more.

Dinner on the bungalow's veranda was delightful. Serge made his excuses and retired, never once letting go of his rosary beads and he was still fingering them as he was escorted by another large man to his room. Bernardu and Kitty spent another hour drinking coffee and cognac before bed. Kitty didn't need any rosary beads.

The next day work began on coating the nets. It all went well but they used twice as much Bug-clean as they had calculated they'd need. Kitty had to ask Bernardu to airfreight in another two hundred litres. He was unamused but the materials arrived two days later.

It hadn't taken long for Kitty and Bernardu to further develop their special relationship and he was taking her out to dinner at local restaurants and introducing her to members of his extended family, all of whom seemed to own the restaurants as well as the bank, petrol station and shops. Even the mayor was a cousin. Meanwhile Serge was relegated to eat with the large suited bodyguard who had swapped his automatic rifle in favour of a more discreet bulge in his jacket.

When Serge and Kitty were alone, he showed her local newspaper full of murders, slayings and attempted murders, mainly of teenagers who had fallen in and out of love, boyfriends killing other boyfriends or husbands killing wives' lovers. Serge was manic. "It's always the vendetta here or strangers who ask too many questions. You must be careful with Bernardu. I am not stupid I can see what is happening. He is something big here and that means he will have enemies or past lovers. We have to get back to the mainland, vitement."

"Oh Serge, stop being a Frenchman. These Corsicans are lovely. I think Bernardu is falling in love with me and I might just stay here and work with him. You're such a scaredy cat. We need to stay anyway to see if the first nets have worked. After that you can go and leave me here."

A week later they were staring at the first cage to have been coated. It had been immersed for two weeks with fish in it. At their request it had been emptied and the cage lifted out of the water. They both looked aghast at the nets. The coating had worn almost completely away and the nets were covered with weed. The man with the rifle frowned and told Serge in French to wait there while he brought Bernardu.

Bernardu was surprisingly calm. "This was the first one we coated, yes? Perhaps the washing machine wasn't working so well. Stay another few days and we shall lift another two nets."

Serge said "I can't stay. I must get back to my laboratory in Lyon."

"That will be impossible. The road back is blocked by a landslide. You will have to stay anyway," Bernardu said with a shrug and turned to walk back to the bungalow.

Serge looked shocked and whispered to Kitty, "There is nothing in the paper about a landslide or on the radio this morning. I think we are prisoners here, Kitty."

"Don't be silly. Bernardu just wants to be sure he gets what he's paid for and we need good or the product is dead."

"It's not the product being dead I am worried about," muttered Serge.

"Oh shut up, silly man. Let's go and have lunch and I'll ring Jack with the bad news,"

Ringing the office wasn't to prove that easy.

"Bernardu, doesn't the phone work? I'm trying to get Jack but nothing is happening," Kitty over lunch on the veranda.

"Oh, that will be the landslide. Only my line works and I'm sorry I can't let you use that. I am expecting an important call from my father in Marseille." Bernardu took a slice of Compte cheese and continued nonchalantly, "Maybe it will be working by the time you have lifted the next nets. There has been some trouble in the town as well – a double shooting - so it's best you don't leave the compound until the police have found out who did it. I can't have anything happening to you, can I?"

Serge choked on his quince jam. Kitty just looked affectionately at Bernardu and said, "That's kind of you. I love it here by the sea. Can we can take a boat out tonight across the bay?"

"That won't be possible, Kitty. I have to head up to Bastia. Jean Paul here will look after you all." And he pointed to the gun man who nodded and frowned. "I'll be driving up after lunch."

Serge looked up from fingering his rosary. "But I thought the road was blocked." He immediately regretted saying anything.

Bernardu just rose to his feet and wiped a few stray crumbs of bread off his trousers and said: "We have other ways to get around that but they are known only to those who need to know." And he left, kissing Kitty affectionately three times on the cheeks.

Three days later although Bernardu had not returned, they lifted the nets in the presence of his manager and the bodyguard. They were all covered in bugs and the coating had largely disintegrated. Everyone looked gloomily at everyone else. Even the bodyguard looked concerned.

Kitty broke the ice. "Where is Bernardu now?" she asked.

"He is on his way back from Marseilles. He will fly into Bastia this afternoon and we will pick him up and bring him back here in time for dinner. You can tell him the bad news then."

Serge's face brightened and he exclaimed in French: "Perhaps I could come with you and take the evening flight to Nice if the road is now open?"

Bernardu's manager shrugged his shoulders and said quietly but firmly, "The road is still closed. And you cannot leave until Bernardu returns and decides what to do about the nets. Please go back to the house and wait."

Despite Serge's Gallic pleadings and emergent histrionics, the bodyguards shuffled him and Kitty back into the bungalow where they waited anxiously until Bernardu's limousine returned, driven by his usual driver alongside a single bodyguard. He was met by the manager and they went off to talk in his private study. The housekeeper ushered the two guests into the sitting room and poured them an aperitif before dinner and eventually Bernardu joined them having changed into casual slacks and a loose shirt.

Kitty hastened over to welcome and kiss him on his cheeks in the French way. He returned the compliment but merely nodded at Serge. The Corsican's demeanour reflected annoyance rather than dislike and he sat down and took a glass of champagne before making his position quite clear to Kitty and Serge. "So, I hear we have a problem with the nets. More accurately, you have a problem with the nets because unless I get my money back and a fee for the labour and the extra washing I now have to do, you will be staying here or in one of my safer places in the mountains. Please explain that to your respective companies in the morning. My father will talk to your boss, Serge. They go back sometime and your boss knows my father is person of power and influence who and his request will not be refused. I expect him to pay his share. So Serge, when I hear from my father, you can leave. The road will be open then. Kitty, my petite; you will talk to whoever in your company can pay. If they do not then you will spend a little more time in my company and I feel for both of us that will not be a hardship."

And he was proven correct the next day when a call from Marseilles confirmed he could release Serge; monies having been transferred from the French country. They were still, however, waiting for KT to agree. Serge said goodbye to Kitty, not particularly reluctantly as he couldn't wait to get out of the country and back to the safety of Lyon. He kissed her and told her not to worry. "Kitty, in the end your company will have to come up with the money. The law doesn't quite work here as it does elsewhere. But I believe you may enjoy your captivity more than your work, so au revoir ma Cherie and come to see me in Lyon; promise me that." And he left in a squeal of tyres from the black limo.

Kitty duly phoned Jack again. Jack was distraught with worry. "I'll have to talk to KT and for sure the police, Kitty. We can't have this man. It's criminal for God's sake; all over a few dog whelks' dicks for ****'s sake."

"Jack, it's not that easy here believe me; look at Serge, they paid in twenty four hours after one call from his Godfather or bloody real dad in Marseilles. They are connected all over France and to be fair to Bernardu, the product was shit. He's not a bad man you know."

"Kitty, I know, I know, but the product was a trial and he knew that. I will call and talk to him before getting the Viking mafia on my back and heaven forbid the Big Yin finds out, he'll be sending Big Tam down to rescue you and sort out the Froggy buggers."

Kitty spoke calmly and persuasively down the phone: "Jack, this is not Glasgow, Big Tam is not the answer, please believe me. I've sat here working and living among them thinking it's a bloody holiday but even I'm not that naïve now. They don't mess about here. I'll get Bernardu to call you. Just talk to KT and pay up. We're at fault Jack. No one is going to take this to court to argue whether this was a trial or a sale. I'm the only witness and I might not be around to testify. For God's sake Jack."

So Jack took the call from Bernardu. "If you pay me 100,000 Francs I will release Kitty unharmed…" The price had gone up and Kitty, it appeared, was the hostage.

He knew this would not go down well with his masters. And sure enough he wasn't disappointed. He was threatened with both broken limbs and career. KT ranted on in an increasing tirade as to violent outcomes for Jack's various soft parts and how Kitty was dispensable anyway. "She's just a girl who'll soon fall in love with a French peasant in the mountains and do what girls do anyway, so forget her".

KT's resolved course of action was to send a lawyer to talk to the police in Bastia and get the whole lot of them arrested .

…Jack tried to explain what Kitty had said but when KT wouldn't listen Jack asked Serge's Chairman to ring KT and explain the facts of life concerning the Union Corse, tentacles, vendettas and fish wrapped in bullet proof jackets.

After the call KT mellowed enough to agree to pay the ransom but there was no question that the research and launch of the product would be cancelled. "And Kitty can stay there for all I care and you, Jack, can join her picking Corsican heather. You're finished, Jack."

Jack immediately called Kitty to say they would fly her out business class back to Bergen and give her two months to sort out her life and return to Britain if she wanted to. Even KT when he calmed down knew she had every right to employment benefits and the law was sacrosanct in Norway - if not in Corsica. To his surprise Kitty turned down the offer and told him she was going to stay and work with Bernardu and to "Please just put what I'm entitled to into my bank account."

Jack put the phone down on Kitty and smiled; Stockholm syndrome was real and Kitty a living example. She had expressed delight that they were paying Bernardu and insisted he had been both a great host and badly done by on the Bug-clean deal. Jack suspected from her complicity in Bernardu's claim of misrepresentation that there was more to her happiness than just being set free. Nor did she seem bothered in the slightest about being fired despite the promising career she had had ahead of her. He promised he'd do all he could to repatriate her and get her compensation before the axe fell on him. She had refused going home and thanked him for the latter before putting the phone down.

He had asked her if she had fallen for the charms of the man and the place and indeed she obviously had. She even told him he should come out and visit them and maybe Bernardu would find Jack a job. "His father is very well connected."

Jack had laughed and said, "Kitty I think I've had enough of mobsters, the mafia and gang warfare. I'm done with corporate business life. I'm setting up my own consultancy and before that I'm taking a break. I might come to your wedding mind, if you invite me. Promise I won't tell Buster Knuckle where you are!"

So Kitty went off to a world of oysters, mullet and dog whelk penises and Jack spent the last month of his employment setting up his own consultancy and arranging his leaving piss up.

Then his mother died.

5
COUNTY DURHAM
MAD JIM

The end

Jack was devastated at her passing but knew it was for the best. She had never really been well for years and had not been right since the death of his father. Of course he needed to return to County Durham for the funeral and wake. He was pleased that so many old colleagues and employees turned up to mourn with him and celebrate her life. The iconic, red-faced Sales Director came down from Glasgow, immaculately dressed in his best tartan for the day and sober to boot. The Big Yin and KT both sent massive wreaths with their condolences and the Yin asked if he wanted Big Tam to come down and make sure there was - 'nae trouble at the wake, big man". Jack politely declined.

His uncle came back to the family after several years of exile and in best mobster tradition he too was dressed up to the nines in a black pin stripe suit, camel hair Crombie overcoat and polished leather shoes. He got on like a house on fire with the Scottish Sales Director; one drinking pints and the other Scotch paid for with his uncle peeling ten pound notes from a roll in his pocket that could choke a horse. Only Jack knew the roll was mainly newspaper. His uncle was always a con man as well as a psychopath and as Jack watched them laughing and drinking with Ernie and the lads from the Boro he mused that maybe his ebullient and dangerous uncle had missed his true vocation - he should have been a contractor.

The funeral car was supplied by Devlin from the Liverpool office.

"The O'Brien brothers you met in Ma Boyle's have fixed it all with the local funeral directors for you Jack. They loved your craic at the Plumbers Ball in the Adelphi last year. Pity you threw up after the last bottle mind. Also the judge says she'll sort any probate issues if you want. And if you need a new suit, the barman says I can pick any one for you and send it up. Sorry but for meself I'm away at Cheltenham with the Irish from the job. We need the cash paid mate. They owe four hundred grand. You know how it is."

"Yes Devlin. You get the money in and thanks for the offer but I've still got the two suits I bought last time I was pissed in Ma

Boyle's. And as for the probate, my mother was penniless and I'm paying for everything so no need for that…but it's very kind of her. I may need her criminal skills mind if the wake ends up like most of them do in my home village. Keep her on hold."

The Mule came and gave him a secret American military handshake and a ring. "This ring cements our band of brothers bond, Jack. Call me if you ever need help. I have skills you may need one day." And he walked off to the bar.

The wake after the funeral was being held in Jack's brother in law's pub. Jack was initially pleased but as he looked around at the crazies he'd been raised up with who still lived in the village he worried for the eventual mayhem that might well erupt with The Mule seemingly on an emotional rollercoaster. But then he calmed down, his nerves cooler, as he realised that even The Mule had probably not met as many damaged people in one room as here in this pub.

Ernie gave him a huge bear hug breaking his spine and slipped two packets into his pockets. "Two Bats and the Merciless thought you might need a pick me up after the loss of your mam. They say give it a shot; one for you and one for your lass. Just call me in future if you ever need any help or anyone upsets you. You know what I mean." And he went over to join The Mule at the bar. By now Jack knew exactly what he meant. He shivered and hoped he didn't have to make the call but it felt good that someone cared for his welfare.

Kitty sent a case of Champagne and Bernardu had packed and flown in four whole smoked sea bass and a whole case of fresh Arcachon oysters with a note: 'Come and see us anytime. The road is now open and the heather is in bloom. Call me anytime if you need anything."

Jack smiled when he read it. And as he looked around in the bar he saw just how many acquaintances and friends he'd made who were willing to offer him help - help he hoped he never needed but was pleased he could call on if he ever did. The odd thing was that none of them were offering him work or a living for his family, just maiming and retribution for anyone who might upset him over a spilt pint or bumped car. He reflected on the fact that there were precious few artists, literary critics, policemen or judges, in the room nor indeed anyone not related to extreme violence or larceny. Maybe he was right to be changing career at this point in his life.

"How man Jack. Ah'm sorry about ya mam. We all loved hor ya kna. Ya kna divn't ya? Ya kna divnt ya? Divn't ya kna?" A small, wiry, lank-haired lad was pulling at Jack's suit jacket and repeating his statement. "Ya kna that Jack, how man, Jack...We loved hor ya kna?"

"Yes, Jaffy I know. I know," Jack tried to cut him off. Sadly the pub was not closed to old school mates or family friends.

"I was ganning to bring our lass but she disn't drink ya kna Jack? Ya kna Jack? she disn't drink, ya kna divn't ya...?"

"Yes, Jaffy I know. She's Thai isn't she? I heard you brought her back from Thailand. Our lad told me." Jack tried to stop Jaffy from tugging and creasing his new suit – one of those he'd bought from the Fagan-like tailor barman at Ma Boyle's. He was distracted by his nephew, a glass of free beer firmly in his hand.

"How man Jack. Jaffy's built hor a ******* mosque out of pallets and an old pigeon cree and put the ******* in the front garden. A ****** mosque! The lads have been hoying bricks at it. They'll burn it doon soon. I keep telling the daft twat. We divn't want mosque's in our council estate for ****'s sake."

Dear God, Jack thought, *how the hell did Jaffy did ever get to Thailand, never mind persuade a beautiful girl to come to this mad house we were brought up in. And a mosque built out of crates and old racing pigeon huts in a council house garden? It's lunacy.* But Jack, born and bred here, knew it would all be true. However he felt he should correct their apparent problems with racial and religious integration.

"Jaffy, Your lass will be a Buddhist. If she comes from Thailand most are. Especially the ones in Bangkok; you should have built a temple man."

Jaffy looked at him, his head cocked to one side. He moved it to the other side to peer at Jack's nephew, who just stood there as blank as usual. Then in a moment of enlightenment he grabbed Jack's suit. He tugged and tugged, turning his head from side to side between Jack and his nephew, repeating his mantra; "How man Jack, how man Jack. That's what I tell them man - the lads...it's a ******* temple not a mosque. She eats real bait man, loves chinkys, pork chop suey as weel. Me mam's pork crackling she loves man. Them Muslims canna eat that stuff, can they?....They eat shite....and she disn't wail and wail in the cree ivry neet and morn like those *******'s dee, she just puts pretty fluoors and oranges and shite on plates for hor God. She winnit even kill a rat when we gan savaging them with our Jack Russells. She's soft that way...all puffs them Thais the lads tells me."

Jack stood looking into space, knowing he'd made the best decision in his life leaving the asylum so many years ago. However, his nephew about finished him off. He pulled at his suit again saying: "How man Jack, so she's not a Muslim then? Then why's he built hor a ****** mosque then? Canna have ******** mosque's here man Jack."

"It's not a mosque it's a...," Jack started to explain but instead gave up the will to live. He had to change the conversation before he lost all brain function in extremis noticed a decent ice breaker and taking a drink of his pint asked: "Where'd you get the England shirt Jaffy?"

The man was wearing a 1966 World Cup winning England red shirt. *Not great funeral wear* Jack thought, *but what the hell, my mam wouldn't have cared, she liked Jaffy.*

Jaffy looked puzzled. Obviously thinking was hard for this mercurial man. Eventually he came out with an explanation of sorts. "How man Jack, How man Jack...this townie gadgy from Sunderland came in last Saturda' and he had a kit bag full of them. He was selling them for five pund each man." Jaffa pulled at his track suit pants and at the obvious semi hard-on he had bulging underneath.

Jack couldn't help noticing. *Why do the lads always have to keep playing with their dicks when they wear track suits. Is it some form of male bonding? Track suits always seem to bring the worst behaviour out of them.*

Jaffa continued after playing with his organ. "How man Jack, he sold the lot of them and for awnly a fiver each. I bought two, one for me and one for the Thai bint."

True love rules, Jack thought. *And I might have had one myself if I'd been there,* he mused. Then he looked again at the shirt and at Jaffy's happy face. It dawned on him what had been puzzling him all along. "Jaffy, I thought there were three lions on the shirt? Like the song." He began singing the anthem, *Three Lions on The Shirt, Jules Rimet still gleaming...*

"There is Jack man; three lions on my short…divn't ya kna that man?" Jaffy replied.

Jack looked again and confirmed his suspicions: "Sorry Jaffy. There are only two on yours you daft twat."

Jaffy looked sideways and back and forwards and finally pulled his shirt out until he could see plainly that indeed there were only two lions on HIS shirt. "For ****'s sake Jack man. That ******* townie fiddled us all .The twat."

Jack laughed and laughed. His nephew looked shocked and couldn't see how funny it was. He pulled at Jack's suit. "How man Jack, How man Jack, what's the matter man. Has the **** cheated Jaffy man. He sold me and ivryone in here them. Should they have three lions on them like?"

"Yes mate, they should have three, "Jack said and stopped laughing. It was pointless. His nephew was renowned for taking things the wrong way which all too frequently ended violently. He looked at the baffled man staring at the two lions on the red shirt shaking his head as if it hurt him to think too deeply about it. It reminded him of being in another pub with his relative meeting a man interested in buying his nephew's car. The man was dodgy and thought he'd got a good deal when he bargained the hapless lad down to a hundred pound. Jack offered to drive both of them back the four miles to his nephew's house to pick the car up. The man, smiling at his fortune, agreed. So they arrived outside his nephew's council house, next door to Jaffy's which would soon have its own adapted pigeon hut mosque…or temple.

The car was a wreck. The tyres were flat and the bodywork rusting all over. The man looked aghast and tried to start it. Nothing happened. From the driver's seat he shouted out of the open car door, "It's *******. How am I going to get this back home?"

Jack's nephew looked shocked and then came to the amazing conclusion that the man might not pay for something he couldn't drive - so he just thumped him and grabbed the hundred pounds the man had already shown him he had in his pocket. "It's a ****** car isn't it. Giz the money you ****." And he hit him again knocking him out. "Howay Jack lets gan to the club its nearly closing time and the last strippers will be on."

As Jack drove away in the rear view mirror he could see the body laid over the steering wheel and the car sitting on its deflated tyres on the road. As he watched, the lads from the street were heading over in response to his nephew's orders, "Mak sure that **** gets out of here afor I get back. And he taks his new car with him." Jack knew there'd be no recriminations. They stuck together in that weird place. *Bit like Zombies*, he mused, *…or wolves. But I don't think a career in sales or after sales service is in the offing for my nephew.*

"So he cheated us. I'll knack the twat when he next comes in here."

His nephew meant the dodgy Mackem townie who'd conned them all. Jack didn't bother enlightening him that a man who had the nous and the bottle to come into a maniac's pub like this to sell two lion shirts to the assembled masses of Mensa rejects might be wise enough to spend his ill-gotten gains elsewhere.

Jack made his excuses from the multi-culturalism of the religious practices of Thailand and the con-man's arts to join The Mule and Ernie. He congratulated himself on stopping The Mule inviting Abdul the Turk to come over. He had a feeling that Abdul would not fit in with the cornucopia of religious and cultural freedom to be found in his brother in law's bar.

The Mule expressed his disappointment that Jack was leaving. He told Jack that he had offered KT to put a small team of Navy SEALs together to raid the fish farm and rescue Kitty but KT'd refused. The Mule was starting to think that KT was losing confidence in him after the incidents over American bridge and the snapping of the client's finger. He and Ernie were thinking of starting up their own personal protection business, "And how about coming in with us, Jack." They both seemed to have become aware that, despite their other particular skills, they struggled to communicate with clients being offensive or rude or challenging towards them. They had learned that maiming them was seldom the answer.

"Yes. Large company clients don't take kindly to being hung, drawn and drowned or having their index finger snapped off at the metacarpal. And heaven forbid you try to get any work from Greenpeace after the drowning incident. I've already been offered a consultancy to help an ex SAS friend of mind to do what you say but I have to say that he and his lads are a little more user friendly with their clients than you and the lads . Maybe you should just stick to the knitting as Jim Collins once said and both expand your doorman business. Why not take over the whole North East? You could do an Amazon. Retain a squad of highly trained psychopaths in each town and when a client presses a button and pays for doormen to move in and batter to unconsciousness high spirited revellers in their establishments, you send in the likes of Mike the Merciless and Two Bats. You could call it: *Mayhem and Extreme Violence on Demand Ltd.* There are a few lads in here that'll join you. I know another maniac, Mad Riv from Consett or Wakey who could well lead a hit squad for you. "

"That's a great idea Jack," said Ernie. "There's a gap in the market in Newcastle after the shooting of Viv. The boys there are getting a bit angry with each other. I was in the pub in the Westgate Road when they threw the West End top boy's father's gravestone through the window the other day. Never seen that in the Boro, A new one on me. And I was just sat talking about a bit of business, you know what a mean?"

"Yes, Ernie, I think I do," answered Jack.

Ernie continued: "Aye, but they're all not that bothered about the pub doors so we might be able to agree a deal with them. What do you think Mule?"

The Mule looked pensive to Jack, which was always a worry, as it usually ended up in blood flow if he thought about things too much. "Ernie, the Toon may be a hard nut to crack buddy. You know the last time we were there on the Quayside? When Jack took out all his site management on the piss."

"Aye: It was pure mayhem, but not our fault, man. Jack, you really shouldn't have invited Dinky to the Toon, you know that don't yeah?" Ernie said.

Jack, with a pint in his hand, shuddered at the memory.

He'd decided to treat his site supervision for doing a good job without committing any grand larceny, disappearing any union men, encouraging raids from the vice and drug squads or inviting prosecution by the Atomic Energy Commission so he invited them all to down to Tyneside's thriving, bohemian Quayside for drinks. Here in the more affluent, multi- cultural environment of the Quayside Jack was trying to explain to the bar owner that his small gang of loyal workers, despite most of them making the Incredible Hulk look like a mere pastry chef and en-masse resembling nothing so much as the cast of a WWF mega show, were really nice guys and only here for the culture. "Perhaps you can clear us four tables near the bar please to keep the team together and private.

A rendition of 'Red Army' from somewhere near the doorway stopped that little white dead lie in its tracks. Immediately he knew it might not have been the wisest course to have invited Dinky.

"Is he one of yours?" The owner asked Jack.

"Sadly, yes," Jack replied. "He's a bit high-spirited. He's from Jarrow."

"He may well be high-spirited, but not in my bar. Shut him up please, before there's trouble." The manager sternly at Jack and the began shouting, "Oh shit, it's kicking off now!"

Jack looked over to see a scuffle breaking out. "Dan go and see what Dinky's doing man and stop it."

Big Dan returned and explained that Dinky's altercation was with the latest French recruit to Newcastle United's football squad. The player had just arrived and it was his first night out in the city. Dinky had spotted him and decided to confront him on why he had chosen his arch enemies over his beloved Sunderland FC. The Frenchman in an inimitably arrogant Gallic way had told Dinky to go away and leave him as he was an important man who demanded respect. Of course Dinky was having none of that - so he pushed him over the table.

"I've sorted it Jack. It's calmed down. There are a couple of other Toon lads with him and they don't want any trouble," Dan said as he returned.

"Thanks Dan. Just can't have bother tonight man. That twat from London is coming up to see us tomorrow. Don't want you lot in jail or in bandages for ****'s sake."

Just as Jack finished thanking Big Dan the dulcet tones of Dinky rose again across the hubbub of a rapidly filling luxury bar. "Red Army, Red Army...Shearer is a ...." Then another scuffle broke out.

The manager looked aghast at Jack and shouted above the noise, "If you can't stop him, my lads will."

Jack saw The Mule take a menacing step towards the manager and Ernie extract a leather cosh from his pocket. Jack muttered just loud enough for the manager to hear. "No Mule, down boy." The manager's face showed abject terror as The Mule retreated and Ernie slowly put his cosh away. Jack tried to further allay his those fears. "Don't worry mate, we'll sort it. Dan, get your arse over man and sort the daft bastard out, will you?"

On his return, Dan provided an update. "Seems that the Frog didn't learn and went over to Dinky demanding an apology. You can guess what happened. I've sorted it. Peter, the Toon captain has had a word with the Frog and it's calmer. Mick the Merciless is mad Toon you know, so I've asked him to get in between Dinky and the Froggie if owt kicks off again."

"See my lads are good uns really. We're only here to have a break from work and some fun. Let me buy you a drink, and the bar staff. Put it on the tab," Jack told the nervously grinning bar owner.

Five minutes later there was yet another scuffle over the doorway but it quickly died down. Dan was sent yet again to calm the troubled waters. He returned with Peter by his side.

Jack asked Dan what had happened.

"Well, Jack. The suicidal Frog had another going at getting respect out of Dinky, who was just now sat enjoying a beer with Mick the Merciless and his fellow psychos..."

"Oh shite and Dinky kicked off again. We'll have to get him out...," Jack nodded to Ernie to come over with him to sort Dinky out but Big Dan seized his arm to stop him.

"Eh, no. Jack it was Mick the Merciless. He ran and grabbed the Frog by the throat and lifted him six inches off the floor and smashed him against the window. Mick shouted that he'd hoy him through the window if he didn't behave in his Toon. And as you know Mick's a nutter for Newcastle but Dinky's one of us. Peter's ordered the Frog to go home and he wants to say sorry to you"

To Jack the Newcastle skipper seemed a lovely bloke and said he hoped the new Gallic acquisition would learn that *not all is as it seems in the 'Toon*. There were plenty worse than Dinky out there.

However, there weren't many worse than Big Tam and the evening wasn't over yet.

The Big Yin had wanted Big Tam to enjoy himself for once. And as he'd never been to Newcastle he'd asked Jack to invite him down but Tam hadn't been there on time because of course he didn't drink. By the time he arrived the full complement of bouncers were manning the door, insistent on searching the wee man. He was resisting and his razor accent, menacing scowl and fixed stance created an impasse. They wouldn't let him in without a search and he wouldn't go away. Then one of the doormen thought he saw a bulge in Big Tam's jacket and went to remove the offending object. A crunching bone and scarlet blood spattering and all hell broke loose.

Again sadly it fell to Mick the Merciless and Two Bats to sort it. "You stay here boss, we'll calm it down." Of course the fatal last words came from The Mule.

They were bailed out the next day and Ernie informed Jack that luckily Big Tam's gun was thrown into The Coaly Tyne before the Old Bill arrived. Jack thought sarcastically, *that was a bit of luck. My whole supervision management locked up: countless bodies strewn around the Quayside: the press phoning me every minute and the new posh boss due here any time now: Yes, that was lucky about the gun! Maybe my idea of an Amazon for doormen was daft after all.*

Leaning on the bar at his brother-in-law's pub, he was broken out of his reverie by a tall good looking man who grabbed his arm and asked if he'd like another drink.

"No thanks John. I'm okay at the moment. Thanks for coming up mate. Where are you stopping?"

"I haven't booked anywhere yet Jack. I've brought the tent in the back of the car though. Was hoping I'd meet a sweet looking maid and someone here to stay with. Slim pickings though if you don't mind me saying, Jack. They're all ****** huge. I wouldn't fancy my chances in a ring with any of the girls in here. That one over there with the tattoos and the biceps, she'd kill me mate."

Jack smiled. "That's my cousin Gore Belle. She's a lovely lass really but don't let her get you in a grip mate. At my wedding she dragged our lass's cousin out of the reception by his neck squealing like a pig and made him make passionate love to her against the chapel wall. He has never been the same since. Never goes out of the house anymore."

Jack took a drink and chuckled remembering how he'd first met his John on Humberside when he'd secured the contract to fix his refinery. John was a strong willed and professional site manager and they'd had several run ins but always managed to make up later, often at 'The Bags' Ball', the iconic dance night held in the Winter Gardens at Cleethorpes, long renowned as the place where the ladies from Grimsby would retire to when their husbands and boyfriends were off on their trawlers in the chilly North Sea fighting Icelandic fishermen during the regular Cod Wars.

The Bags' Ball was the place for contractors to find a woman who fancied something more exotic than a wet codfish and John was a master at wooing them. He carried his courting kit with him in his car boot. His main tool was his tent for lunchtime sessions when he left the site, supposedly to eat lunch back at his digs. The tent he'd put up anywhere on a piece of grass or woodland (a bit of a rarity around Humberside) and meet his conquest of *The Bag's Ball* there for a mid-day break from welding valves together. He also carried things like chocolate paint to coat his ladies with, the odd whip or mask, and odd-looking bulbous beads. He had had many a close shave when shagging ladies back at their place after *'The Ball'* when a boat landed early and an irate husband returned unexpectedly, loaded up with cod fillets and fish cakes for their lonely and devoted wife back home.

Jack chuckled to himself when he noticed that John still had the limp from being gnawed by a Staffordshire bull terrier one husband had set on him as he raced for the bedroom window. He never did get his trousers back.

"John if I were you just for once I'd forget the shagging and just enjoy the beer. Here girls are much more dangerous than the men mate."

"Yup. For once I think you're right Jack. I'll book into a bed and breakfast in Durham. Mind you that one looks sexy," and he headed off to romance the vicar's young wife of the vicar. *Incorrigible* Jack thought as the engineer went off on his ecumenical crusade, fingering the string of anal beads in his suit pocket.

"Dan's doon Jack!"

Jack looked over to the door where the shout had originated. It was the proposals manager he had played hangman with all those years ago. *Oh shit* Jack thought, *not again*. Sadly Dan, who was now well over twenty stone, could drink pints without swallowing, his huge fist grasping the glass and hurling the beer down in one slurp. He would drink like this continuously for about two hours and then go onto litres of wine. Jack recalled the last time he was 'doon'. He'd done his usual and swallowed the gallons and Jack said goodbye to him in a pub car park as he climbed into a taxi. The next morning he got a call from Dan hoping Jack didn't mind if he was bit late for work.

"It's ok Dan. No worries mate. What's the problem, sore head?"

"No mate, I woke up in intensive care. I have no idea how I got there but it seems I was lying comatose in the car park you left me in so someone called an ambulance. They thought I'd had a heart attack, the size and clip of me…hah hah…"

"And had you? Jack asked concerned.

"Well they phoned wor lass and told her that I had, so she drove down fast from the Toon and when she got here they let her in to see me. She took one look at the clip and smelt the beer and the doctors said she just said, **** *him. He's pissed. He always does this. I'm off.*" And Dan guffawed loudly down the phone, "Ha ha ha. They took me back to a normal ward and I must have sobered up about five. I had to get a taxi home and I just got in. She's not talking to me."

Now Dan was *doon* again.

Jack smiled to himself as he walked over to see what had happened recalling Dan's wife telling him that last New Year, he had gone out and got legless again leaving her home with their two young sons. One of the boys heard a noise at the patio doors and went to see if it was the cat. "It was Dan, legless staring through the window with one eye focused on the lock, trying to open it and the other closed in drunken sympathy. *Mam, Dad's only got one eye!* the son screamed as he ran into his mother's arms. *I thought the bastard had been in a fight and lost his bloody eye, so I screamed too and ran to help him. I saw him staggering trying to focus his one open eye, the other just closed through the drink. Pissed again! I locked the door and left him to fall over comatose on the grass. He was still there the next day. Happy bloody New Year!"*

This time Dan had collapsed on the street outside the pub after a meagre ten pints and three bottles of wine.

"Get him up man!" Jack shouted to the proposals manager.

"I can't lift the bastard man. You'll need Coles' cranes to dee that. Giz a hand."

The two of them struggled to lift the big man but finally with the help of Gore Belle, who tucked most of Dan's bulk under one arm, they got him inside and propped up against the bar. Dan woke grunting like a Cape buffalo. Indeed his head was the size of a buffalo's. Dan always said his heed was *a snipers dream*. He spotted the snacks on the bar and began to scoop them up in a huge hand, clearing ten bowls of crisps and two plates of sandwiches, swallowing their contents whole.

"For ****'s sake. Stop that big bastard. He'll be sick all ower me bar, man," shouted Jack's brother in law.

"Nah, he'll be alright. He's been on his diet again. This is just grazing for the big man," said Jack calmly. "Let's fetch him a cab and get him home."

The taxi arrived and Jack and the proposals manager took him out, staggering with Dan's bodyweight, Dan with the last pork pie in his fist.

"I'm not taking that drunken bastard. He'll be sick in me , man," said the driver through his open window.

"He's never sick son. He won't be, take my word on it," Jack explained, "And he's comatose now anyway. He's harmless when he's asleep. He'll sleep till you get him home."

They opened the door and piled Dan in, fast asleep and sprawled on the back seat. "How much to Newcastle mate?" Jack asked the taxi man.

"Where in Newcastle?" the car driver asked sensibly.

Jack looked at his proposals manager and he looked back at Jack. They shrugged their shoulders. Jack replied: "Buggered if I know mate. Just take him there man. Wake him up and he'll tell yeah. Here's twenty quid. That'll more than cover it."

"If I wake him, he might get violent. Look at the size of the bastard, man."

"He'll not get violent mate. He just tired and emotional man. Just take him for ****'s sake," Jack shouted and the sound brought Mick the Merciless out.

"You got some bother boss!" Mick said menacingly. The driver looked at the crazed eyes and muscles and decided that poking a comatose buffalo awake was the better part of valour and drove off.

Later Jack phoned Dan's home to see if he was okay. His long suffering wife said she'd just a few minutes ago answered a doorbell and there he was lying on the doorstep. How the taxi driver found out where he lived remained a mystery.

As the day wore on into night Jack realised that this may well be the last time he'd ever have all his pets in one zoo. It made him sad to think he was now looking for work and maybe a whole new life away from the madness of contracting. His wife had left for home early on as the ways of the pub were not hers and she had problems with their dog at home and was taking it to the PDSA. Better her than him. His last and only visit remained scarred on his mind.

"Name?" the stern faced lady behind the counter had asked him as he rocked up in his suit and tie with a small hamster in a cage.

"Jack," he replied confidently, looking around at the assembled tattooed and shaven-headed men holding on to their associated *killing dogs*, growling and slavering in the small waiting room. He noticed with some apprehension that there were no pussies or budgies or small furry animals, just large, potentially lethal ones. He stood out a mile in his suit and he was anxious to seem as macho as the rest.

"No the bloody hamster man," the stern lady shouted. The men all glowered at Jack. He could feel the stares in his back. A bull terrier growled angrily. He looked around nervously, turned back and whispered to his nemesis as quietly as he could in the silent waiting room, "Hammy…"

"What did you say? Speak up man, I can't hear you…" the woman shouted far too loudly for Jack. He turned again and saw all the fixed stares on him. He leaned over the counter towards the woman and spoke a little bit louder. "Hammy…"

"Hammy!! It's called Hammy. That's a girl's name for a hamster. Is it yours son?"

Some of the men laughed. Others obviously too thick or just psychotic just glared at him.

"No it's bloody not. It's my wife's from the school and it's sick," he stammered out trying to be positive and re-establish some street cred.

"Well ok then. Just take poor Hammy over there with you and take a seat next to the nice man with the Rottweiler."

Jack sat with the cage on his knee. The Rottweiler kept sniffing the cage and scratching at Jack's leg, the owner ignoring him, smoking and reading The Sun. The hamster lay there comatose oblivious to the risk of impending death by swallowing. Jack thought *Why didn't I just chuck the bloody hamster out into the field next to school and let it take its chances with Mother Nature? What a daft sod having to put up with this humiliation…all for a bloody rodent.*

His turn came to take Hammy in to see the vet. The vet looked at the unconscious furry critter. "How long's he been like this?" he asked, opening the cage.

"About two days I think. It's my wife's school's class pet. It's not mine, you do know that, I hope," Jack pleaded, trying to disown the embarrassment.

"Uhm." The vet murmured, picking up the prostrate critter. He turned Hammy over and back again. He then put his hand around his body and squeezed. Even Jack thought that was cruel. Throwing him onto the field at the mercy of weasels, cats and Jack Russells, was as nothing compared to squeezing the poor thing to death. The vet squeezed yet again and suddenly a small pellet came out of the rodent's backside quickly followed by two more and finally one last one. "It's as I thought. He was just constipated. He'll be fine now."

And sure enough Hammy was. He perked up and started running around his cage. Jack thanked the vet and couldn't wait to get out. He walked through the surgery door and into the waiting room with Hammy in his cage running on his wheel, resurrected Lazarus- like. The nurse followed him out and he paid his donation to the stern faced receptionist.

"Well Hammy looks fine now. What was wrong with him then?" she shouted at Jack.

The men all looked up. The killing dogs cocked their heads too, listening. Before Jack could whisper anything, the young nurse just shouted across the room, "He was constipated. Just needed a shite!"

Jack could still hear the laughter and the comments as he hurried out of the room. "Soft twat!" And, "******** hamster needing a shite; should have wrung it's ****** neck, the puff," and finally, the ultimate insult, "I think he was a Mag." And the Rottweiler made one final lunge at the cage as he slammed the door shut.

Back in the present; "What the **** are you laughing at?"

Jack turned to see a grizzled older man on a stool at the end of the bar. His face resembled something that someone had been sharpening chisels on or using as a chopping board. Half his nose was missing and he was scowling at Jack in pure hatred. The casual observer would have thought he was about to launch a violent assault on the hapless mourner but Jack just grinned back at the angry man.

"What fettle Jim? I was just remembering happier times."

The grizzled old man took a drag of his cigarette and blew the smoke in Jack's face before replying. "You know nowt about happy times. You and your Tory mates in your ****** crystal palace glass mansion houses know nowt about what we working lads call happy times. *******. Tories the lot of yeah!"

Jack smiled again. This was Mad Jim. It had taken him years to convince Jim that because he had gone off to University and finally bought himself a house with a heavy mortgage that he wasn't a Tory or had a silver spoon in his mouth. Jim was irascible and angry all the time. Jack had tried to make friends with him every time he arrived at the bar. Everyone had told him not to bother as he was the angriest person known to man. "Joe Pesci in *Goodfellas* was Mother Theresa compared to Mad Jim." But Jack never learned. Ever the optimist he set himself the goal of winning over Mad Jim and making him, if not a friend, at least not an enemy. So he persevered taking humiliation and abuse every time he stood next to the crazy man.

"Canny day today Jim. The wind a bit wild mind?" Jack said one day as he entered the bar and ordered a beer standing next to Mad Jim.

"Is it ****. What do you lot know about canny days? All you posh ********'s just sit in your crystal palaces with your central heating and know **** all about what wind was like when we worked down the pit. ******* windy! My arse blows more out than what is out there today you soft twat."

Jack took his beer and smiled, deciding to talk about one of Jim's pet subjects. It seems he had been a champion boxer in the army and he would sometimes talk boxing to his peers although even his old workmates from down the pit struggled to talk to him without a fight breaking out so normally he sat alone at the bar. "Canny fight last night Jim. Did you watch it?" Jack, not having watched the fight but having read the rave reviews about the contest.

"Canny fight....! Was it shite! What the **** were you watching you soft bastard. Two puffs trying to fight and couldn't punch ******** blancmange. In my day I'd have knacked the two together. You know **** all you."

Jack let Mad Jim raged on and considered his options, as he had done many times over the past few months trying to enamour himself to the demonic retired pitman. Perhaps gardening would be non- controversial. "How's your allotment doing? My spuds are not so good this year. I tried to put some seaweed in the trench with them but wondering if that's messed them up a bit."

"What the **** would Tories like you know about growing spuds? You posh ******* should stick to buying them in shops. You've got plenty money to dee it. Yaeh thieving bastards ya's. Nye Bevan was reet; vermin the ******* lot of yaeh." Jim howled and then calmly took a drink of his beer and continued. "Spuds need lots of hoss shite, you daft twat. Where did you get your seed potatoes?"

Jack seeing a glimmer of hope grabbed the proverbial straw. "I bought them at a garden centre near Durham, Jim. Did I not get the right ones then?"

"You daft bastard! Typical Tory, loads of money from hard working lads and you ****** piss it away on luxuries. Your Uncle would have told yeah to buy them from our allotment club you stupid twat. I give up."

Jim turned his head and stared at the person at the bar on the other side of him who obviously he didn't like and rhetorically said: "Thowt I told yeah to **** off when I'm sat in the bar."

"Sorry Jim didn't see yeah there. I'm just ordering man and ganning to play dominoes ower with the dole lads."

"Well get ya pint and **** off." Jim growled and turned back to stare at the walls.

And so it had gone for months. Jack coming in and trying to be polite and Jim assassinating his manhood, politics, gardening, fishing, boxing, football, working skills - you name it and he was shite at it.

He did discover some of Mad Jim's history from other people though. Brian the Lion told him Jim had been pretty violent all his natural life. One night four hard men from town had arrived to beat him up for some reason long forgotten. They entered to find Jim leaning against the mantelpiece. The biggest man came on and Jim grabbed him, hit him with an uppercut and pulled him down head first into the fire. Jim then stood the assailant who was howling in pain as the fire burned him. Jim faced the others. "Come on then. I'll tak the three of yeah!" Brian the Lion said the three looked at the fallen man being incinerated in the fire and listening to his terrifying screams while Jim just stood there, fists clenched and foot firmly planted on the immolated man's head. They wisely turned and ran. In thirty years Jim had changed little Jack thought.

Brian also explained the missing part of Mad Jim's gnarled nose. It had been bitten off in a boxing match in the army against a black opponent which ended up in a brawl. From then on Jim had nursed a passionate hatred of tinted people and was known to threaten anyone of any colour who entered his territory. One unfortunate Sikh carpet salesman who ploughed his lonely furrow selling rugs in oriental patterns to drunken persons in the bars of the North East happened to come across Jim. He found himself knocked out, rolled up in his carpet and thrown down the steps into the street.

Now at his mother's wake, Jack took one last look at the chisel-faced, racist old psychopath and shook his head, wondering why he had tried so hard to ingratiate himself with the man. A masochistic tendency to align with homicidal maniacs? Well, that was possible as he'd gone on to do that most of his working life. Or was it a deep need to show some form of kindness to the afflicted and animals of the world? Nope he concluded - he was just shit scared of the lunatic.

But his perseverance had paid off! One day there was a knock on the door. Jack opened it and there was Mad Jim. Jack immediately reached behind the hat stand for the sawn off shotgun he kept for such emergencies, as you do but Jim just growled at him and handed over a tray of young cabbages. "You are so shit at gardening I've grown these seedlings for you useless twat. Dig plenty hoss shite in with them and they'll graw. Even you Tories can't **** that up. I'm ganning to the Club. You can buy me a pint. Looking at this ******* glass mansion, you can afford it you twat." Jim turned and walked off, flat cap on his head, carrying his leaded walking stick to assist the gout and also batter any unsuspecting Tories to death.

Yes Jack thought, *I did well with that one didn't I? Maybe that will be my new career? - converting homicidal maniacs to altruistic behaviours that benefit mankind.* He was broken out of his stupor and foolishness by a large man who stood next to him and Mad Jim laughing loudly.

"Heh Jack, that Jock you brought down from Scotland is a character. Canny lad that one son and **** me he can drink. Let me buy you a beer Jim. I see you and our Jack are getting on well again marra. Jack's still smiling."

"What fettle Kenny. Aye your lad is alreet for a ******* Tory," Jack tried to interrupt Jim for the thousandth time in his short acquaintance and show him his membership of the Workers Revolutionary Party and letter of affiliation from Vanessa Redgrave but was cut off in his attempt by the usual abuse. "He's a ******* useless gardener as well marra and soft as shite. Canna believe he's your sister's son."

"Aye Jim, "Kenny said, "His fatha wanted him to read and write and not go down the pit, daft bugger that he was. He's soft as shite. He even took their lasses ******** hamster to the vet for ****'s sake the other week."

Jack looked from his Uncle to Mad Jim and back feeling that he might as well been a wardrobe for all they cared about hurting his obviously soft feelings.

"A ******* hamster! Dear God Kenny, what the hell have yeah brought up man? He should have been there the day we hoyed the ram off the cliff."

"Aye Jim that was a laugh wasn't it. I've nivva laughed so much since we kicked olwd Ralphie's pig to death. Ha...ha...ha..." Kenny laughed loudly in the raucous way he always did when in a good mood - usually after conning someone or fooling his mates into thinking he'd pay for their beer and dinner before leaving by the back door or the toilet window.

"You threw a ram off a cliff? Why do that for God's sake?" Jack decided to join the conversation.

"Coz we could you soft shite," Jim snarled at Jack and turning to Kenny, "Towld ya he's soft as shite."

Kenny laughed again. "Aye, it was a laugh mind. We were down Whitburn cliffs the coast on the Club trip and pissed, had a walk along the cliff and saw some sheep. I said to Jim, let's kill one for dinner and tak it back to the lads on the coach. So Jim went to get one but a ram decided to protect the flock the daft sod. So when he charged Jim he just grabbed his horns and hoyed him off the cliff. We looked down but couldn't see it so we climbed down expecting to see it deed on the rocks, but nee sign, just blood on the rocks. I said to Jim, *Gan in and see if it's crawled in the cave to die.* So Jim crawled into the cave head first The ram was still fit as a lop and had backed up to the back wall and when it saw Jim crawl head first in it charged him and head butted the daft bastard full on the nose-hah...hah....hah!"

Kenny howled again and took a drink. Jim just scowled and Jack noticed what was left of his nose seemed to twist on its own like a misshapen banana. He didn't dare stare too much so he interrupted Kenny, careful not to laugh himself as he could still see Jim's horrible face glowering.

"What happened then Kenny?"

"The bugger broke his nose - blood everywhere, lost a tooth too! Hah..hah..hah. I've nivva laughed so much." Kenny carried on laughing for a few moments and then without any emotion at all he concluded the tale of the unfortunate sheep. "Jim just crawled after the bugger, dragged it out by its horns and we kicked the twat to death...best club trip I've been on in years - hah..hah..hah..."

Jack thought he saw Mad Jim's lips move slightly into a smile, something he'd never seen in any conversation up to now, but then realised it might just be gas from the beer. He decided he needed some air to clear his head. This was his mother's wake after all and the madness surrounding him was finally taking its toll. "Kenny I'm going to take a walk mate. It'll be good to see the old house maybe for one last time. I hope you'll give a song for mam soon. Everyone has asked if you will."

Kenny put his pint down and smiled: "Aye Jack, we'll see. We'll see how it gans."

Jim slurred out of the side of his mouth as Jack moved to walk away. "See, I towld yeah he was soft as shite. ******* needs air? The soft twat. He could nivva drink. All Tories canna hold their drink. But he's alreet Kenny, I like the lad."

Jack stopped in his tracks. He thought about turning around and shaking Jim's hand or giving him a hug as a mate. He'd finally made it. But then he remembered the ram, the poor Moghul carpet salesman and the townie with the burnt bonce and decided to bank the one and only utterance of affiliation and compassion he'd ever had from the irascible psychopath.

He walked down the front street past several deranged people who offered their condolences and to buy a drink for him but he strolled on to his old council house where now there was nothing but the memories of a wonderful childhood. The coalhouses and coal lets they used as football goals, the wooden posts and their yellow fluorescent lamps they used as target practice for their air rifles and as stages for Stakalaka road races, the hen houses, pigeon crees, steel bins full of fire ashes they used as cricket wickets, all were gone in some daft council modernisation scheme. He thought *maybe this was progress* but he couldn't really believe it. Life would never be the same. The pits were long gone; the pitmen condemned to a life on the dole, their kids leading lives of crime, drugs and indolence if they couldn't move on. All the front and back doors were now locked. What cars hadn't been stolen or torched were clamped up with enough steel protection and locks to keep the inmates of Alcatraz incarcerated but they were still stolen.

Jack leaned against the wooden fence that surrounded his old house and remembered how his mother was forever leaning on the old rickety home-made gate and chatting to all the other women in the street. No one called anyone by their first names then; everyone was Mrs or Mr even if they were great friends and long term neighbours. He could hear his mother's quiet, timid voice, talking about the latest fight. "Eee, the poor lad's mother will be in a mess. He wouldn't have kicked him to half to death if he hadn't been full of the drink you knar. Poor mother, now he'll probably have to do time."

No mention of the poor boy maimed by the poor mother's lad. Jack shook his head. The culture he had grown up was unique. You had to say that for it.

The night was drawing on and it was starting to freeze up all around him. He didn't feel the cold lost as he was in the happier times of his past. He moved off the fence and decided it was now time to drop everything and take up whatever the new challenge was. He didn't believe in God, fate or karma but he would take up his own cross and pin it to the next stage of his career, wherever that might lie. All that mattered was his family and now he'd lost his last link to his own parents, it made him more determined to give his own family everything that he had shared with his parents and sisters and the people he'd known and grown up with in these two grimy little streets. *Well*, he corrected himself, *not the rampant poverty, the icy windows, the extreme violence and all those other wonderful things of the time before Thatcher.*

He shuddered as the cold finally bit into his body and he said his goodbyes to the house, the street and their memories and walked back to the pub. As he entered his nephew grabbed his suit jacket again.

"How man Jack, how man Jack….our Kenny is ganna sing man…he's ganna sing man…dae yeah knar man…he's ganna sing …"

Jack brushed away the tattooed hand and put his arm around his nephew. He loved him a lot. A simple, strong-willed man and with a strong compass for what he believed was right or wrong. He would do someone a good turn rather than a bad one and that to Jack was the best moral and value he could have. Yes he loved the lad.

"Aye son, I knew he would. He promised your Nana one day he'd sing for her again. He just never got the chance when she was alive."

His brother in law came over to repeat the news. "Heh Jack, Kenny's gonna sing. What the **** have yeah done with him man. He never sings now."

And he was correct. Kenny had been a wonderful singer. He had given up a potential glittering career onstage to go back down the pit and to fall into a life of gambling, crime and fun. An enigmatic man with very little emotion or love in his heart except for his sister, Jack's mother. This would be a momentous event. Hard men used to cry at his voice. He was much older now, and fresh out of jail for using a knuckle duster on someone his own age – sixty-eight. Kenny was closing out a family feud from many years before. And no one had heard him sing in twenty years.

Jack's nephew went around the people in the pub telling them to shut up and keep quiet as his uncle was about to sing for his nana. He had no fear of The Mule, Ernie and the likes because, like the lad *who bought a flute for 50 pence…he had no sense* and like most from that village, no fear. But everyone quietened down and Kenny stood on the raised area at the back of the small bar. Despite all the alcohol he was still immaculate in his suit (stolen from Binns), patent leather shoes (stolen from Fenwicks) and silk tie (stolen from Bainbridges). He said only one thing: "This is for our Edie," and sang only one song, *Sweet Sixteen.*

Women cried. Men cried. Jack cried. The Scottish Sales Director said he'd never heard anything like it.

Then Kenny came over to Jack and asked him outside where he had a taxi waiting for him. He looked at Jack, who still had tears in his eyes, shook his hand and as he got into the taxi, spoke for the first time, "Son, I won't be back. Now our Edie's gone, there's no point. She was the only one I ever loved. Keep your timma in son, I always liked you."

And was gone. Jack never saw him again.

The night ended without a fight. That was a personal win for Jack because that simply never ever happened in the village but he had asked everyone to respect his mam and not cause mayhem and it had worked.. Everyone had respect for his mam there anyway and even his own personal lunatics from work were nothing but amicable and friendly. Jack even briefly considered whether he should stay and try to set up his own contracting business with them all. Then he saw Ernie arm wrestling the village idiot or l one of them and Two Bats showing his nephew how to use the back handed Yamasuki move with the bat to crush the testicles of anyone daft enough to even look at him in the wrong way, and he thought, *No, let's keeping climbing up this mountain and move on to Eden. Please if there is a God at the top of Mount Purgatory, get me away from Beelzebub and give me a glimpse of Paradise.* God must not have heard him as the next day he met The Iron Chancellor.

BOOK FIVE

JACK'S PARADISE GLIMPSED

VISIONS OF HEAVEN

1

LONDON
THE IRON CHANCELLOR

The beginning of Paradise...

KT had called him before the funeral to say that the crazy Dane, Knut, he of The Mule's inspector monkey-hanging incident and the horrible liquorice drink *Gamell Dansk*, had heard that Jack was free and that his boss could well be looking for someone with Jack's skills.

"But the Dane told me his boss was the devil incarnate, a nightmare?" Jack retorted.

"**I** am a ******* nightmare but you worked for me didn't you?" KT said truthfully.

"Well yes, but best the devil you know as they say and for ****'s sake you'd take some beating in the burning inferno stakes."

KT laughed down the phone. "You twat! I was the making of you. Look what you've become."

"Yes KT, I'm on the dole, another kid on the way and skint. Thanks mate."

"Now Jack, let's move on, my friend. I'm trying to help. When you've finished with your mother's funeral, and you only need an afternoon off for that, make the ******* call. The world's gone soft. When I ran everything no one got more than three hours off for funerals and only if it was their kids. Now the daft bastards are giving my staff time off for babies, and for ****'s sake, the men get it as well. It's time to get out, Jack. The Big Yin had it right. Sell the lot and go and farm Highland cattle and slaughter them for some fun. There's no fun left in the business. I bet you're pleased I fired you now."

Jack just kept quiet. By now he knew his boss. He probably thought he had done Jack a favour throwing him to wolves and then dumping him in the shite. Jack held his own counsel. He had got too comfortable and too confident, too bored he guessed. The challenge had gone. Counting scaffold fittings, Dog Whelk penis's, daily conflict with his bosses, clients and staff, crazed killers and sociopaths (and these were only his clients), relentless pursuit of profit and cash had all taken their toll and he had not responded well in the latter years. Maybe KT had actually done him a favour. *Bugger it,* he thought, *it's time to take up a new challenge.*

"If I'm honest KT, maybe it's for the best. The fun had gone out of it all, mate. I guess I went with it. Give me the guy's number and I'll call him. Oh, by the way, why do they call him the Iron Chancellor?"

"Because he's German. Knut doesn't like the Germans that's all. You'll get on alright with him. You English are not much different to them. They were Saxons and shagged your women the same as we did. So if you're not half Viking, you'll be half ******* German. Jack, all my respects for your mother and hope it works out for you. Tell that sales manager he'd better be back at work tomorrow. I'm not the Big Yin. He was too soft on the bastard. And don't let him drink the bar dry. He's got to get the Minister for Energy pissed Wednesday night and persuade him to let us rape and pillage Russia again after The Mule upset the KGB. If you get the job with the oil company and the big project in Asia, remember your friends and who looked after you and took you to Zurich. We can visit again if things work out. You know the craic. See you Jack."

Jack put the phone down. Yes, he knew the craic, even when wiped out emotionally, unemployed and in extreme distress one had to remember one's friends when new work came up. Scratching backs, however, after having one's own whipped to bare bones was not in Jack's new plan. Look after number one and the family was his goal and maybe the Iron Chancellor could help with that mission. So he went to London.

"I have researched your career and taken up references. I have to say as a person who purports to be an intelligent man and with post graduate qualifications you have made a mess of your life. Your choice of employers has been abysmal up to now. You seem to fall from one crisis to another. This may well be a flaw in your character."

Dear God Jack thought as he sat opposite his potential new employer *this guy makes Mad Jim seem like Oprah Winfrey.*

The Iron Chancellor carried on. "However, quite a few of the people I respect tell me that you are not as bad as your career seems to suggest. So I may well give you the opportunity to benefit from my experience and leadership and perhaps reset your lost career. Obviously as you are not an engineer you cannot do anything that is really important or valued. Only engineers have much worth on projects but people like you are useful in a peripheral way."

Jack sat staring at the white shirted, tall, thin German with the red tie. He was sitting upright, looking supremely confident and superior, his slightly greying hair belying that his youthfully fit-looking looking body. The man continued. " On projects, engineers do the work and get paid much more. Others like you will support them and as you are worth less you will get paid less but on this project I am about to lead to greatness, I feel I may well need someone to help me. It is a mega project spread over many countries, many of which are very foreign and Asian. Also we have chosen an American contractor to do the work. As you should know by now, Americans are Neanderthals and I need someone to help me torture the contactor. But this time I want to torture them nicely. I want to work….as…well….as…."

He was struggling to get out anything that sounded remotely friendly Jack realised, so he butted in. "You want to work with them like a partnership? Friends? An alliance type contract?"

The Iron Chancellor scrutinised Jack across his tidy desk. He peered over his spectacles, weighing up what he had said. His face grimaced and he nodded slightly.

"Yes. You are not concise in your deduction but yes, I want to work together with them and all the suppliers and subcontractors. Not because it's normal to work closely with inferior intellects and so many foreigners but because that is the best way I have decided to deliver this project. And I will deliver it. I always do."

The Teutonic project director crossed his arms and focused on Jack.

"You have little experience for delivering mega projects so I will educate you. On projects you can make things happen. Or you can watch things happen. Or you can say what the **** happened. On my project I will only have people who make things happen. If they watch things happen I run them off. I have decided you will help me deliver this and if you don't I will run you off."

Jack thought that perhaps he should say something like *maybe I don't want to make things happen for you* or *I'm not letting anyone run me off pal without a fight* but he decided to keep quiet and let this run its course.

"So even though you look like a bricklayer with a PhD, I believe you can build these teams and stop them failing to deliver. I would like to you to go to Houston and begin to communicate with these Stone Age construction men. I expect them to provide execution plans by your return. If they don't I will cancel the contract and ask their Vice President to run them off. If you can't do that I will run you off. After that you will come to Singapore with me."

He looked as if he was about to stand up with the interview over so Jack stammered out his questions.

"But what about my family? The salary? The schools and things for the kids?"

The Iron Chancellor settled back down and leaned over his desk, facing Jack.

"I guess you need to know those things. I believe in looking after my team. You can pick up your contract from my lady's desk outside. I pay my staff much higher than the market rate. I know what you have been paid in your lesser jobs and I can assure you this is much more and you can bring your wife, your brood and your dog to Singapore at our cost, schools paid for and all expenses. The company pays all personal tax due to the relevant authorities and you will receive a large loyalty bonus if I don't run you off in the four years. I look after my team for one reason only; if they are not happy at home then they may well be unhappy at work. That means I will have to run them off and even I get tired of running people off all the time, so it's best you work with me to make them happy. For some reason I struggle with that. Anyway, I can't waste time with you. Go away and sign your contract and provide me with a plan by the time you get to Houston. It will be a test of competence. If you fail, I will tear up the contract and run you off back to that Northern dump you people call home. I really am looking forward to a great four years with you Jack....as we sing in Germany, *We'll invade again, Don't know where, don't know when, But I know we'll invade again, One stormy trooper day*...hah. .hah...hah. Close the door after you, Goodbye."

And that was that.

Singapore awaited him. He had not paid Charon the Ferryman the devil's coins to cross the River Styx to Hades because he had paid him off with real wedge, the coin of the realm, in true contractor style, to take him and Kitty elsewhere.

210

Jack's Inferno, Mount Purgatory had finally gone...and a glimpse of Paradise had been offered.

Well that's what he thought...

FICTION FROM APS BOOKS
(www.andrewsparke.com)

HR Beasley: *Nothing Left To Hide*
Lee Benson: *So You Want To Own An Art Gallery*
Lee Benson: *Where's Your Art gallery Now?*
Lee Benson: *'Now You're The Artist…Deal With It'*
Nargis Darby: *A Different Shade Of Love*
Jean Harvey: *Pandemic*
Michel Henri: *Mister Penny Whistle*
Michel Henri: *The Death Of The Duchess Of Grasmere*
Michel Henri: *Abducted By Faerie*
Hugh Lupus *An Extra Knot*
Ian Meacheam: *An Inspector Called*
Tony Rowland: *Traitor Lodger German Spy*
Andrew Sparke: *Abuse Cocaine & Soft Furnishings*
Andrew Sparke: *Copper Trance & Motorways*
Phil Thompson: *Momentary Lapses In Concentration*
Paul C. Walsh: *A Place Between The Mountains*
Michael White: *A Life Unfinished*
TF Byrne: *Damage Limitation*

Printed in Great Britain
by Amazon